Science Fiction Story Index

1950-1968

Science Fiction Story Index

1950-1968

Frederick Siemon

ALA

American Library Association
Chicago 1971

International Standard Book Number 0-8389-0107-7-(1971)
Library of Congress Catalog Card Number 70-162470

Printed in the United States of America

CONTENTS

INTRODUCTION

Upon first noting Science Fiction Story Index, the librarian or informed science fiction reader may well say, "Oh, another author-title index—why?" The question is a valid one and deserves an answer, for several other approaches to the literature of science fiction short stories, which duplicate in part the material covered by this book, are already available to libraries. Perhaps the best known is the Short Story Index and its supplements, published by the H.W. Wilson Company. Other extant works include the Fiction Catalog and its supplements, and the various specialized bibliographies for aid in choosing the "best" books for readers of various age levels, such as the High School Catalog and the Children's Catalog, both published by Wilson. These specialized bibliographies have sections devoted to science fiction literature and make some attempt at listing the contents of anthologies analytically.

Comparison with Other Works

However, the competing bibliographies do not begin to equal Science Fiction Story Index in breadth (number of anthologies covered) or in depth (completeness of indexing). For example, the Short Story Index, the most significant contender, does not index joint authors, editors, poetry, novels, or novellas. Science Fiction Story Index does. Short Story Index covers only thirteen of the eighteen years covered by Science Fiction Story Index, and in these thirteen years it indexed only about 1,800 separate stories under the representative headings, compared to the more than 3,400 in the present volume.

What about other relevant reference works? There are

several, some still in print, that attempt to offer an author-title approach to science fiction literature. In the main they reflect the approach used by nonlibrarians, being almost too specific and giving too much information. They are also less comprehensive. The interested reader is referred to the excellent guide to the literature of science fiction, written by Neil Barron, in the January 1970 issue of Choice magazine (pages 1536 ff.). Mr Barron's article gives a comprehensive listing of extant indexes, as well as a listing of subject collections, criticism, and works of evaluation.

Scope

Although the first science fiction anthology, Amazing Stories Annual, was published in 1927 by the indomitable and prescient Hugo Gernsback, it was not until the early 1950s that publishers generally appreciated the commercial value of bringing together the most noteworthy or important stories from a representative science fiction magazine (or, for that matter, from any source) and publishing them in a collection. Indeed, science fiction as a literary or bibliographical form was not really recognized until the Library of Congress established a separate subject heading for science fiction in its 1950-54 listing of Books: Subjects. The comprehensive English-language bibliography Cumulative Book Index began to use the subject heading "Science Fiction" in 1953.

The works included in this index reflect the availability of the bibliographic information given in the above lists; if the anthology was published within the eighteen-year period from 1950 to 1968, it was a candidate for inclusion in Science Fiction Story Index. In most cases, a copy of the anthology was available to the author; if not, then a photocopy of the table of contents. In some few regrettable cases information had to be taken from a secondary source, such as a communication with the publisher of the book or the analytical entries shown on a library catalog card.

It is pertinent to compare the production of anthologies during the 1950-68 period and the number listed in Science Fiction Story Index. Exact figures for the total number published are difficult to come by, but perhaps the entries under the subject heading "Science Fiction" in the Cumulative Book Index for the years covered may give an approximation. One must take into account, however, the fact that Cumulative Book Index, while it attempts to list all publications in the English language, cannot distinguish between original publications and reprints subtly disguised by alternate titles, subtitles, or other alterations. For example, it is not unusual for a British publisher to produce an anthology which is almost simultaneously published in America with the same stories but under a slightly different title. Contrary to the happy mythology perpetrated by library schools and given credence by what purports to be the publishing history of the work on the verso of the title pages, publishers do not always advise readers about the ancestry of their products; indeed, the lineage of some anthologies may be suspect of the taint of bastardy or incest. Hence, the statistics given in Cumulative Book Index can be taken, in specific terms, only with a grain of salt; they may, however, have some validity as general indicators of trends or ratios. Another complicating factor is the difficulty of establishing whether or not a certain title is, in fact, an anthology; editors and compilers tend toward coyness in this regard.

An educated guess must thus be gauged as shown below:

Year	Total Adult Science Fiction Monographic Entries in CBI	Number Definitely Identifiable as Anthologies	Number Included in SFSI
1948-52	No SF subdivision		
1953-56	271	64	46
1957-58	118	17	16
1959-60	91	19	16
1961-62	103	30	23
1963-64	129	42	29
1965-66	206	76	62
1967-68	208	73	45
	1,126	321	237

A very soft interpretation of the statistics given in the table would indicate that about 74 percent (237/321) of the works identifiable as anthologies have been indexed in Science Fiction Story Index. The remainder—the alterations, the duplications, the products of minor publishers, the quickly out-of-print, the impossible to locate works—have not.

Organization

Science Fiction Story Index consists of three distinct parts. The first, "Author-Title Index," is arranged alphabetically by author, and under each author's name alphabetically by title. Each title entry refers directly to a code number or numbers which designate the anthologies in which the particular story appears. The second part, "Bibliography of Indexed Anthologies," is an alphabetical listing of the indexed anthologies arranged by code number and with complete bibliographic citations for each. Most of these citations are preceded by one or more symbols which designate reading level and in-print status. These symbols are explained on page 133. The third part, "Title-Author and Anthology-Code Index," refers either from story title included in the indexed anthologies to the story's author, or in the entries for titles of indexed anthologies to the code numbers.

The compiler personally supervised the composition of the book.

Science Fiction Story Index

1950-1968

AUTHOR-TITLE INDEX

Since most people know a story by the pen name or pseudonym of a writer (if he uses one), the listing of stories in this index is by pseudonym. This policy conforms to Rule 40 of the Anglo-American Cataloging Rules (A.L.A., 1967). For example, stories by Samuel L. Clemens will be found under Twain, Mark, pseud., rather than under Clemens.

Initials and acronyms are placed at the beginning of the alphabet to which they belong; for example, the story IBM is placed at the beginning of I section.

Abbreviations and numbers are arranged as if spelled out:

Dr. is arranged as if spelled Doctor.
Mr. is arranged as if spelled Mister.
St(e). is arranged as if spelled Saint(e).
1937 is arranged as if spelled Nineteen Thirty...
5,271,009 is arranged as if spelled Five Million...

AUTHOR–TITLE		ANTHOLOGY
Aandahl, Vance.		
It's a Great Big Wonder Universe		M235
The Unfortunate Mr. Morky		M630
When Lilacs Last in the Dooryard Bloomed		M245
Abernathy, Robert.		
Axolotl	B590	D580
The Canal Builders		D575
Deep Space		D580
Grandma's Lie Soap		M600
Heirs Apparent	B590	M205
Heritage		C785
Junior		M595
Peril of the Blue World	G225	W870
Single Combat		K705
Ackerman, Forrest J.		
The Mute Question		C960
Adams, Louis J.A.		
Dark Conception		M255
Aickman, Robert.		
The Cicerones		D450
Aiken, Conrad.		
Oneiromachia		M625
Aldiss, Brian W.		
Afterword [Knights of the Paper Space Ship]		H320
Ahead		A375
Amen and Out		W900
Basis for Negotiation		A375
Best Fantasy Stories [Editor]		A360
Best SF: 1967 [Joint Editor]		H320
But Who Can Replace a Man?	K700	W725
Comic Inferno		G175
Dumb Show		A375
Full Sun		0645
Heresies of the Huge God		G185
Hothouse		W735
The Impossible Star		A375
Intangibles Inc.		A360
Jungle Substitute		G180
A Kind of Artistry	A375	M245

AUTHOR–TITLE	ANTHOLOGY
Analog Science Fact and Science Fiction.	
Analog I	A535
Analog 2	A540
Analog 3	A545
Analog 4	A550
Analog 5	A555
The Astounding Science Fiction Anthology	A875
Prologue to Analog	A560
Anderson, Karen.	
In Memoriam: Henry Kuttner	M225
Landscape with Sphinxes	M245
Origin of the Species	M225
The Piebald Hippogriff	M630
Six Haiku [poems]	A835
Treaty in Tartessos	M250
Anderson, Poul.	
The Adventure of the Misplaced Hound	A565 S420
Backwardness	M225
Ballade of an Artificial Satellite	A835
The Barbarian	M215
Brain Wave	B755
Butch	D445
Call Me Joe	A520 B605 K700
Critique of Impure Reason	A575
The Disinherited	O640
Don Jones	A565
Door to Anywhere	G185
The Double-Dyed Villains	G830
Earthman's Burden	A565
Epilogue	A 575
Escape from Orbit	A575
Eve Times Four	A575
Flandry of Terra	A570
Flight to Forever	Y395
The Game of Glory	A570
Garden in the Void	M925
Genius	C765
Gypsy	D575

AUTHOR–TITLE		ANTHOLOGY
Anderson, Poul [Cont'd]		
The Helping Hand	C775	C795
Hiding Place		A580
The Immortal Game		M205
In Hoka Signo Vinces		A565
Innocent Arrival		D310
Inside Earth		G140
Interloper		D435
Journey's End		M220
Kings Who Die		M630
The Last Monster		L640
Life Cycle		S585
The Live Coward		C750
The Long Remembering		K850
The Longest Voyage		A840
The Man Who Came Early		M215
The Martian Crown Jewels	B750	S420
The Martyr	C950	M235
The Master Key		A580
A Message in Secret		A570
Mysterious Message		A565
Night Piece		M655
No Truce with Kings		A575
The Plague of Masters		A570
Sam Hall	C830	C835
The Sheriff of Canyon Gulch		A565
The Sky People		M270
A Sun Invisible		A585
Sunjammer		A550
Swordsman of Lost Terra		W885
Terminal Quest		T290
Territory		A580
The Three Cornered Wheel		A585
The Tiddlywink Warriors		A565
Time and Stars		A575
Time Heals		S595
Time Lag		M240
The Tinkler		D455

AUTHOR–TITLE	ANTHOLOGY
Anderson, Poul [Cont'd]	
Trader to the Stars	A580
Trespass !	B570
The Trouble Twisters	A585
Turning Point	A575
The Un-Man	G800
Yo Ho Hoka!	A565
Andrew, William.	
The Right Thing	O140
Anmar, Frank.	
The Fasterfaster Affair	N785
Anonymous.	
Missing One's Coach: An Anchronism	D430
Tale of a Chemist	D430
Anthony, John.	
The Hypnoglyph	D440 M270
Anvil, Christopher.	
Gadget vs. Trend	A525
The Hunch	A535
Mind Partner	G200
Not in the Literature	A545
Pandora's Planet	A560
Philosopher's Stone	A540
The Prisoner	C950
A Rose by any Other Name	M620
Apostolides, Alex.	
Civilized [Joint Author]	D440
Crazy Joey [Joint Author]	M580
What Thin Partitions [Joint Author]	M920
Arkin, Alan.	
People Soup	C820
Arr, Stephen [pseud]	
See Rynas, Stephen A.	
Arthur, Robert.	
Evolution's End	C960
Postpaid to Paradise	M190
The Wheel of Time	B880

AUTHOR–TITLE	ANTHOLOGY
Ash, Paul.	
Big Sword	A530 C750
The Wings of a Bat	W900
Ashby, Richard.	
Commencement Night	A530 C765
Master Race	S640
Ashton-Smith, Clark.	
See Smith, Clark Ashton.	
Asimov, Isaac.	
All the Troubles of the World	A855 W745
Anniversary	R820
The Author's Ordeal	A830
Belief	A560 M580
Blind Alley.	C775
Breeds There a Man...?	D420
Bridle and Saddle	G820
Buy Jupiter!	F220
Catch That Rabbit	A845
The Caves of Steel	A860
Christmas on Ganymede	C960
The Chute	G145
The Currents of Space	A870
The Dead Past	A830
Death Sentence	D435
The Deep	A850
Dreaming Is a Private Thing	A830 B665 M595
Dreamworld	M210
The Dying Night	A885
Earth Is Room Enough	A830
Each an Explorer	M600
Escape!	A845
Evidence	A845 N785
The Evitable Conflict	A845
Eyes Do More Than See	M260 M645
The Feeling of Power	A515 A855
Fifty Short Science Fiction Tales	A835
First Law	A860 F215
Flies	C825
Foreword [To Worlds Beyond]	S590
The Foundation of Science Fiction Success	A830 M205

AUTHOR–TITLE		ANTHOLOGY
Asimov, Isaac [Cont'd]		
Franchise		A830
The Fun They Had	A830 A835 B670 C790	L885
Galley Slave	A860 C855	G215
The Gentle Vultures	A855	S585
Gimmicks Three		A830
Hell-Fire		A830
Homo Sol		C785
Hostess		G140
The Hugo Winners		A840
I, Robot		A845
Ideas Die Hard		G150
I'm in Marsport without Hilda		A855
The Immortal Bard		A830
"In a Good Cause—"		H435
Introduction [to All About the Future]		G800
Introduction [to More Soviet Science Fiction]		P965
Introduction [to Soviet Science Fiction]		D980
It's Such a Beautiful Day		P780
Jokester		A830
The Key		M265
Kid Stuff		A830
The Last Question		A855
The Last Trump		A830
Lenny	A860	P760
Let's Get Together	A860	M605
Liar!	A845 J330 M585 M915	M935
The Little Man on the Subway [Jt. Author]		F700
Little Lost Robot	A845	C935
Living Space	A830	W730
A Loint of Paw		M220
The Machine That Won the War		M240
Marooned off Vesta		R820
The Martian Way	A850	K730
The Message		A830
Misbegotten Missionary	C765	H505
Mother Earth		G815
The Naked Sun		A860

AUTHOR–TITLE	ANTHOLOGY
Asimov, Isaac [Cont'd]	
Nightfall	A875 . H430 K690
Nine Tomorrows	A855
Not Final!	C640 C795
"Nobody Here But—"	P770
The Pause	D445
Pebble in the Sky	A870
Profession	A855
Reason	A845 K700
The Red Queen's Race	P910
Rejection Slips	A855
The Rest of the Robots	A860
Risk	A860
Robbie	A845 . C830 C835
Robot AL-76 Goes Astray	A860
Runaround	A845 M910
Satisfaction Guaranteed	A830 A860
Science Fiction Tales of Our Own Planet	A830
The Singing Bell	M210
Someday	A830
Spell My Name with an S	A855
Star Light	C303
The Stars, Like Dust	A870
Strikebreaker	C845
Sucker Bait	A850
The Talking Stone	D310
Thiotimoline and the Space Age	M620
The Thunder-Thieves	M610
Tomorrow's Children	A865
Trends	D590 G820
Triangle	A870
The Ugly Little Boy	A855 . A865 M655
Unto the Fourth Generation	M270
The Up-to-Date Sorcerer	M225
Victory Unintentional	A860 L640
The Watery Place	A830
What If...	C800 C810
What Is This Thing Called Love?	C820

AUTHOR–TITLE	ANTHOLOGY
Asimov, Isaac [Cont'd]	
Youth	A850
Astounding Science Fiction Magazine	
The Astounding Science Fiction Anthology	A875
Atherton, John.	
Waste Not, Want Not	P720
Auerbach, Arnold M.	
The Day Rembrandt Went Public	M630
Bacon, Francis.	
The New Atlantis	D425
Bade, William L.	
Ambition	C800
Baker, Russell.	
Ms. Found in a Bus	M630
A Sinister Metamorphosis	M640
Bakhnov, Vladlen.	
Mutiny	M277
The Robotniks	M277
Ballard, J.G.	
The Assassination of John Fitzgerald Kennedy Considered as a Downhil Motor Race	H320
Billenium	K705 W735
Build-Up	B670
Chronopolis	C410
The Drowned Giant	M645 N360
The Drowned World	B185
End Game	B190
The Garden of Time	M245
The Illuminated Man	M255
The Insane Ones	M630
The Last World of Mr. Goddard	B190
Minus One	B190
Now Wakes the Sea	B190 M250
Prima Belladonna	M600
The Sound Sweep	M615
Souvenir	P720
The Subliminal Man	B190
The Sudden Afternoon	B190

AUTHOR–TITLE		ANTHOLOGY
Beaumont, Charles.		
Blood Brother		P720
The Crooked Man		P720
Keeper of the Dream		D445
Last Rites		N785
The Last Word		M210
Mourning Song		M635
The Vanishing American	D245	M210
You Can't Have Them All		A360
Becker, Stephen.		
The New Encyclopaedist		M640
Belayev, Alexander.		
Hoity-Toity		D980
Invisible Light		M275
Bell, Eric Temple.		
The Ultimate Catalyst		C810
Bellamy, Edward.		
The Blindman's World		D425
Benedict, Myrle.		
Sit by the Fire		F215
Benet, Stephen Vincent.		
The Angel Was a Yankee.		M575
By the Waters of Babylon		K705
Nightmare for Future Reference: A...Poem .		T290
The Place of the Gods	A865	S250
Bennett, Keith.		
The Rocketeers Have Shaggy Ears		G830
Bennett, Kem.		
A Different Purpose		M230
The Soothsayer		M195
The Trap.		S250
Berdanier, Paul F., Illustrator.		
At the Earth's Core		B970
Bermel, Albert.		
The End of the Race		G175
Berry, John.		
The One Who Returns		M240

AUTHOR–TITLE	ANTHOLOGY
Berryman, John.	
Berom	B645
Space Rating	C795
Special Flight	A510
The Trouble with Telstar	A545
Bester, Alfred.	
Adam and No Eve	H430
Disappearing Act	B670 P765 P775
5,271,009	P750
Fondly Fahrenheit	A520 M205
Hobson's Choice	C935 M195
The Men Who Murdered Mohammed	C410 M225 S595
My Private World of Science Fiction	M655
Oddy and Id	B570
Of Time and Third Avenue	B575 K700
The Pi Man	M230
Starlight, Star Bright	M200
The Stars, My Destination	B755
They Don't Make Life Like They Used To	M250 M635
The Trematode, a Critique of Modern S-F	B580
Will You Wait?	M270
Bevan, Alistair.	
Susan	M645
Beynon, John [Pseud. of John Beynon Harris]	
No Place Like Earth	C305
Survival	C305
Technical Slip	C790
Bierce, Ambrose.	
The Damned Thing	K950
Moxon's Master	B890 C830 K700 L885
Biggle, Lloyd, jr.	
And Madly Teach	M265
Monument	A535
Round Trip to Esidarap	W730
A Slight Case of Limbo	M635
The Tunesmith	B605
Binder, Eando.	
I, Robot	M910 M920

AUTHOR–TITLE	ANTHOLOGY
Binder, Eando [Cont'd]	
Via Asteroid	M925
Via Death	D590
Via Etherline	D585
Bixby, Jerome.	
Angels in the Jets	P750
The Holes Around Mars	C775 C790
It's a Good Life	A865 C945 J330 P765 P775
Old Testament	I230
One Way Street	B590
Page and Player	N880
Bleiler, Everett F.	
The Best Science Fiction Stories:1951 [Editor]	B570
Imagination Unlimited [Editor]	B645
Men of Space and Time [Editor]	B645
Year's Best Science Fiction Novels 1952 [Editor]	Y395
Year's Best Science Fiction Novels 1953 [Editor]	Y400
Year's Best Science Fiction Novels 1954 [Editor]	Y405
Blish, James.	
Battle of the Unborn	C805
Beanstalk	C965
Beep	N885 S645
The Box	C785
Bridge	A 515
A Case of Conscience	C930
Common Time	D655
The Dark Night of the Soul	B665
FYI	P775
The Genius Heap	G165
How Beautiful with Banners	O640
A Matter of Energy	M210
Mistake Inside	K710 P910
New Dreams This Morning [Editor]	B665
Okie	K705 S645
Solar Plexus	M575
Sunken Universe	K730
Surface Tension	C850 G145 Y400
The Testament of Andros	D440

AUTHOR–TITLE	ANTHOLOGY
Blish, James [Cont'd]	
Who's in Charge Here?	M245
A Work of Art	B665 . K850 M655
Bloch, Alan.	
Men Are Different	A835 . C830 C835
Bloch, Robert.	
Crime Machine	G170
Daybroke	P765
The Fear Planet	D430
The Hell-Bound Train	A840
I Do Not Love Thee, Doctor Fell	B595
Nightmare Number Four	K850
One Way to Mars	M940
The Strange Flight of Richard Clayton	M935
A Way of Life	F215
Word of Honor	P720
Block, Lawrence.	
Make a Prison	M615
Boardman, Tom V.	
Connoisseur's Science Fiction [Editor]	B670
Bolsover, John.	
Jackson Wong's Story	O140
Bond, Nelson S.	
The Abduction of Abner Green	B880
And Lo! The Bird	D430
Conqueror's Isle	G225 P910
The Day We Celebrate	C795
Magic City	B775
Pilgrimage	R820
This Is the Land	D435 D440
Bone, J.F.	
Insidekick	C750 G165
On the Fourth Planet	M635
A Prize for Edie	M625
Triggerman	A560 L885 M610
Borges, Jorge Luis.	
The Circular Ruins	M645
Borgese, Elisabeth Mann.	
True Self	G165

AUTHOR–TITLE		ANTHOLOGY
Borgese, Elisabeth Mann [Cont'd]		
Twin's Wail		P765
Boucher, Anthony [Pseud. of W.A.P. White]		
The Ambassadors	A835	C965
The Anomaly of the Empty Man		S420
Balaam	C945	H440
Barrier	A525	C850
Before the Curtain [Preface to Anthology]		B750
The Best from Fantasy and Science Fiction [Editor]		M190
First – Eighth Series	M195 . M200	M205
	M210 . M215 . M220	M225
Books		M635
The Chronokinesis of Jonathan Hull		C530
The Compleat Werewolf		M575
Conquest		P775
Gandolphus		M270
The Ghost of Me		M580
The Greatest Tertian		C780
Introduction [to New Tales of Space and Time]		H435
Nellthu	K710	M210
Nine-Finger Jack		B575
The Other Inauguration		C825
Public Eye		D310
Q.U.R.		H430
The Quest for Saint Aquin	C950 . H435	M655
Science Fiction Still Leads Science Fact		M605
Sherlock Holmes and Science Fiction		S920
Snulbug		M200
The Star Dummy		C785
Starbride		S645
Transfer Point		C960
A Treasury of Great Science Fiction v. 1		B750
A Treasury of Great Science Fiction v. 2		B755
Bova, Ben.		
Fifteen Mules		H320
Where Is Everybody?		M635
Bowen, Elizabeth.		
The Cherry Soul		M195

AUTHOR–TITLE	ANTHOLOGY
Boyd, Felix.	
The Robot Who Wanted to Know	F215
Boyd, Lyle, and William C. Boyd.	
Chain Reaction [See Also Boyd Ellanby, pseud.]	P760
Boy's Life [Periodical]	
The Boy's Life Book of Outer Space Stories	B970
Brackett, Leigh.	
All the Colors of the Rainbow	D320 F220
Enchantress of Venus	M330
The Moon That Vanished	W885
The Other People	B605
Retreat to the Stars	C960
Terror Out of Space	W875
Bradbury, Ray.	
All Summer in a Day	A865 B825 B840 M205
Almost the End of the World	B800 B815
And So Died Riabouchinska	B815
And the Moon Be Still as Bright	B820
And the Rock Cried Out	B800
And the Sailor, Home from the Sea	B815
The Anthem Sprinters	B815
The April Witch	B805 B840
Asleep in Armageddon	C795
The Beggar on the O'Connell Bridge	B815
The Best of All Possible Worlds	B815
The Big Black and White Game	B805 B840
The Black Ferris	K710
Boys! Raise Giant Mushrooms in _Your_ Cellar!	B815
Changelling	N785
Chrysalis	B835
The City	B810
Come into My Cellar	B835 C845 G170
The Concrete Mixer	B810
Dark They Were, and Golden-Eyed	B800 B825 B835 B840
The Day It Rained Forever	B800 B825 B840
Death and the Maiden	B815
Doodad	M940

AUTHOR–TITLE	ANTHOLOGY			
Bradbury, Ray [Cont'd]				
The Dragon	B800	B825	B830	B840
The Drummer Boy of Shiloh				B815
Dwellers in Silence				B565
The Earth Men				B820
El Dia de Muerte				B815
Embroidery			B805	B840
En la Noche			B805	B840
The End of the Beginning		B800	B825	B830
			B840	K850
The Exiles		B810	B830	D425
Fever Dream		B800	B825	B840
The Fire Balloons			B810	C930
The First Night of Lent			B825	B840
A Flight of Ravens				B815
The Flying Machine		B805	B835	B840
The Fog Horn		B805	B830	B840
Forever and the Earth				C760
The Fox and the Forest			B570	B810
Frost and Fire				B830
The Fruit at the Bottom of the Bowl			B805	B840
The Garbage Collector			B805	B840
The Gift	B800	B825	B830	B840
The Golden Apples of the Sun		B805	B830	B840
The Golden Kite, the Silver Wind			B805	B840
The Great Collision of Monday Last			B825	B840
The Great Fire			B805	B840
The Great Wide World Over There			B805	B840
The Green Morning				B820
Hail and Farewell		B805	B835	B840
The Headpiece		B800	B825	B840
Here There Be Tygers		B800	B830	H435
The Highway				B810
Holiday				D430
I See You Never			B805	B840
Icarus Montgolfier Wright		B800	B825	B835
			B840	M215

AUTHOR–TITLE				ANTHOLOGY
Bradbury, Ray [Cont'd]				
The Illustrated Man				B810
The Illustrated Woman				B815
In a Season of Calm Weather			A360	B800
			B825	B840
In This Sign				L640
Interim				B820
Invisible Boy	B805	B835	B840	D245
Kaleidoscope		B810	C775	C785
King of the Grey Spaces			C815	W465
The Last Night of the World				B810
The Lifework of Juan Diaz				B815
A Little Journey				G140
The Little Mice		B800	B825	B840
The Locusts				B820
The Long Rain			B810	B830
The Long Years				B820
The Luggage Store				B820
The Machineries of Joy				B815
The Man	B565	B810	B835	B970
Marionettes, Inc.				B810
The Marriage-Mender		B800	B825	B840
Mars Is Heaven!				K730
The Martian				B820
The Meadow			B805	B840
A Medicine for Melancholy			B825	B840
The Million-Year Picnic	B820	B835	K690	P910
A Miracle of Rare Device		B815	M630	M655
The Murderer			B805	B840
The Musicians				B820
The Naming of Names		B820	F700	S795
Night Meeting			B820	C800
No Particular Night or Morning				B810
The Off Season				B820
The Old Ones				B820
One Who Waits			B815	D430
The Other Foot			B810	D320
The Other Foot	B575	B805	B835	B840

AUTHOR–TITLE	ANTHOLOGY
Bradbury, Ray [Cont'd]	
The Pedestrian	B840
Perchance to Dream	B800
Perhaps We Are Going Away	B815
Pillar of Fire	B750 B835
The Playground	D440
Powerhouse	B805 B840
Punishment Without Crime	C825
R Is for Rocket	B830
Referent	B645 B800
The Rocket	B810 B830
The Rocket Man	B810 B830
Rocket Summer	B820
S Is for Space	B835
A Scent of Sarsaparilla	B800 B825 B840 S645 P770
The Screaming Woman	B835
A Serious Search for Weird Worlds	M620
The Settlers	B820
The Shape of Things	G830
The Shore	B820
The Shoreline at Sunset	B825 B840 M615
The Silent Towns	B820
The Small Assassin	T290
The Smile	B800 B825 B835 B840 D455
Some Live Like Lazarus	B815
The Sound of Summer Running	B830
A Sound of Thunder	B805 B830 B840 C310
The Strawberry Window	B800 B825 B830 B840 P780
Subterfuge	P750
The Summer Night	B820
Sun and Shadow	B805 B840
The Sunset Harp	B800
The Taxpayer	B820
There Will Come Soft Rains	B820 B890 C410 C960
The Third Expedition	B820
Time in Thy Flight	B835

AUTHOR–TITLE			ANTHOLOGY
Bradbury, Ray [Cont'd]			
The Time Machine			B830
The Time of Going Away	B800	B825	B840
To the Chicago Abyss			B815
The Town Where No One Got Off	B800	B825	B840
The Trolley			B835
Twice Twenty-Two [Anthology]			B840
Tyrannosaurus Rex			B815
Uncle Einar			B830
Usher II			B820
The Vacation		B815	P720
The Veldt	B810	D655 J330	M580
Vignettes of Tomorrow			D430
The Visitor			B810
Wake for the Living			M935
The Watchers			B820
Way in the Middle of the Air		B820	D320
The Wilderness	B805	B840	S645
The Wonderful Ice-Cream Suit	B800	B825	B840
Ylla		B820	D435
Zero Hour	B810	B835	C935
Bradley, Marion Zimmer.			
The Wind People			K700
Brand, Jonathan.			
Long Day in Court			I230
Bretnor, R.			
All The Tea in China			M625
The Doorstep			M600
Genius of the Species			H440
The Gnurrs Come from the Voodvork Out			B570
Gratitude Guaranteed			D440
Little Anton			H435
The Man on Top			M620
Maybe Just a Little One			M200
Mrs. Pigafetta Swims Well			M635
Mrs. Poppledore's Id			C820
The Past and Its Dead People			D310

AUTHOR–TITLE	ANTHOLOGY
Breuer, Miles J., M.D.	
The Appendix and the Spectacles	C815
A Baby on Neptune [C.W. Harris]	W870
The Gostak and the Doshes	C800 C810
The Hungry Guinea Pig	C805
Man with the Strange Head	C760
Man without an Appetite	C770
Briarton, Grendel.	
Through Time and Space with Ferdinand Feghoot	M225
Brode, Anthony.	
The Better Bet	M225
The Watchers	M225
Broderick, Damien.	
The Sea's Furthest End	N530
Broughton, Rhoda.	
Behold It Was a Dream	M580
Brown, Bill.	
Medicine Dancer	M580
The Star Ducks	B570
Brown, Fredric.	
Abominable	M620
All Good BEMS	B885
The Angelic Angleworm	B875
Angels and Spaceships	B875
Answer	B875 C940
Arena	C760 C825
Armageddon	B875
Come and Go Mad	B885
Crisis, 1999	B885 D310
Daisies	B875
Dark Interlude [Mack Reynolds]	B575 D320 G140
Daymare	B885
Double Standard	M635
Earthmen Bearing Gifts	G170
Etaoin Shrdlu	B875 P910
Expedition	M220
Gateway to Darkness	M330
Hall of Mirrors	P750
The Hat Trick	B875
Honeymoon in Hell	D590 G140

AUTHOR–TITLE	ANTHOLOGY
Brown, Fredric [Cont'd]	
Imagine: a Poem	M210
Immortality	C410
Keep Out	C805
Knock	B885
The Last Martian	B570 G140
Letter to a Phoenix	B875 G815
Mouse	B565
Nightmare in Time	M625
Nothing Sirius	B885
Paradox Lost	B880
Pattern	B875
Pi in the Sky	B885
Placet Is a Crazy Place	B875 C935 G830 W720
Politeness	B875
Preposterous	B875
Puppet Show	M630 P720
Reconciliation	B875
Rustle of Wings	D440
Science Fiction Carnival [Editor]	B880
Search	B875
Sentence	B875
Solipsist	B875
Something Green	B885 M925
Space on My Hands	B885
Star Mouse	B885 H430
Too Far	M210
The Weapon	A835 C310 C785
The Waveries	B670 B875 C780
The Yehudi Principle	B875
Brown, J.G.	
From Frankenstein to Andromeda [Editor]	B890
Brown, Rosel George.	
David's Daddy	M620
Flower Arrangement	G165
Browning, John S.	
Buring Bright	G825
Brownlow, Catherine.	
Voice from the Gallery	O140
Brunner, John.	
Badman	B895 W740

AUTHOR–TITLE		ANTHOLOGY
Brunner, John [Cont'd]		
A Better Mousetrap		I230
Coincidence Day		A555
Elected Silence		B895
Fair		B895
The Iron Jackass		B895
The Last Lonely Man	M640	W890
No Future in It		B895
Out of Order		B895
Protect Me from My Friends		B895
Puzzle for Spacemen		B895
Report on the Nature of the Lunar Surface		B890
	B895	M620
Stimulus	B895	W745
Such Stuff	A525	M630
Wasted on the Young		G180
The Windows of Heaven		B895
Brunner, K. Houston.		
Thou Good and Faithful		N880
Brust, John C.M.		
The Red White and Blue Rum Collins		C410
Buchan, John.		
Space		D425
Buchwald, A.		
Mars Is Ours!		M645
Buck, Doris Pitkin.		
Epithalamium		M225
From Two Universes [Poem]		M260
Mickey Finn [Poem]		M265
Budrys, Algis.		
And Then She Found Him		F220
Chain Reaction		C885
The Congruent People		P775
The Edge of the Sea	K730	M605
The Executioner		A510
For Love		G170
The Frightened Tree		P750
Lower Than Angels		S585

AUTHOR–TITLE		ANTHOLOGY
Budrys, Algis [Cont'd]		
Man in the Sky		D575
The Man Who Always Knew		B595
Nightsound		B605
Nobody Bothers Gus		M595
Riya's Foundling		M585
Silent Brother		M600
Wall of Crystal, Eye of Night		G185
Bulfinch, Thomas.		
Daedalus		L885
Bulichev, Kirill.		
Life Is so Dull for Little Girls		M277
Bulmer, Kenneth.		
The Adjusted		M265
Bunch, David R.		
Investigating the Bidwell Endeavors		M645
Training Talk		M640
Burks, Arthur J.		
Escape into Yesterday		F700
Burroughs, Edgar Rice.		
At the Earth's Core		B970
Beyond the Farthest Star		B990
The Chessmen of Mars		B995
A Fighting Man of Mars		B985
The Land That Time Forgot		B975
Lost on Venus		B980
A Martian Glossary		B995
The Master Mind of Mars		B995
The Moon Maid		B975
Pellucidar		B970
The Pirates of Venus		B980
A Princess of Mars		B985
The Resurrection of Jimber-Jaw	B990	M930
Skeleton Men of Jupiter		M940
Tales of Three Planets		B990
Tanar of Pellucidar		B970
Three Martian Novels		B995
Thuvia, Maid of Mars		B995

AUTHOR–TITLE **ANTHOLOGY**

Burroughs, Edgar Rice [Cont'd]
  The Wizard of Venus B990
Butler, Bill.
  Letter to a Tyrant King [Poem] M265
Byram, George.
  The Wonder Horse. M605
Byrne, Johnny.
  Yesterday's Gardens. M645
Campanella, Giovanni Domenico.
  City of the Sun. D425
Campbell, J. Ramsey.
  The Cellars D450
Campbell, John W.
  Analog Science Fact and Science Fiction I-5 A535
    [Editor] A540 A545 A550 A555
  The Astounding Science Fiction Anthology [Editor] A875
  The Idealists H440
  Night. M935
  Prologue to Analog [Editor] A560
  "Scientists Are Stupid!" A555
  "What Do You Mean...Human?" M615
Cantine, Holley.
  Double, Double, Toil and Trouble . . M235 M620
Capek, Karel.
  The Absolute at Large K695
  R.U.R. [Rossum's Universal Robots] . . C830 K950
  System [Josef Capek] M930
Capote, Truman.
  Miriam T290
Caravan, T.P.
  The Court of Tartary. M255
  Random Sample A835
Carlson, Esther.
  Museum Piece P910
Carmel, Carl.
  The Year after Tomorrow [Jt. Ed. L. Del Rey]. D360
Carnell, John.
  Gateway to the Stars [Editor] C290

AUTHOR–TITLE — **ANTHOLOGY**

Carnell, John [Cont'd]
  Gateway to Tomorrow [Editor] C295
  New Writings in SF 1-9 [Editor] N530 . N535 N540
    N545 N550 N555 N560 . N565 N570
  No Place Like Earth. C305
Carr, John D.
  Introduction [to The Poison Belt] D755
Carr, Robert Spencer.
  Easter Eggs. B565
Carr, Terry.
  Hop-Friend M245
  Science Fiction for People Who Hate Science
    Fiction [Editor] C310
  Touchstone M255
  World's Best SF: 1965-67 [Editor] W890 . W895 W900
Carter, Paul A.
  The Man Who Rode the Trains. D450
  An Ounce of Prevention D430
Cartier, Edd, Illustrator.
  Travelers of Space G830
Cartmill, Cleve.
  The Green Cat D435
  Huge Beast M190
  The Link. H430
  Number Nine L530
  Oscar. A835
  Overthrow G815
  You Can't Say That H435
Cartur, Peter.
  The Mist A835 C800
Cassill, R.V.
  The War in the Air M655
Causey, James.
  The Felony B590
  The Show Must Go On. N785
  Teething Ring A835 G145
Cawood, Hap.
  Synchromocracy. M640

AUTHOR–TITLE **ANTHOLOGY**

Cerf, Christopher.
  The Vintage Anthology of Science Fantasy [Editor] C410
Chambers, Robert W.
  The Demoiselle D'Ys M920
Chandler, A. Bertram
  See also George Whitley, pseud.
  The Cage M220
  Castaway C800
  Fall of Knight F215
  False Dawn G815
  A Finishing Touch C295
  Giant Killer P910
  The Left-Hand Way H320
Chatrian, Alexandre.
  Hans Schnap's Spy Glass [Emile Erckmann] . . M940
Choron, Jacques.
  Epilogue [to The Weigher of Souls] M455
Christie, Agatha.
  The Last Seance. M580
Christopher, John [Pseud. of C.S. Youd]
  Balance B575 C305
  Colonial W740
  Conspiracy C290
  The Drop C295
  A Few Kindred Spirits M265
  Man of Destiny G140 L640
  The New Wine C930
  Socrates M575 S645
Ciardi, John.
  Love Letter from Mars [Poem]. M260
  A Magus M645
Clark, Walter Van Tilburg.
  The Portable Phonograph C960
Clarke, Arthur Charles.
  Across the Sea of Stars. C590
  All That Glitters C610 C620
  All the Time in the World C610 C620
  An Ape About the House C635

AUTHOR–TITLE	ANTHOLOGY
Clarke, Arthur Charles [Cont'd]	
Armaments Race	C590 C600
An Arthur C. Clarke Omnibus	C595
At the End of the Orbit	P760
The Awakening	C625 C630
Before Eden	C615 C635 M915 M935
Big Game Hunt	C625
Breaking Strain	C305 C590
	C595 C600 C605 W720
The Call of the Stars	C610 C615 C620
Castaway	M940
Childhood's End	C590 C595 C600
The City and the Stars	C610
Cold War	C625
Cosmic Casanova	C610 C620
Critical Mass	C625
The Curse	B890 C615 C625 C630
Death and the Senator	C615 C635
The Deep Range	B890 C610
	C765 K690 P765 P780
Dial "F" for Frankenstein	P720
Dog Star	C615 C635
The Earth and the Overlords	C595
Earthlight	C590
Encounter at Dawn	C590 C595 C600 C615
Exile of the Eons	C605 C625
Expedition to Earth	C595 C605
Feathered Friend	C610 C620
The Fires Within	C590 C600 C630 C815 D455
The Forgotten Enemy	C625 C630 S645
Freedom of Space	C610 C620
From the Ocean, From the Stars	C610
The Golden Age	C595
Green Fingers	C610 C620
Hate	C635
The Haunted Space Suit	A835
Hide and Seek	C295 C590 C595
	C600 C605 C615 S640

AUTHOR–TITLE	ANTHOLOGY
Clarke, Arthur C. [Cont'd]	
History Lesson	C590 . C600 . C605 C785
I Remember Babylon	C615 . C635 . M620 P720
"If I Forget Thee, Oh Earth"	C590 C595 . C600 . C605 C615
Inheritance	C590 . C595 . C600 C605
Inside the Comet	W735
Into the Comet	C635
Jupiter Five	C590 . C600 C630
The Last Generation	C595
Let There Be Light	C635
Loophole	C595 . C605 C870
Maelstrom II	M645
The Man Who Ploughed the Sea	C625
Moving Spirit	C625
Nemesis	C595
The Next Tenants	C590 C600
The Nine Billion Names of God	C610 C615 C620 . C935 . P770 . S645 W745
No Morning After	C610 . C615 . C620 D445
The Other Side of the Sky	B755 . C610 C620
The Other Tiger	D440
Out of the Cradle, Endlessly Orbiting	C635 C770
Out of the Sun	C610 C615 . C620 S585
The Pacifist	C590 . C600 F215
The Parasite	C625 C630
Passer-By	C610 C620
Patent Pending	C410 C615
The Possessed	C615 . C625 C630
Prelude to Mars	C625
Prelude to Space	C595 C625
Publicity Campaign	C610 C620
A Question of Residence	C610 C620
Reach for Tomorrow	C630
Refugee	C610 C620
The Reluctant Orchid	C590 . C600 C615
Rescue Party	C590 C600 C615 C630 C870 W860

AUTHOR–TITLE	ANTHOLOGY
Clarke, Arthur C. [Cont'd]	
The Road to the Sea	C635
Robin Hood, F.R.S.	C610 C620
The Sands of Mars	C625
Saturn Rising	C635
Second Dawn	C595 C605 C625
Security Check	C610 C620
Seeker of the Sphinx	Y395
The Sentinel	A520 C590 C595 C600 C605 C615 K730
The Shining Ones	M640
Silence, Please	C590 C600
A Slight Case of Sunstroke	C635
The Songs of Distant Earth	C610 C620
Special Delivery	C610 C620
The Star	A840 C310 C610 C615 C620 C950 D655 K700
Starting Line	C610 C620
Summertime on Icarus	C615 C635 C810
Sunjammer	W895
Superiority	C590 C595 C600 C605 C615 D455
Take a Deep Breath	C610 C620 C640
Tales of Ten Worlds	C635
Technical Error	C590 C600 C630
Thirty Seconds–Thirty Days	S795
This Earth of Majesty	M210
Time Probe [Editor]	C640
Time's Arrow	C590 C600 C630
Transcience	C610 C615 C620 L640
Transition–From Fantasy to Science	M605
Trouble with the Natives	C625 C630
Trouble with Time	C615 C635
The Ultimate Melody	C625
Venture to the Moon	C610 C620 M220
A Walk in the Dark	C615 C625 C630 C775 C795
The Wall of Darkness	C610 C615 C620 M920
Watch This Space	C610 C620

AUTHOR–TITLE			ANTHOLOGY
Clarke, Arthur C. [Cont'd]			
What Goes Up			C625
Who's There?.	C615	C635	W730
Claudy, Carl H.			
The Land of No Shadow			D360
The Master Minds of Mars			D360
Tongue of Beast			D360
Cleeve, Brian.			
Angela's Satyr			M630
Clement, Hal.			
Answer			C830
Attitude			G830
Cold Front			G820
Critical Factor			P775
Hot Planet	A525	G175	M635
Proof			C795
Clifton, Mark.			
Civilized [Alex Apostolides]			D440
Clerical Error			B595
The Conquerer		B580	C785
Crazy Joey [Alex Apostolides]			M580
Hang Head, Vandal!			M630
Sense from Thought Divide		A515	M595
Star Bright		A865	G145
What Have I Done?			M575
What Now, Little Man?			M615
What Thin Partitions [Alex Apostolides]			M920
A Woman's Place			G220
Clingerman, Mildred.			
Birds Can't Count		M210	M595
First Lesson			M270
The Last Prophet			M210
Letters from Laura			B755
Minister Without Portfolio		C780	S645
Mr. Sakrison's Halt			M215
Stair Trick		A835	M195
Stickeney and the Critic			D440

AUTHOR–TITLE	ANTHOLOGY	
Clingerman, Mildred [Cont'd]		
The Wild Wood		M220
The Word		D440
Clinton, Ed M., jr.		
The Small World of M-75		C805
Cloete, Stuart.		
The Blast		C850
Clough, Roy L., jr.		
Bait		N885
Coblentz, Stanton A.		
The Scarlet Lunes		F700
Sunward		W870
Cogswell, Theodore R.		
The Big Stink		D320
Blowup Blues		M620
Limiting Factor	C805	G150
Minimum Sentence		G145
Radiation Blues		M620
The Specter General		N890
The Wall Around the World		M580
You Know Willie		M605
Cole, Everett B.		
Exile	B590	D580
Colladay, Morrison.		
The Planetoid of Doom		C760
Collier, John.		
Evening Primrose		M655
Incident on a Lake		A360
Interpretation of a Dream		M580
The Invisible Dove Dancer of Strathpheen Island		D245
Man Overboard		M235
Meeting of Relations		M270
Rope Enough		M585
Conklin, Groff.		
Another Part of the Galaxy [Editor]		C750
Big Book of Science Fiction [Editor]		C760
Essay on Sturgeon		S935
Fifty Short Science Fiction Tales [Joint Editor]		A835

AUTHOR–TITLE **ANTHOLOGY**

Conklin, Groff [Cont'd]
  Giants Unleashed [Editor] C765
  Great Science Fiction about Doctors [Editor] . C770
  Great Science Fiction by Scientists [Editor] . C810
  Great Stories of Space Travel [Editor] C775
  Introduction [to Human and Other Beings] . . D320
  Invaders of Earth [Editor] D780
  Omnibus of Science Fiction [Editor]. C785
  Operation Future [Editor] C790
  Possible Worlds of Science Fiction [Editor]. . C795
  Science-Fiction Adventures in Dimension [Editor] C800
  Science-Fiction Adventures in Mutation [Editor] C805
  Science Fiction by Scientists[Editor]. C810
  The Science Fiction Galaxy [Editor]. C815
  Science Fiction Oddities [Editor] C820
  Science Fiction Terror Tales [Editor] C825
  Science Fiction Thinking Machines [Editor]. . C830
  Selections from Science Fiction Thinking Machines [Editor] C835
  Seven Come Infinity. C840
  Seven Trips Through Time and Space [Editor] . C843
  17x Infinity[Editor] C845
  Six Great Short Novels of Science Fiction [Editor] C850
  Six Great Short Science Fiction Novels [Editor] C855
  A Treasury of Science Fiction [Editor]. . . . C870
  A Way Home [Compiler] S950
Conquest, Robert.
  Spectrum I-V [Joint Editor] A510
  A515. A520 . A525 A530
Cooper, Ralph S.
  The Neutrino Bomb C810
Coppard, A.E.
  Adam and Eve and Pinch Me T290
Coppel, Alfred.
  The Dreamer B580
  The Exile S645
  Last Night of Summer W860
  What Goes Up F700

AUTHOR–TITLE ANTHOLOGY

Correy, Lee [Pseud. of G. Harry Stine]
"And a Star to Steer By" D575
The Council of Four.
See The Science Fictional Sherlock Holmes.
Counselman, Mary Elizabeth.
A Handful of Silver D450
Coupling, J.J.
Mr. Kincaid's Pasts M580
Courtney, Robert.
A Rover I Will Be D575
Cowie, George R.
Demobilization F700
Cox, Arthur J.
The Blight D445
Cox, Irving, jr.
Hole in the Sky D445
Like Gods They Came S640
Crane, Robert.
The Purple Fields P775
Crispin, Edmund [Pseud. of R.B. Montgomery]
Best Science Fiction Stories I-5 [Editor] . . . C930
C935 C940 C945 C950
Crossen, Kendell F.
Adventures in Tomorrow C960
Assignment to Alderbaran Y405
The Closed Door N885
Future Tense C965
Houyhnhnms and Company [Introduction] . . . C960
Restricted Clientele C960
Things of Distinction C965
Tomorrow Is Here to Stay [Introduction] . . . C965
Cummings, Ray.
The Girl in the Golden Atom M330
The Gravity Professor W865
Curtis, Betsy.
A Peculiar People. B575
Cuthbert, Chester D.
The Sublime Vigil M920

AUTHOR–TITLE **ANTHOLOGY**

Dahl, Roald.
The Great Automatic Grammatisator C410
In the Ruins M645
Daley, John Bernard.
The Man Who Liked Lions M600
Dance, Clifton, jr., M.D.
The Brothers C770
Danzig, Allan.
The Great Nebraska Sea A525 M635
Davenport, Basil.
Invisible Men [Editor] D245
To the End of Time [Compiler] S790
The Vision of Olaf Stapledon S790
Davidson, Avram.
Apres Nous M235
The Best from Fantasy...12th Series [Editor] . M245
The Best from Fantasy...13th Series [Editor] . M250
The Best from Fantasy...14th Series [Editor] . M255
The Bounty Hunter F215
Bumberboom W900
The Certificate M270
Dagon M230
The Golem . . . . J330 . K710 . M210 M595
The Grantha Sighting M225
Help! I Am Dr. Morris Goldpepper G150
The House the Blakeneys Built M260
King's Evil M215
Love Called This Thing [L. Goforth] . . C310 G165
Mr. Stillwell's Stage M220
My Boy Friend's Name Is Jello M205
No Fire Burns M615
Now Let Us Sleep . . . . F220 . M605 M655
Or All the Seas with Oysters A840 C410 . G155 M610
Or the Grasses Grow D310 K850
The Singular Events Which Occurred in the
Hovel on the Alley off of Eye Street M245
Sacheverell M255
The Sensible Man P720

AUTHOR–TITLE		ANTHOLOGY
Davidson, Avram [Cont'd]		
The Sources of the Nile		M240
The Tail-Tied Kings		G170
Take Wooden Indians		G160
The Teeth of Dispair [Sidney Klein]		C820
What Strange Stars and Skies		M250
Davis, Chan.		
Last Year's Grave Undug		C810
Letter to Ellen	C830	C835
Davis, Chandler.		
Adrift on the Policy Level		P760
Davis, Dorothy Salisbury.		
The Muted Horn.		F215
De Bergerac, Cyrano [i.e. Rostand, E.]		
Voyage to the Moon.		M930
De Camp, Lyon Sprague.		
The Animal-Cracker Plot.		D290
Aristotle and the Gun		D300
The Black Ball		M195
The Blue Giraffe	H430	P910
The Command.	M915	M935
Conan the Adventurer [R.E. Howard]		H857
Conan the Warrior [R.E. Howard]		H859
The Continent Makers, and Other Tales		D290
Cornzan the Mighty		D300
The Egg		D300
Employment		B645
The Exalted		A875
Finished		D290
The Galton Whistle		D290
Gavagan's Bar		M190
Git Along!	D290	D435
The Gnarly Man		M585
Gratitude		D300
The Guided Man		D300
A Gun for Dinosaur	D300	G220
Hyperpilosity		C785
Impractical Joke		D300

AUTHOR–TITLE		ANTHOLOGY
De Camp, Lyon Sprague [Cont'd]		
In-Group		D300
The Inspector's Teeth		D290
Internal Combustion		D300
Judgment Day	B595	D300
Lament by a Maker		M210
Language for Time Travelers		G805
Let's Have Fun		D300
New Arcadia		D300
Perpetual Motion		D290
Summer Wear	B570	D290
Tales of Conan [R.E. Howard]		H860
A Thing of Custom	D300	F215
Throwback		D300
The Untimely Toper [F. Pratt]		M200
The Weissenbroch Spectacles [F. Pratt]		D245
De Courcy, Dorothy and John.		
Rat Race		C760
Dee, Roger.		
Problem on Balak		G145
Unwelcome Tenant	A835	M575
Defoe, Daniel.		
The Friendly Demon		M190
De Ford, Miriam Allen.		
The Eel		G160
Rope's End		D310
Space, Time and Crime		D310
Throwback		C965
De Graeff, Allen		
Human and Other Beings [Editor]		D320
De Graw, Pat.		
Memo to Secretary [Poem]		M265
Dell, Dudley [Pseud. of H.L. Gold]		
The Biography Project		G140
Del Rey, Lester.		
Alien		P780
And It Come Out Here	C800	S595
Day Is Done		C790

AUTHOR–TITLE	ANTHOLOGY
Del Rey, Lester [Cont'd]	
Dead Ringer	G150
For I Am a Jealous People!	P785
Helen O'Loy	J330 M575 M910 P750
Idealist	P770
Instinct	C785
Into Thy Hands	G825 L640
Introduction [to The Fantastic Universe Omnibus]	F215
Kindness	D360 M935
The Luck of Ignatz	D360 W875
The Monster	H505
Nerves	H430
Over the Top	A875
A Pound of Cure	P775
Psalm	M620
Return Engagement	G170
Seat of Judgment	F220
The Still Waters	W725
Though Dreamers Die	G825
To Avenge Man	G180
The Wings of Night	C760 C775
The Year afterTomorrow	D360
"The Years Draw Nigh"	D420
Deming, Richard.	
The Shape of Things That Came	B750
Derleth, August W.	
The Adventure of the Ball of Nostradamus [Mack Reynolds]	S420
The Adventure of the Snitch in Time [Mack Reynolds]	D310 S420
Beachheads in Space [Editor]	D420
Beyond Time and Space [Editor]	D425
Far Boundaries [Editor]	D430
McIlvaine's Star	D455
The Outer Reaches [Editor]	D435
Portals of Tomorrow [Editor]	D440
Time to Come [Editor]	D445
Travelers by Night [Editor]	D450

AUTHOR–TITLE			ANTHOLOGY
Derleth, August W. [Cont'd]			
"Who Shall I Say Is Calling?"			M585
Worlds of Tomorrow [Editor]			D455
Deutsch, A.J.			
A Subway Named Mobius		C785	C945
Deutsch, R.H.			
The Watchers.			F700
De Vet, Charles V.			
Special Feature			C840
Dewey, G. Gordon			
The Tooth			M195
Dick, Philip K.			
Expendable			K850
The Father-Thing		A865	B750
Foster, You're Dead			P780
The Golden Man			M580
If There Were No Benny Cemoli			G175
Impostor	C825	C935	W860
Jon's World			D445
Oh, to Be a Blobel!.			W890
Second Variety		A515	Y405
We Can Remember It for You Wholesale . . .			M265
		N365	W900
Dickens, Charles.			
The Rat That Could Speak			M190
Dickinson, Joseph.			
Three for the Stars.			M245
Dickson, Gordon R.			
The Adventure of the Misplaced Hound [Poul Anderson]		A565	S420
Ballad of the Shoshonu.			M620
Black Charlie			G160
Call Him Lord			N365
Computers Don't Argue		A555	N360
Don Jones [Poul Anderson]			A565
The Dreamsman			M615
Earthman's Burden [Poul Anderson]			A565
Half a Hoka-Poul Anderson			S420

AUTHOR–TITLE	ANTHOLOGY
Dickson, Gordon R. [Cont'd]	
The Haunted Village	M240
Hilifter	A545
Home from the Shore	M630
In Hoka Signo Vinces [Poul Anderson]	A565
Lulungomeena [Sic]	L640
Mysterious Message [Poul Anderson]	A565
Sleight of Wit	A535
Steel Brother	N890
Trespass [Poul Anderson]	B570
Warrior	M645
Yo Ho Hoka! [Poul Anderson]	A565
Dighton, Ralph.	
Sierra Sam	M615
Dikty, Thaddeus Eugene.	
The Best Science Fiction Stories: 1950–53 [Joint Editor]	B565 B570 B575 B580
The Best Science-Fiction Stories and Novels: 1955–1956. [Editor]	B590 B595
The Best Science-Fiction Stories and Novels, Ninth Series	B605
Earth's Natural Satellite	D590
Every Boy's Book of Outer Space Stories [Editor]	D575
Five Tales from Tomorrow	D580
Great Science Fiction Stories about Mars [Editor]	D585
Great Science Fiction Stories about the Moon [Editor]	D590
Imagination Unlimited [Joint Editor]	B645
The Red Planet	D585
The Science-Fiction Year [1955, 1956, 1958]	B590 B595 B605
The Year's Best Science Fiction Novels, 1952–1954	Y395 Y400 Y405
Disch, Thomas M.	
Descending	M640
5 Eggs	O640
Nada	M255
Now Is Forever	W890

AUTHOR–TITLE | ANTHOLOGY

Disch, Thomas M. [Cont'd]
The Roaches M645
Dnieprov, Anatoly.
The Heroic Feat M277
The Maxwell Equations M275
Siema P965
Doar, Graham.
Who Knows His Brother M585
Outer Limit C760
Doherty, G.D.
Second Orbit [Editor] D655
Donovan, Francis.
The Short Life C945
Dorman, Sonya.
Splice of Life O640
When I Was Miss Dow N365
Dos Passos, John.
Three Epologues and an Epilogue. M625
Doyle, Arthur Conan.
The Blurring of the Lines D755
The Dead World D755
A Diary of the Dying D755
The Disintegration Machine L885
The Great Awakening D755
The Great Keinplatz Experiment C770
The Los Amigos Fiasco M930
The Lost World [Selections] B890
The Maracot Deep K950
The Poison Belt. D755
The Professor Challenger Stories [Bibliography] D755
Submerged D755
The Tide of Death. D755
Drake, David.
Denkirch D450
Draper, Hal.
Ms Fnd in a Lbry [Sic] C845
Dressler, Daniel.
The White Army G225 W865
Driscoll, Dennis.
Going Up! M605

AUTHOR–TITLE	ANTHOLOGY
Drury, Allen.	
Something	M235
Du Bois, William Pene.	
The Poison Belt [Illustrator]	D755
Dudintsev, Vladimir.	
A New Year's Fairy Tale.	M275
Dunsany, Edward J., Lord.	
Misadventure	M205
Durrell, Lawrence.	
High Barbarry.	M625
Dutt, Violet L.	
Soviet Science Fiction [Translator]	D980
Dyalhis, Nietzin.	
When the Green Star Waned	D425
Dye, Charles.	
Syndrome Johnny	G140
Earl, Stephen.	
Walkabout	O140
Edmondson, G.C.	
The Galactic Calabash	C820
Rescue	M220
Edwards, Dolton.	
Meihem in Ce Klasrum [Sic]	A875
Edwards, Kelley.	
Counterspy.	C940
Eisenberg, Larry.	
The Pirokin Effect.	M640
Elam, Richard M.	
By Jupiter	E375
The Day the Flag Fell	E375
Expedition Pluto	E380
The First Men Into Space.	E380
Flight of the Centaurus	E380
The Ghost Ship of Space	E380
Hands Across the Deep	E375
The Iron Moon	E375
Lunar Trap	E375
Mercy Flight to Luna	E380
Mystery Eyes Over Earth	E380
The Peril from Outer Space	E380

AUTHOR–TITLE	ANTHOLOGY
Elam, Richard M. [Cont'd]	
Project Ocean Floor	E375
Race around the Sun	E380
Red Sands	E375
Sol's Little Brother	E375
Space Steward	E380
The Strange Men	E375
Teen-Age Science-Fiction Stories	E375
Teen-Ague Super Science Stories	E380
Venusway	E375
What Time Is It?	E375
Ellanby, Boyd [Pseud. of Lyle and William Boyd]	
Category Phoenix	Y400
Chain Reaction	P760
Ellern, W.B.	
Moon Prospector	D590
Elliot, John.	
A for Andromeda [Fred Hoyle]	B890
Elliott, Bruce.	
The Battle of the S...S	C965
The Devil Was Sick	C960
Fearsome Fable	M190
Elliott, Chandler.	
A Day on Death Highway	G175
Inanimate Objection	A510
Elliott, George P.	
Among the Dangs	M625
Faq'	M655
The Invasion of the Planet of Love	M230
The NRACP	D320
Sandra	B750
Elliott, Rose Bedrick.	
Baby Killers	C965
Ellis, H.F.	
The Space-Crime Continuum	C820
Ellison, Harlan.	
See also Hart, Ellis, Pseud.	
All the Sounds of Fear	M630
Back to the Drawing Boards	E460

AUTHOR–TITLE	ANTHOLOGY
Ellison, Harlan [Cont'd]	
Battle Without Banners	E460
Blind Lightning	S585
A Friend to Man	E460
From the Land of Fear	E460
In Lonely Lands	F215
Lufe Hutch	E460
My Brother Paulie	E460
Pretty Maggie Moneyeyes	H320
"Repent, Harlequin, Said the Ticktockman	G185 N360 W895
The Sky Is Burning	E460
Soldier [Originally, Soldier from Tomorrow]	E460
The Time of the Eye	E460
The Voice in the Garden	E460
We Mourn for Anyone	E460
Emmett, Elizabeth.	
Enchantment	M620
Emshwiller, Carol.	
Day at the Beach	M615
Hunting Machine	B605
Pelt	M610
Emtsov, M.	
The Mystery of Green Crossing [E. Parnov]	M277
Endore, Guy.	
Men of Iron	M270
Erckmann, Emile.	
Hans Schnap's Spy-Glass [A. Chatrian]	M940
Ernst, Paul.	
The Microscopic Giants	C825
"Nothing Happens on the Moon"	C785
Etchison, Dennis.	
The Country of the Strong	C303
The Fires of Night	N785
Odd Boy Out	C300
Evans, E.E.	
The Shed	S645

AUTHOR–TITLE ANTHOLOGY

AUTHOR–TITLE			ANTHOLOGY
Fenton, Frank.			
The Chicken or theEgghead			H440
Tolliver's Travels [Joseph Petracca]			H435
Ferman, Edward L.,			
The Best from Fantasy and Science Fiction, 15th and 16th Series [Editor]		M260	M265
Ferman, J.W.			
No Limits			F220
Fessier, Michael.			
The Fascinating Stranger			L530
Fink, David Harold, M.D.			
Compound B		C770	H440
Finney, Charles G.			
The Captivity			M240
Finney, Jack.			
Behind the News			F225
Contents ot the Dead Man's Pocket			F225
Cousin Len's Wonderful Adjective Cellar		A360	F225
A Dash of Spring			F225
Double Take			P720
The Face in the Photo			M630
I'm Scared		F225	H505
Of Missing Persons		F225	M595
The Other Wife			M615
Quit Zoomin' Those Hands Through the Air . .			B670
	C790	F225	L885
Second Chance			F225
Something in a Cloud			F225
Such Interesting Neighbors			F225
The Third Level	A835	F225	M195
Fischer, Michael.			
Misfit			M910
Fisher, Leonard Everett.			
The Weigher of Souls [Illustrator]			M455
Fitzgerald, F.S.			
The Curious Case of Benjamin Button			K950
Fitzpatrick, E.D.			
The Shadow Lay			O140

AUTHOR–TITLE				ANTHOLOGY
Fitzpatrick, E.M.				
Venus and the Rabbit				O140
Fitzpatrick, R.C.				
The Circuit Riders.			A540	M630
Fleher, Paul.				
The Hated.				G155
We Never Mention Aunt Nora				G160
Fontenay, Charles L.				
The Silk and the Song				M215
Ford, Garret.				
Science and Sorcery [Compiler].				F700
Forster, E.M.				
The Machine Stops . . .	C815.	C845	.K705	K950
The Story of a Panic.				T290
Free, Colin.				
The Weather in the Underworld				W890
Friborg, Albert Compton.				
Careless Love		B590	D580	M205
Push-Button Passion				D580
Friedberg, Gertrude.				
The Wayward Cravat				A865
Friedman, Bruce Jay.				
A Foot in the Door				P720
The Killer in the TV Set				P720
Friedman, Stuart.				
Beautiful, Beautiful, Beautiful! . . .			A835	D455
Friend, Oscar J.				
The Giant Anthology of Science Fiction [Editor]				M330
The Impossible Highway				L530
Frisch, O.R.				
On the Feasibility of Coal-Driven Power Stations				P760
Fritch, C.E.				
Geever's Flight				N785
Furnas, J.C.				
The Laocoon Complex				M580
Fyfe, H.B.				
Afterthought				M575
Bureau of Slick Tricks				G830

AUTHOR–TITLE	ANTHOLOGY
Fyfe, H.B. [Cont'd]	
Implode and Peddle	N890
In Value Deceived	C795 G225 S645
Locked Out	G820
Manners of the Age	C785
Moonwalk	K730 N880
Protected Species	A875
Ransom	M195
Star-Linked	N890
The Well-Oiled Machine	B880
Galaxy Science Fiction Magazine.	
Bodyguard and Four Other Short Novels	G190
The Eighth Galaxy Reader	G175
The Fifth Galaxy Reader	G160
Five Galaxy Short Novels	G195
The Fourth Galaxy Reader	G155
The Galaxy Reader of Science Fiction [First]	G140
Mind Partner and 8 Other Novelets	G200
The Ninth Galaxy Reader	G180
The Second Galaxy Reader	G145
The Seventh Galaxy Reader	G170
Six Fingers of Time	G210
The Sixth Galaxy Reader	G165
The Tenth Galaxy Reader	G185
The Third Galaxy Reader	G150
Time Waits for Winthrop and Four Other Novels	G215
The World That Couldn't Be and 8 Others	G220
Gallagher, John.	
Tree Trunks	M635
Gallant, Joseph.	
Stories of Scientific Imagination [Editor]	G225
Gallun, Raymond Z.	
Asteroid of Fear	N880
Derelict	M910
Old Faithful	B645
Operation Pumice	C795
Return of a Legend	N890
The Scarab	C830

AUTHOR–TITLE	ANTHOLOGY
Gallun, Raymond Z. [Cont'd]	
The Seeds of the Dusk	H430
Trail Blazer	N880
Galouye, Daniel F.	
The City of Force	G190
Sanctuary	M205
Sitting Duck	G210
Gamow, George.	
The Heart on the Other Side	P760
Gardner, Martin.	
The Island of Five Colors	C965
No-Sided Professor	C410 M190
Garrett, Randall.	
All about "The Thing"	M600
The Best Policy	S585
A Case of Identity	A550
Fighting Division	A555
Hot Argument	M615
Sound Decision [Robert Silverberg]	A560
Tin Lizzie	D585
Gary, Romain.	
Decadence	M640
Gault, William Campbell.	
Made to Measure	G140
Title Fight	F215
Geer, Charles H.	
Teen-Age Science Fiction Stories [Illustrator]	E375
Gehman, Richard.	
Hickory, Dickory, Kerouac	M610
Geier, Chester S.	
Environment	C785
Genberg, Mort	
IBM	M635
Gernsback, Hugo.	
Extra Sensory Perfection	M930
Gibson, Walter B.	
Rod Serling's The Twilight Zone [Adaptor]	S490

AUTHOR–TITLE				ANTHOLOGY
Gilbert, Robert Ernest.				
Footprints				F700
Gilien, Sasha.				
Two's a Crowd				M245
Gironella, Jose Maria.				
The Death of the Sea				C410
The Red Egg				M640
Godwin, Francis.				
The Man in the Moone.				D425
Godwin, Tom.				
The Cold Equations . . .	B590.	C940 .	D580	J330
The Last Victory.				B605
Mother of Invention				A530
You Created Us.				B595
Goforth, Laura.				
Love Called This Thing [Avram Davidson] . .				C310
Goggin, Richard.				
Frances Harkins				C845
Gold, H.L.				
See also Dudley Dell, pseud.				
Bodyguard and Four Other Short Novels [Editor]				G190
The Day They Got Boston				C845
The Enormous Room [Robert Krepps] . . .			W755	Y405
The Fifth Galaxy Reader [Editor]				G160
Five Galaxy Short Novels [Editor]				G195
The Fourth Galaxy Reader [Editor]				G155
How to Write Science Fiction.				G165
Love in the Dark				D245
Man of Parts				H440
The Man with English		C310	P765	P770
A Matter of Form			C760	P750
Mind Partner and 8 Other Novelets [Editor] .				G200
Perfect Murder				C800
Personnel Problem.				G165
The Second Galaxy Reader [Editor]				G145
The Sixth Galaxy Reader [Editor]				G 165
The Third Galaxy Reader [Editor]				G150
Trouble with Water				K710

AUTHOR–TITLE		ANTHOLOGY
Gold, H.L. [Cont'd]		
The World That Couldn't Be [Editor]		G220
Goldstone, Herbert.		
Virtuoso	C830	C835
Goodale, Earl.		
Success Story		G165
Gor, Gennady.		
A Dweller in Two Worlds		M277
Gordon, W.J.J.		
The Nobel Prize Winners		M635
Goulart, Ron.		
Badinage		N785
Calling Dr. Clockwork		W895
Experiment in Autobiography		M265
Into the Ship	A525	M255
Letters to the Editor		M195
McNamara's Fish		M250
A New Lo!		M225
Please Stand By.		M245
Rake		M260
Ralph Wollstonecraft Hedge: a Memoir		M230
The Recurrent Suitor		D310
Terminal		M645
Graves, Robert.		
The Shout		M195
Gray, Will H.		
The Bees from Borneo		C785
Green, Joseph.		
The Creators		C300
Haggard Honeymoon [James Webbert]		N530
Treasure Hunt		N550
Green, Robert M., jr.		
Apology to Inky		M265
Greenberg, Martin.		
All about the Future [Editor]		G800
Coming Attractions [Editor]		G805
Five Science Fiction Novels [Compiler]		G810
Journey to Infinity [Editor]		G815

AUTHOR–TITLE	ANTHOLOGY
Greenberg, Martin [Cont'd]	
Men Against the Stars [Editor]	G820
The Robot and the Man [Editor]	G825
Travelers of Space [Editor]	G830
Greene, Graham.	
The End of the Party	T290
Proof Positive	M270
Greer, William W.	
Quads from Vars	B970
Gregor, Lee, pseud.	
See also Milton A. Rothman.	
Heavy Planet	H430
Grendon, Edward.	
Crisis	C780
The Figure	A835
Trip One	C765 S640
Open Sesame	D430
The Song of the Pewee	D430
Gresham, W.L.	
The Star Gypsies	M200
Griffith, A.W.	
Captive Audience	M200
Griffith, Ann.	
Zeritsky's Law	C785
Grimm, Christopher.	
Bodyguard	G190
Grinnell, David.	
Extending the Holdings	B575
The Lysenko Maze	C805
Malice afore Thought	M580
The Rag Thing	A835 C785
Top Secret	C780
Gross, Marion.	
The Good Provider	A835 C800
Grove, Walt.	
John Grant's Little Angel	P720
Groves, J.W.	
Robots Don't Bleed	C305
Grow, Julian F.	
The Fastest Gun Dead	M625

AUTHOR–TITLE		ANTHOLOGY
Grunert, Karl.		
Enemies in Space		C780
Guin, Wyman.		
Beyond Bedlam	A515	G140
Trigger Tide		C785
Volpla		G150
Gunn, James E.		
The Cave of Night		M595
The Misogynist		G145
Wherever You May Be		G195
Gurevich, G.		
Infra Draconis	D980	W755
Guttridge, Len.		
Aunt Millicent at the Races		M260
Haggert, W.T.		
Lex		G165
Haldane, J.B.S.		
The Gold-Makers		C810
Hale, Edward Everett.		
The Brick Moon		M930
Hale, Robert Beverly		
Immediately Yours		M625
Hall, Donald.		
The Wonderful Dog Suit		M640
Hall, Steve.		
A Round Billiard Table		C300
Hallstead, William F. III		
Space Lane Cadet		B970
Hamilton, Edmond.		
The Conquest of Two Worlds		W865
The Dead Planet	D455	M925
Exile		L640
Fessenden's Worlds		D425
The Forgotten World		M330
In the World's Dusk		W860
Kaldar, World of Antares		W885
The Man Who Saw the Future		M940
The Pro		D590
Requiem		M935
Sunfire		R820

AUTHOR–TITLE ANTHOLOGY

Hamilton, Edmond [Cont'd]
What's It Like Out There? . . . C310 K700 S795
Harding, Lee.
The Liberators N550
Harmon, Jim.
Name Your Symptom G155
The Place Where Chicago Was G185
Harness, Charles L.
The Chessplayers C820
Child by Chronos M200
The New Reality B570
Harper, Richard.
The Samaritan B970
Harris, C.W.
A Baby on Neptune [M.J. Breuer] W870
Harris, John Beynon.
See also John Beynon, pseud.
See also John Wyndham, pseud.
The John Wyndham Omnibus W990
The Lost Machine R820
Never on Mars C290
Time to Rest D430
Harris, Larry M.
Mex F215
Harrison, Harry.
Best SF: 1967 [Brian W. Aldiss] H320
Captain Honario Harpplayer, R.N. M250
Final Encounter. G175
How the Old World Died. G180
Nebula Award Stories: Two [Joint Editor] . . N365
Portrait of the Artist B665
The Toy Shop. M630
Trainee for Mars D655
The Velvet Glove F215
Hart, Ellis, pseud of Harlan Ellison.
Mourners for Hire E460
Harvey, Frank.
The Death Dust S250

AUTHOR–TITLE		ANTHOLOGY
Hasse, Henry.		
The Eyes		F700
He Who Shrank		H430
Hatcher, Jack.		
Fuel for the Future		G805
Hawkins, Peter.		
Circus		C290
Life Cycle		C295
Hawkins, William.		
The Dwindling Sphere		J330
Hawthorne, Nathaniel.		
The Birthmark		L885
Rappaccini's Daughter	C770	M940
Healy, Raymond J.		
Adventures in Time and Space [J.F. McComas]		H430
Famous Science Fiction Stories [J.F. McComas]		H430
The Great Devon Mystery		H440
New Tales of Space and Time [Editor]		H435
Nine Tales of Space and Time [Editor]		H440
Heard, Gerald.		
B M—Planet 4		H435
Heard, Henry Fitz-Gerald.		
The Collector		M190
Cyclops		C965
The Great Fog		C870
Wingless Victory		D425
Heinlein, Robert A.		
"All You Zombies—"	M230	M655
And He Built a Crooked House		C640
Assignment in Eternity		H470
The Black Pits of Luna	C795 G225 H475	H490
Blowups Happen	A875 C935	H490
By His Bootstraps	A510 H485	M330
Columbus Was a Dope	A835	H485
Coventry	C850 H490	K690
Delilah and the Space-Rigger	H475	H490
Elsewhen		H470
Gentlemen, Be Seated	H475	H490

AUTHOR–TITLE				ANTHOLOGY
Heinlein, Robert A. [Cont'd]				
Goldfish Bowl				H485
The Green Hills of Earth		H475	H490	S250
Gulf			H470	K695
"If This Goes On—"				H490
Introduction [to All about the Future]				G800
Introduction [to The Best from Startling Stories]				S795
It's Great to Be Back	C870	H475	H490	K705
Jerry Was a Man				H470
"Let There Be Light"				H480
Life Line				H490
Logic of Empire			H475	H490
The Long Watch		D425	H475	H490
Lost Legacy				H470
Magic, Inc.			H500	H510
The Man Who Sold the Moon		B755	H480	H490
The Menace from Earth		A865	H485	H490
Methuselah's Children				H490
Misfit			C765	H490
Ordeal in Space	H475	H490	K730	W750
Our Fair City				M575
The Past Through Tomorrow				H490
Project Nightmare				H485
The Puppet Masters				H500
Requiem	H430	H480	H490	J330
The Roads Must Roal	H430	H480	H490	L885
Searchlight				H490
Sky Lift			H485	K700
Space Jockey			H475	H490
They		C825	K710	P910
Three by Heinlein				H500
Tomorrow the Stars				H505
Waldo		B750	H500	H510
Water Is for Washing				H485
"We also Walk Dogs"		H475	H490	M935
The Year of the Jackpot	C310	G145	H485	W860
Henderson, Gene L.				
Tiger by the Tail				B970

AUTHOR–TITLE	ANTHOLOGY
Henderson, Zenna.	
And a Little Child	H515
Angels Unawares	H520
The Anything Box	H515 H600
Ararat	B580 W730
Captivity	M225 W755
Come on, Wagon!	H515 M195
Deluge	H520 M250
Food to All Flesh	C940 H515
Gilead	A865
The Grunder	H515
Hush!	H515
Jordan	M270
The Last Step	H515
No Different Flesh	H520 M260
The People: No Different Flesh	H520
Pottage	M210 M595
Return	H520
Shadow on the Moon	H520
Something Bright	G170 H515 M620
Stevie and the Dark	H515
Subcommittee	H515 M630
The Substitute	H515
Things	H515
Troubling of the Water	H520
Turn the Page	H515
Walking Aunt Daid	H515
Wilderness	M605
Henneberg, Charles.	
The Blind Pilot	M235
Henry, O. [Pseud of W.S. Porter]	
Roads of Destiny	P910
Herbert, Frank.	
A-W-F Unlimited	C845
Cease Fire	K700
The Mary Celeste Move	A550
Nightmare Blues	B590
The Primitives	G185

AUTHOR–TITLE	ANTHOLOGY
Household, Geoffrey.	
The Lost Continent	S250
Houston, James D.	
Gas Mask	M640
Howard, Ivan.	
Escape to Earth [Editor]	H850
Howard, Robert E.	
Beyond the Black River [L.S. De Camp] . . .	H859
The Black Stone	H865
The Blood-Stained God	H860
The Cairn on the Headland	H865
The Coming of Conan	H855
Conan the Adventurer [L.S. De Camp] . . .	H857
Conan the Warrior [L.S. De Camp]	H859
Drums of Tombalku [L.S. De Camp]	H857
The Fire of Asshurbanipal	H865
The Flame Knife	H860
The Frost-Giant's Daughter.	H855
The God in the Bowl.	H855
Hawks over Shem	H860
The Horror from the Mound	H865
The House of Arabu	H865
The Hyborian Age.	H855
An Informal Biography of Conan the Cimmerian	H855
Jewels of Gwahlur [L.S. De Camp]	H859
The King and the Oak	H855
Letter to P. Schuyler Miller	H855
The Mirrors of Tuzun Thune	H855
The People of the Black Circle [L.S. De Camp]	H857
The Pool of the Black One [L.S. De Camp]. .	H857
Queen of the Black Coast	H855
Red Nails [L.S. De Camp].	H859
The Road of the Eagles	H860
Rogues in the House	H855
The Shadow Kingdom	H855
The Slithering Shadow [L.S. De Camp] . . .	H857
Tales of Conan [L.S. De Camp].	H860
The Tower of the Elephant	H855

AUTHOR–TITLE		ANTHOLOGY
Howard, Robert E. [Cont'd]		
The Valley of the Worm		H865
Wolfshead		H865
Hoyle, Fred.		
A for Andromeda [Selections] [John Elliot]		B890
Agent 38		H870
The Ax		H870
The Black Cloud	B890	P760
Blackmail	H320	H870
Cattle Trucks		H870
Element 79		H870
The Judgment of Aphrodite		H870
A Jury of Five		H870
The Magnetosphere		H870
The Martians		H870
The Operation		H870
The Play's the Thing		H870
Pym Makes His Point		H870
Shortsighted		H870
Welcome to Slippage City		H870
Zoomen		H870
Hubbard, L. Ron.		
Tough Old Man		N885
When Shadows Fall		G820
Hubbard, P.M.		
Botany Bay		M210
The Golden Brick		M250
Manuscript Found in a Vacuum		M200
Hugi, Maurice A.		
Mechanical Mice		H430
Hull, E.M.		
Competition		G820
The Flight That Failed		C800
The Patient		C805
Hunter, Mel.		
The Year After Tomorrow [Illustrator]		D360
Hurlbut, Kaatje		
A Passage from the Stars		M625
Huxley, Aldous.		
Brave New World	K950	T290

AUTHOR–TITLE		ANTHOLOGY
James, E.R.		
Emergency Working		C295
Six-Fingered Jacks		W735
Jameson, Malcolm.		
Admiral's Inspection		J310
Blind Alley		L530
Blind Man's Buff	B645	D575
Blockade Runner		J310
Brimstone Bill		J310
Bullard of the Space Patrol		J310
Bullard Reflects	B755	J310
The Bureaucrat		J310
Hobo God		G800
Lillies of Life		C795
Pride		M575
The Sorcerer's Apprentice		C790
Space War Tactics		G805
Orders		J310
White Mutiny		J310
Janifer, Laurence M.		
Master's Choice		J330
Janvier, Ivan.		
Things		B595
Jarry, Alfred.		
Two Letters to Lord Kelvin		M645
Javor, Frank A.		
Interview		M635
Jenkins, William F.		
See also Murray Leinster, pseud.		
Doomsday Deferred	B565	S250
The Little Terror	A865	S250
Jennings, Gary.		
A Murkle for Jesse		M260
Jerome, Jerome K.		
The Dancing Partner		B890
Johnson, Doris.		
Russian Science Fiction [Translator]		M275

AUTHOR–TITLE	ANTHOLOGY
Johnson, Robert Barbour.	
Far Below	M920
Johnson, S.S.	
The House by the Crab Apple Tree	M255
Jonas, Gerald.	
Imaginary Numbers in a Real Garden [Poem]	M265
Jones, A.E.	
Created He Them	M210
Jones, Elis Gwyn.	
When the Engines Had to Stop	W735
Jones, N.R.	
Hermit of Saturn's Ring	W870
Jones, Raymond F.	
Correspondence Course	H430
Discontinuity	C840
Doomsday's Color-Press	H850
The Farthest Horizon	N880 S645
Noise Level	A530 C950 S645
Pete Can Fix It	C800
Production Test	L640
A Stone and a Spear	C785
Tools of the Trade	S640
Jorgensson, A.K.	
Coming-of-Age Day	M645
Joyce, Michael.	
Perchance to Dream	A360
Kaempffert, Waldemar.	
The Diminishing Draft	C760
Kafka, Franz.	
Metamorphosis	P910
Kagan, Norman.	
The Mathenauts	M640
Kahn, Bernard I.	
Command	N890
For the Public	N890
Kane, Harry.	
The Boy's Life Book of Outer Space [Illustrator]	B970

AUTHOR–TITLE					ANTHOLOGY
Kersh, Gerald [Cont'd]					
The Copper Dahlia					C935
River of Riches					M610
Somewhere Not Far from Here					M645
The Unsafe Deposit Box				M630	S250
Whatever Happened to Corporal Cuckoo?				P765	P780
Keyes, Daniel.					
Crazy Maro					M235
Flowers for Algernon	A840		C945	M230	M615
The Quality of Mercy					F945
Kidd, Virginia.					
Kangaroo Court					O640
King, Marshall.					
Beach Scene					M620
King, Vincent.					
Defence Mechanism					N570
Kingston, John.					
Manipulation					N540
Kipling, Rudyard.					
Easy as A.B.C.				C815	C845
The Finest Story in the World					P910
MacDonough's Song					C845
The Mark of the Beast					P910
Wireless					L885
Kippax, John.					
The Dusty Death					W725
Friday					W720
Kirkland, Jack.					
The Wall of Fire					M920
Kirs, Alex.					
Better than Ever.					M645
Klass, Philip.					
See William Tenn, pseud.					
Klein, Sidney.					
The Teeth of Dispair [Avram Davidson]					C820
Kline, Otis Adelbert.					
The Stolen Centuries					M920
A Vision of Venus					W885

AUTHOR–TITLE	ANTHOLOGY
Knight, Damon.	
Anachron	K715
The Analogues	C410
An Ancient Madness	G180
Ask Me Anything	G140
Auto-Da-Fe	G185 K725
Babel II	K715 M655
Backward, O Time	K725
Beyond Tomorrow	K690
The Big Pat Boom	G170 K725
Cabin Boy	A865 C775 G140 K715
Catch That Martian	C785
A Century of Great Short Science Fiction Novels	K695
A Century of Science Fiction	K700
Cities of Wonder	K705
Collector's Item	K725
The Country of the Kind	B665 M595
Damon Knight's Orbit 2	0645
The Dark Side	K710
Don't Live in the Past	G140 K725
The Dying Man	K720
The Enemy	K715
Eripmav	K725 M225
Extempore	K715
An Eye for What?	G220 W755
Far Out; 13 Science Fiction Stories	K715
Four in One	C940 G145 W740
The Handler	M615
Idiot Stick	K715
The Last Word	K715
A Likely Story	K725
Maid to Measure	K725
Man in the Jar	G150 K725
Mary	K725
Natural State	G215 G800 K720
Nebula Award Stories, 1965 [Editor]	N360
The Night of Lies	K725
Not with a Bang	A835 C310 C760 K715
Orbit I [Editor]	O640

AUTHOR–TITLE			ANTHOLOGY
Knight, Damon [Cont'd]			
Orbit 2			0645
Rule Golden		C855	K720
Semper Fi			K725
Special Delivery		C790	K715
Stranger Station	A525	M600	S585
Thing of Beauty		G165	K715
Three Novels			K720
Ticket to Anywhere			K850
Time Enough			K715
To Serve Man		B570	K715
To the Pure			K725
Turning on			K725
What Rough Beast?			M230
World without Children			G195
Worlds to Come			K730
You're Another		K715	M210
Knight, David C.			
The Amazing Mrs. Mimms			F215
Knight, N.L.			
Crisis in Utopia			G810
Koch, Howard.			
Invasion from Mars			C780
Kornbluth, Cyril M.			
The Advent on Channel Twelve			P765
The Adventurer		K845	P750
The Altar at Midnight	A835	C935	K840
The Cosmic Expense Account		M215	M600
Critical Mass [Frederik Pohl]			G175
Dominoes		P770	S595
The Education of Tigress Macardle			F220
The Events Leading Down to the Tragedy			K845
Everybody Knows Joe			K845
The Explorers			K840
Friend to Man			K840
Gomez		B750	K840
The Goodly Creatures			K840
I Never Ast No Favors			M205
Kazam Collects			K845

AUTHOR–TITLE	ANTHOLOGY
Kornbluth, C.M. [Cont'd]	
The Last Man Left in the Bar	K845
The Little Black Bag	C640 C770 K845
The Luckiest Man in Denv	K705
MS. Found in a Chinese Fortune Cookie	M220
Make Mine Mars	K845
The Marching Morons	A525 B575
The Meddlers	K845
A Mile Beyond the Moon	K845
The Mindworm	B570 K840
Nightmare with Zeppelins [Frederik Pohl]	G160
The Only Thing We Learn	C760
Passion Pills	K845
The Quaker Cannon (and Pohl, F.)	M625
The Remorseful	P775
The Rocket of 1955	C410 K840
Shark Ship	K845
The Silly Season	H505
The Slave	K845
That Share of Glory	D575 K730 K840 N890
Theory of Rocketry	J330 M225
Thirteen O'Clock	K840
Time Bum	K845
Time Travel and the Law	G805
Two Dooms	K845
Virginia	K845
With These Hands	B665 D655 K840
The Words of Guru	K845 T290
The World of Myrion Flowers	D320
Kornbluth, Mary.	
Science Fiction Showcase [Editor]	K850
Krenkel, Roy G.	
Tales of Three Planets [Illustrator]	B990
Krepps, Robert W.	
The Enormous Room [H.L. Gold]	W755 Y405
Five Years in the Marmalade	B565
Kruse, Clifton B.	
Dr. Lu-Mie	W865

AUTHOR–TITLE		ANTHOLOGY
Kubilius, Walter.		
The Other Side		B575
Second Chance [Fletcher Pratt]		S640
Kuebler, Harold W.		
The Treasury of Science Fiction Classics [Editor]		K950
Kummer, F.A., jr.		
The Forgiveness of Tenchu Taen		G830
Kurosaka, Bob.		
Those Who Can, Do		M645
Kuttner, Henry.		
Absalom		H505
Ahead of Time		K970
By These Presents		K970
Camouflage		K970
The Children's Hour [C.L. Moore]		B750
Cold War		C805
A Cross of Centuries		P765
De Profundis		K970
Deadlock		K970
Don't Look Now		J330
Dream's End		C965
The Ego Machine		B880
Ghost		K970
Happy Ending		K690
Home Is the Hunter		K970
Home There's No Returning		M595
Jesting Pilot		K705
Near Miss		M605
Or Else	C930	K970
Piggy Bank		B755
Pile of Trouble		K970
Private Eye		B565
Shock	D435	K970
Sword of Tomorrow		M330
Those Among Us		N785
Vintage Season		A515
The Voice of the Lobster		C960
We Guard the Black Planet!		M935

AUTHOR–TITLE	ANTHOLOGY
Kuttner, Henry [Cont'd]	
A Wild Surmise [C.L. Moore]	P770
Year Day	K970
Kuykendall, Roger.	
We Didn't Do Anything Wrong, Hardly	A560
Kyle, David.	
The Interstellar Zoo	G830
Lack, G.L.	
Rogue Leonardo	C300
La Farge, Oliver.	
John the Revelator	M190
Spud and Cochise	M270
Lafferty, R.A.	
Among the Hairy Earthmen	N365
Hog-Belly Honey	M260
The Hole on the Corner	0645
Nine Hundred Grandmothers	W900
Rainbird	G170
Seven-Day Terror	J330 M630
The Six Fingers of Time	G210
Slow Tuesday Night	G180 M645
Snuffles	G200
What's the Name of That Town?	C820
Lamport, Felicia.	
A Sigh for Cybernetics	M620
Lang, Allen Kim.	
Blind Man's Lantern	A540
Cinderella Story	F945
An Eel by the Tail	C780
Thaw and Serve	M255
Lang, Daniel.	
Man in Space	M610
Langart, Darrel T.	
What the Left Hand Was Doing	M615
Langdon, George.	
Of Those Who Came	C295
Langdon, John.	
Hermit on Bikini	D440

AUTHOR–TITLE	ANTHOLOGY
Langelaan, George.	
The Fly	M605 P720
Lanier, Sterling E.	
Join Our Gang?	A535
Latham, Philip, pseud.	
See also R.S. Richardson.	
The Blindness	C640
The Dimple in Drace	0645
The Xi Effect	B645 C930
Laumer, Keith.	
A Bad Day for Vermin	G175
The Brass God	L375
The Castle of Light	L375
Cocoon	L380
Courier	L375
Dinochrome	L380
Doorstep	L380
End as a Hero	L380
The Frozen Planet	F945
Galactic Diplomat	L375
Hybrid	L380
The King of the City	G170
The Last Command	H320
The Long Remembered Thunder	L380
Native Intelligence	L375
Nine by Laumer	L380
Placement Test	L380
The Prince and the Pirate	L375
Protest Note	L375
Saline Solution	L375
Trick or Treaty	I2 30
A Trip to the City	L380
Ultimatum	L375
The Walls	L380
Wicker Wonderland	L375
Worlds of the Imperium	K700
Lawrence, D.H.	
The Rocking-Horse Winner	T290

AUTHOR–TITLE		ANTHOLOGY
Lawrence, Margery.		
The Terror of the Anerly House School		D450
Lawson, Jack B.		
The Competitors		W890
Leahy, John Martin.		
Voices from the Cliff		F700
LeBlanc, Maurice.		
The Invisible Prisoner		D245
Lee, William.		
Junior Achievement	A540	A865
Lees, Gene.		
Stranger from Space		C290
Leiber, Fritz, jr.		
Answering Service		H320
Appointment in Tomorrow		B575
A Bad Day for Sales	A835 . B810	G145
Be of Good Cheer		M640
The Beat Cluster		G170
The Big Engine		G175
The Big Trek		M220
Business of Killing		C800
Coming Attraction	B570 . G140 . J330	M935
A Deskful of Girls		M225
Destiny Times Three		G810
The Enchanted Forest		D455
Four Ghosts in Hamlet		M260
The Foxholes of Mars		M575
The Last Letter		G160
Later Than You Think	C950	D430
The Man Who Made Friends with Electricity		M630
The Man Who Never Grew Young		K710
Mariana		M615
The Mechanical Bride		C830
The Moon Is Green		B580
Moonduel		M645
The Night He Cried		P770
The Number of the Beast		G165
A Pail of Air	A865 . G145	N880

AUTHOR–TITLE				ANTHOLOGY
Leiber, Fritz, jr. [Cont'd]				
Poor Superman				H505
Rump-Titty-Titty-Tum-TAH-Tee				C820
Sanity				C760
The Secret Songs				A525
The Ship Sails at Midnight				D435
The 64-Square Madhouse				I230
Smoke Ghost				M585
Space-Time for Springers			M610	P765
Taboo				G815
Time in the Round				G150
Try and Change the Past				D310
237 Talking Statues, etc.				M635
Wanted—an Enemy				D425
What's He Doing in There?				G155
When the Change-Winds Blow				W890
Leimert, John.				
John Thomas' Cube				C785
Leinster, Murray, pseud.				
See also William F. Jenkins.				
The Ailiens				W745
The Corianis Disaster				C840
Cure for a Ylith				C790
De Profundis			D430	L535
Doctor				W755
The Ethical Equations			C765	C870
Exploration Team			A520	A840
First Contact			A875	S645
The Fourth Dimensional Demonstration				L535
The Gadget Had a Ghost				Y400
Great Stories of Science Fiction [Editor]				L530
Historical Note				A875
If You Was a Maklin				G140
Jezebel				D440
The Journey				P770
Keyhole			H505	T290
The Lifework of Professor Muntz			B565	C815
A Logic Named Joe	B880	L535	M915	M935

AUTHOR–TITLE			ANTHOLOGY
Leinster, Murray [Cont'd]			
A Martian Adventure			C810
Med Service			K850
The Middle of the Week After Next	B580	C800	W720
The Mole Pirate			L540
Nobody Saw the Ship			C760
The Other Now			G140
The Other World			C850
Pipeline to Pluto			C825
The Plague			C785
The Plants			G820
Politics			J330
The Power	D435	L535	L640
Propagandist	C775	C795	G225
Proxima Centauri			L535
Ribbon in the Sky			C770
The Runaway Skyscraper			R820
The Sentimentalists			Y405
Sidewise in Time			L535
Skag with the Queer Head			C805
The Strange Case of John Kingman			L530
Symbiosis		G225	L530
Things Pass By			M330
This Star Shall Be Free			C780
Three Stories by Murray Leinster et al			L540
The Wabbler	C640	C940	M575
Lernet-Holenia, Alexander.			
Baron Bagge			A360
Lesser, Milton.			
Black Eyes and the Daily Grind			S645
Looking Forward			L640
Pen Pal			C780
Lewis, Clive S.			
Ministering Angels			M225
The Shoddy Lands			M215
Unreal Estates [B.W. Aldiss & K. Amis]			A525
Lewis, Jack.			
Who's Cribbing?		A835	S795

AUTHOR–TITLE	ANTHOLOGY
Lewis, Oscar.	
The Lost Years	B755
Ley, Willy.[Also writes under Pseud. of Robert Willey]	
Geography for Time Travelers	G805
Introduction [to Men Against the Stars]	G820
Introduction [to Travelers of Space]	G830
The Invasion	P760
A Letter to the Martians	G805
Space War	G805
V-2 Rocket Cargo Ship	H430
Where Do We Go from Here?	M605
Leyson, Burr.	
Trail to the Stars [Introduction to anthology]	E375
Lightner, A.M.	
Best Friend	B 970
A New Game	B970
Lindner, Robert.	
The Jet-Propelled Couch	A360
Livingston, Herb.	
See H.B. Hickey, pseud.	
Locke, Robert Donald.	
Dark Nuptial	S795
Lockhard, Leonard.	
The Lagging Profession	M620
London, Jack.	
The Scarlet Plague	C785
The Shadow and the Flash	D245
Long, Amelia Reynolds.	
Omega	W860
Reverse Phylogeny	C800
Long, Frank Belknap.	
And Someday to Mars	M920
Cones	C795
The Critters	D435
The Great Cold	D455
Humpty Dumpty Had a Great Fall	D425
Invasion	D430

AUTHOR–TITLE		ANTHOLOGY
Long, Frank Belknap [Cont'd]		
The Mercurian		W870
Red Storm on Jupiter		W870
To Follow Knowledge		C800
Two Face		B570
Longdon, George.		
Of Those Who Came		N885
Loomis, Noel.		
"If the Court Pleases"		H850
The Long Dawn		C760
Loran, Martin.		
An Ounce of Dissension [sic]		W750
Lord, Glenn.		
Wolfshead [Editor]		H865
Lory, Robert.		
Rundown		C820
The Star Party		W890
Loughlin, Richard L.		
Journeys in Science Fiction [Editor]		L885
Lovecraft, Howard P.		
The Color Out of Space	C785	M930
From Beyond		D455
The Horror from the Middle Span		D450
Letter to Donald Wollheim		H855
The Shadow Out of Time		W880
The Whisperer in Darkness		M940
Lowenkopf, Shelly.		
The Addict		N785
Lowndes, Robert W.		
Highway		L640
Lucian.		
A True History		D425
Lukodyanov, I.		
Formula for the Impossible [E. Voisunsky]		M277
McAllister, Bruce.		
The Faces Outside		M635
MacApp, C.C.		
And All the Earth a Grave		G175

AUTHOR–TITLE **ANTHOLOGY**

AUTHOR–TITLE			ANTHOLOGY
MacDonald, John D. [Cont'd]			
Ring Around the Redhead			C800
Spectator Sport		A835	C785
Susceptibility			G140
MacDonald, Philip.			
The Hub			M190
Private–Keep Out			P910
McDowell, Emmett.			
Veiled Island			C805
MacFarlane, Wallace.			
Dead End		C830	C835
MacGregor, James J.			
See J.T. McIntosh, pseud.			
McGregor, R.J.			
The Perfect Gentleman			S795
McGuire, John J.			
The Queen's Messenger			B605
The Return [H. Beam Piper]			S420
McIntosh, J.T. [Pseud. of J. J. MacGregor]			
The Bliss of Solitude			C945
First Lady		C750	C930
Hallucination Orbit			G145
Machine Made	C305	C765	W725
Made in U.S.A.	B670	D320	G195
Poor Planet			C843
Stitch in Time			C290
Venus Mission			W875
You Were Right, Joe			G155
Mackelworth, R.W.			
The Expanding Man			N550
The Final Solution			N565
A Touch of Immortality			C306
McKenna, Richard.			
Casey Agonistes	K710	M230	M610
Fiddler's Green			0645
Hunter, Come Home		K695	M250
Mine Own Ways		M235	M620
The Secret Place		N365	O640

AUTHOR–TITLE		ANTHOLOGY
McKenty, Jack.		
$1,000 a Plate		G160
MacKenzie, Jonathan Blake.		
Overproof	A555	C843
Thin Edge		A 545
McKettrig, Seaton.		
A World by the Tale		A545
McKimmey, James.		
The Eyes Have It		D310
MacKin, Edward.		
Key to Chaos		N530
The Unremembered		W890
Macklin, Edward.		
The Trouble with H.A.R.R.I.		C820
McKnight, John P.		
Prolog		A835
McLaughlin, Dean.		
The Brotherhood of Keepers		M620
The Permanent Implosion		A550
MacLean, Katherine.		
And Be Merry		C785
Contagion	B570	C795
Defense Mechanism	C760	M580
The Fittest		M575
Games		C790
Incommunicado		C855
Interbalance		M235
The Origin of the Species		T290
Pictures Don't Lie	C780	C930
The Snowball Effect		G145
Unhuman Sacrifice	A510	K700
McMorrow, Fred.		
The Big Wheel		S250
McMorrow, Thomas.		
Mr. Murphy of New York		C760
Maddux, Rachel.		
Final Clearance		M215

AUTHOR–TITLE					ANTHOLOGY
The Magazine of Fantasy and Science Fiction.					
The Best from Fantasy and Science Fiction, 1st–					M190
16th Series	M195	M200	M205	M210	M215
	M220	M225	M230	M235	M240
	M245	M250	M255	M260	M265
A Decade of Fantasy and Science Fiction					M270
Magidoff, Robert.					
Russian Science Fiction [Compiler]					M275
Russian Science Fiction 1968 [Compiler]					M277
Malamud, Bernard.					
The Jewbird					M635
Malcolm, Donald.					
Potential					N550
Twice Bitten					W735
Malec, Alexander.					
Diehl					M280
Extrapolasis					M280
Landmark					M280
Matayama					M280
Monsignor Primo Macinno					M280
Once Was					M280
Opaxtl					M280
Project Inhumane				M280	M645
Proof Positive					M280
Remote Incident					M280
10:01 A.M.					M280
Thing-Thing					M280
To Relieve the Sanity					M280
Mallette, Mose.					
The Seven Wonders of the Universe					M265
Malpass, E.L.					
The Return of the Moon Man					O140
When Grandfather Flew to the Moon					M600
Manhattan, Avro.					
The Cricket Ball					A835
Manning, Lawrence.					
Good-Bye, Ilha!				C765	M575
The Living Galaxy					C815

AUTHOR–TITLE **ANTHOLOGY**

Margulies, Leo.
The Giant Anthology of Science Fiction [Editor] M330
Marks, Winston K.
Call Me Adam C790
Double Take A835
John's Other Practice B590
Mate in Two Moves C770
The Water Eater C820
Marlowe, Stephen.
Lion's Mouth L640
Marlowe, Webb.
Flight into Darkness H430
Marquis, Don.
Ghosts. M585
Marsh, W.
The Ethicators M595
Marti-Ibanez, Felix.
Nina Sol M250
Martino, Joseph P.
Pushbutton War A560
To Change Their Ways W750
Masefield, John.
The Sealman M270
Mason, Douglas R.
Folly to Be Wise N570
The Man Who Missed the Ferry C306
Masson, David I.
Traveller's Rest M645 S595
Matania, Fortunino.
The Pirates of Venus [Illustrator] B980
Mateyko, G.M.
On Handling the Data [H. Hirshfield] C950
Matheson, Richard.
Born of Man and Woman B570 T290
Dance of the Dead P765 P780
Dress of White Silk M190
The Jazz Machine M635
Lover When You're Near Me G145 B580

AUTHOR–TITLE	ANTHOLOGY
Matheson, Richard [Cont'd]	
Mantage [sic]	K850
One for the Books	G220
Pattern for Survival	M210
SRL AD [sic]	B880
Shipshape Home	C785
Steel	N785
The Test	M205
Third from the Sun	G140
Through Channels	C825
The Waker Dreams	G140
Witch War	B575
Matschat, Cecile.	
The Year after Tomorrow [Joint Editor]	D360
Maurois, Andre.	
The Earth Dwellers	M455 M635
The War Against the Moon	C785
The Weigher of Souls	M455
May, Julian.	
Dune Roller	B645 S645
Star of Wonder	D575
Mayan, Earl E.	
Rod Serlings The Twilight Zone [Illustrator]	S490
Mayne, Isobel.	
The Place of the Tigress	O140
Meadows, Patrick.	
Countercommandment	A555
Merliss, R.R.	
The Stutterer	M595
Merril, Judith.	
Barrier of Dread	G815
Beyond Human Ken	M575
Beyond the Barriers of Space and Time	M580
A Big Man with the Girls [James MacCreigh]	H850
Daughters of Earth	P945
Dead Center	B755
The Deep Down Dragon	G170
Exile from Space	F215

AUTHOR–TITLE **ANTHOLOGY**

Merril, Judith [Cont'd]
- The 5th Annual of the Year's Best S-F M615
- How Near Is the Moon? M605
- Human? M585
- Project Nursemaid C855
- Rockets to Where? M610
- S-F: The Year's Greatest Science Fiction and Fantasy, 1956-59 . . . . . M600 M605 M610 M595
- So Proudly We Hail P770
- Survival Ship. H505
- That Only a Mother P910 T290
- The Year's Best S-F; the 6th-11th Annuals. . . M620 M625 M630 M635 M640 M645

Merritt, A.
- The Peoples of the Pit M930

Merwin, Sam jr.
- Exiled from Earth C960
- Exit Line C795
- Judas Ram G140

Metcalfe, John. D450

Middleton, Richard.
- Shepherd's Boy M200

Miles, Hamish.
- The Weigher of Souls [Translator] M455

Miller, Lion.
- The Available Data on the Worp Reaction A835 C940

Miller, P. Schuyler.
- As Never Was H430
- The Sands of Time H430 S595
- Status Quondam H435
- Trouble on Tantalus G830

Miller, R. Dewitt.
- Swenson, Dispatcher B595
- Within the Pyramid H430

Miller, Walter M., jr.
- Blood Bank G800
- A Canticle for Leibowitz . . . B595 C410 M210
- Command Performance B580 G145

AUTHOR–TITLE ANTHOLOGY

Miller, Walter M., jr. [Cont'd]
Conditionally Human Y400
Crucifixus Etiam A530 M585
The Darfsteller A840
Dumb Waiter C830 C835 K705
The Hoofer M595
Izzard and the Membrane Y395
The Little Creeps L640
Momento Homo B590 J330 M655
No Moon for Me S640
Vengeance for Nikolai F220
The Will B590
Wolf Pack M580
Mills, Robert P.
The Best from Fantasy and Science Fiction, 9th–11th series [Editor] M235 M230 M240
A Decade of Fantasy and Science Fiction. . . M270
The Last Shall Be First M270
The Worlds of Science Fiction M655
Mines, Samuel.
Blueprint for Tomorrow [Foreword to Anthology] S795
Mirrieless, Edith.
Introduction [to World of Wonder]. P910
Mitchell, J.A.
The Last American D430
Monig, Christopher.
Love Story C965
Monroe, Lyle.
Columbus Was a Dope G830
Montgomery, Robert Bruce.
See Crispin, Edmund, pseud.
Moorcock, Michael.
Behold the Man. W900
Flux S595
Moore, C.L.
The Bright Illusion J330
The Children's Hour [Henry Kuttner] B750
Doorway into Time M915 M935

AUTHOR–TITLE	ANTHOLOGY
Moore, C.L. [Cont'd]	
Home There's No Returning	M595
No Woman Born	C930 L530
Scarlet Dream	C965
Shambleau	C960
There Shall Be Darkness	G815
A Wild Surmise [Henry Kuttner]	P770
Moore, Hal R.	
Sea Bright	M260
Moore, Ward.	
Adjustment	M220
Dominions Beyond	B590
The Fellow Who Married the Maxill Girl	M235 M620
Flying Dutchman	C960
It Becomes Necessary	M625
Lot	M200
Lot's Daughter	M270
No Man Pursueth	M215
Peacebringer	C760
The Second Trip to Mars	S250
We the People	C965
More, Thomas.	
Utopia	D425
Morgan, Dan.	
Emreth	N540
Parking Problem	C303
Morris, Gouverneur.	
Back There in the Grass	P910
Morrison, D.A.C.	
Another Antigone	O140
Morrison, William, pseud.	
See also Joseph Samachson.	
Bedside Manner	C770
Country Doctor	P765 P770
A Feast of Demons	G160
The Inner Worlds	B590
The Model of a Judge	G150
The Sack	H505
The Sly Bungerhop	G200

AUTHOR–TITLE	ANTHOLOGY
Moskowitz, Samuel.	
The Coming of the Robots [Editor]	M910
Doorway into Time and Other Stories	M915
Editor's Choice in Science Fiction	M920
Exploring Other Worlds	M925
The Golden Pyramid	F215
The Lost Chord	F700
Man of the Stars	M925
Masterpieces of Science Fiction	M930
Modern Masterpieces of Science Fiction	M935
The Sense of Wonder	L 540
Strange Signposts [Roger Elwood]	M940
Moudy, Walter F.	
The Survivor	M645
Mugnaini, Joe.	
The Golden Apples of the Sun [Illustrator]	B805
Mulisch, Harry.	
What Happened to Sergeant Masuro?	W890
Munro, H.H.	
See Saki, pseud.	
Murphy, Robert.	
Fallout Island	S250
The Phantom Setter	S250
The Replacement	M235
Nash, Ogden.	
A Tale of the Thirteenth Floor	M270
Nathan, Robert.	
Digging the Weans	M600
A Pride of Carrots	C820
Neal, H.C.	
Who Shall Dwell	P720
Nearing, H., jr.	
The Cerebrative Psittacoid	C930
The Hyperspherical Basketball	M195
The Maladjusted Classroom	M200
The Mathematical Voodoo	M190
Nelson, Alan.	
Narapoia	A835 M190

AUTHOR–TITLE		ANTHOLOGY
Nelson, Alan [Cont'd]		
The Shopdropper		C770
Silenzia		C845
Nelson, Ray.		
Eight O'Clock in the Morning	M250	M635
Nesvadba, Josef.		
The Last Secret Weapon of the Third Reich		M640
Neville, Kris.		
Bettyann	H435	S645
Cold War		A875
Experiment Station		C805
The Forest of Zil		H320
Franchise		S645
Gratitude Guaranteed		D440
Hold Back Tomorrow		B645
Old Man Henderson		M190
Overture		H440
Shamar's War		C843
Underground Movement		M575
Newman, Louis.		
License to Steal		G165
Neyroud, Gerard E.		
The Terra-Venusian War of 1979		C820
Nissenson, Hugh.		
The Mission		P720
Niven, Larry.		
Becalmed in Hell	N360	W895
Flatlander		C843
Wrong-Way Street	G180	S595
Nolan, William F.		
The Joy of Living		N785
One of Those Days		M630
The Pseudo-People [Editor]		N785
Norbert, W., pseud.		
See Norbert Wiener		
Norton, Andre [Pseud of Alice Mary Norton]		
Bullard of the Space Patrol [Editor]		J310
Mousetrap		B590

AUTHOR–TITLE	ANTHOLOGY
Norton, Andre [Cont'd]	
People of the Crater	W885
Space Pioneers	N880
Space Police	N885
Space Service	N890
Norton, Henry.	
The Man in the Moon	C780
Nourse, Alan E., M.D.	
Brightside Crossing	G220 . K690 N935
The Canvas Bag	N930
Circus	N930
The Coffin Cure	C820 N935
The Compleat Consummators	M255
The Counterfeit Man	N930
The Dark Door	N930
The Expert Touch	N930
Family Resemblance	C770 . C805 N935
Hard Bargain	P720
High Threshold	C785
Image of the Gods	N930
Letter of the Law	N935
The Link	N930
Love Thy Vimp	N935
Meeting of the Board	N930
A Miracle Too Many [Philip H. Smith]	M640
My Friend Bobby	N930
The Native Soil	N935
Nightmare Brother	C825 . N935 S640
An Ounce of Cure	N930
PRoblem [sic]	N935
Second Sight	N930
Tiger by the Tail	A835 C800 . G145 N935
Novotny, John.	
On Camera	C820
A Trick or Two	M270
O'Brien, Fitz-James.	
What Was It?	D245 K700
The Wondersmith	M930

AUTHOR–TITLE		ANTHOLOGY
The Observer [London]		
A.D. 2500; The Observer Prize Stories		O140
O'Donnell, Lawrence.		
Clash by Night		A875
O'Donnevan, Finn.		
The Gun without a Bang		G155
A Wind Is Rising		G150
Offutt, A.J.		
Blacksword		G200
Okhotnikov, Vadim.		
The Fiction Machines	M275	W740
Oliver, Chad.		
The Ant and the Eye		S645
Any More at Home Like You?		P780
Between the Thunder and the Sun		M220
Blood's a Rover		C790
The Boy Next Door		M585
Didn't He Ramble		B605
The Field Expedient		W875
The Last Word [Charles Beaumont]		M210
Let Me Live in a House		C825
The Life Game		N785
The Mother of Necessity		C810
Of Course		B590
Rite of Passage		C840
Win the World		L640
Oliver, J.T.		
The Peaceful Martian		F700
Olsen, Bob [Pseud. of Alfred John Olsen]		
The Four-Dimensional-Roller-Press		W865
Osborne, Robertson.		
Action on Azura		G830
Contact, Incorporated		C760
Ottum, Bob, jr.		
Ado about Nothing		M645
Owen, Mably.		
Out of This World 1-7 [Joint Editor]	W720	W725
W730 W735 W740	W745	W750

AUTHOR–TITLE			ANTHOLOGY
Owen, Mably [Cont'd]			
Worlds Apart [Joint Editor]			W755
Owsley, Cliff.			
Confessions of the First Number			M635
Padgett, Lewis.			
Compliments of the Author			P125
The Cure			P125
Deadlock			G825
Endowment Policy			C800
Ex Machina			P130
Exit the Professor			P125
Gallegher Plus			P130
A Gnome There Was		M575	P125
The Iron Standard			G820
Jesting Pilot			P125
Line to Tomorrow			D455
Margin for Error			C760
Mimsy Were the Borogoves		C870	P125
Open Secret			L530
The Piper's Son			T290
Project			C790
The Proud Robot		H430	P130
Rain Check			P125
Robots Have No Tails			P130
See You Later			P125
This Is the House			P125
Time Locker		H430	P130
The Twonky		H430	P125
We Kill People			L640
What You Need		C785	P125
When the Bough Breaks	A875	D425	H865
The World Is Mine			P130
Page, Gerald W.			
Guardian Angel			N570
Spacemen Live Forever			N565
Page, N.W.			
But Without Horns			G810

AUTHOR–TITLE ANTHOLOGY

AUTHOR–TITLE		ANTHOLOGY
Poe, Edgar Allan [Cont'd]		
Facts in the Case of M. Valdemar		C770
Hans Phaall—a Tale		M930
Mellonta Tauta		M940
Note on "Hans Phaall"		M930
Richard Adams Locke		M930
The Thousand-and-Second Tale of Scheherazade		D425
Pohl, Frederik		
Assignment in Tomorrow		P750
The Bitterest Pill		G160
The Census Takers		M215
The Children of Night	G180	P757
Critical Mass [C.M. Kornbluth]		G175
Day Million	N365	W900
Digits and Dastards		P757
Earth Eighteen		P757
The Eighth Galaxy Reader [Editor]		G175
The Expert Dreamers		P760
Father of the Stars	I230	P757
The Fiend	N540 . P720	P757
The Five Hells of Orion		P757
The Gentlest Unpeople		G155
The Haunted Corpse		G150
How to Count on Your Fingers	G805	P757
The If Reader of Science Fiction [Editor]		I230
Introduction [to Bodyguard]		G190
The Man Who Ate the World		K850
The Martian Star-Gazers		M630
The Midas Plague	A510	G800
My Lady Green Sleeves		D320
Nightmare with Zeppelins [C.M. Kornbluth].		G160
The Ninth Galaxy Reader [Editor]		G180
On Binary Digits and Human Habits		P757
Punch	C820	P720
The Quaker Cannon (& C. M. Kornbluth)		M625
The Seventh Galaxy Reader [Editor]		G170
Star of Stars [Editor]		P765
Star Science Fiction Stories 1-3	P770 . P775	P780
Star Short Novels		P785

AUTHOR–TITLE	ANTHOLOGY
Pohl, Frederik [Cont'd]
The Tenth Galaxy Reader [Editor]	G185
Third Offense	D310
Three Portraits and a Prayer	G170
Time Waits for Winthrop [Editor]	G215
The Tunnel Under the World	G185
What to Do Until the Analyst Comes	C845
Whatever Counts	G190
With Redfern on Capella XI	P757
The Wizards of Pung's Corners	B670
The World of Myrion Flowers [C.M. Kornbluth]	D320
Popp, Lilian M.
Journeys in Science Fiction [Joint Editor]	L885
Porges, Arthur.
Emergency Operation	C770
The Fly	A835 B580 M575
Guilty as Charged	B590
$1.98	M205
Problem Child	M640
The Rats	B575
The Ruum	B890 C930 W720
Porter, William S.
See O.Henry, pseud.
Powers, William T.
Meteor	A875
Poyer, Joe.
Mission "Red Clash"	A555
Pratt, Fletcher.
The Black Ball [L.S. De Camp]	M195
Gavagan's Barr [L.D. De Camp]	M190
Hormone	P775
Introduction [to Journey to Infinity]	G815
Introduction [to Beyond Human Ken]	M575
The Long View	P945
Official Record	P750
Pardon My Mistake	D435
The Roger Bacon Formula	C760
Second Chance [Walter Kubilius]	S640
The Thing in the Woods [B.F. Ruby]	C785
The Untimely Toper [L.S. De Camp]	M200

AUTHOR–TITLE	ANTHOLOGY
Pratt, Fletcher [Cont'd]	
The Weissenbroch Spectacles [L.S. De Camp]	D245
World of Wonder [Editor]	P910
Presslie, Robert.	
Another Word for Man	W725
The Day Before Never	N555
The Night of the Seventh Finger	C306
Price, E. Hoffman.	
Clark Ashton Smith; a Memoir	S650
Price, Roger.	
An Inquiry Concerning the Curvature of the Earth's Surface and Divers Investigations of a Metaphysical Nature.	M615
J.G.	M620
Priestly, J.B.	
Mr. Strenberry's Tale	K950
Prokofieva, R.	
More Soviet Science Fiction [Translator]	P965
Purdy, Ken.	
The Noise	P720
Rabelais, Francois.	
Phalanstery of Theleme	D425
Rackham, John.	
Advantage	N555
Computer's Mate	N565
Hell Planet	C300
Poseidon Project	N570
Rankine, John.	
Maiden Voyage	C300
Six Cubed Plus One	C306
Two's Company	N530
Ransom, James.	
Fred One	M255
Raphael, Rick.	
A Filbert Is a Nut	A560
Sonny	A545 M640
Raspe, Rudolf.	
The Adventures of Baron Munchausen [Selections]	B890

AUTHOR–TITLE	ANTHOLOGY
Ray, Robert.	
The Heart of Blackness	W745
Rayer, Francis G.	
Sands Our Abode	W730
Ready, W.B.	
Devlin	M200
Redgrove, Peter.	
The Case	M645
Mr. Waterman	M635
Reed, Kit.	
Automatic	M640
Automatic Tiger	M255
The Food Farm	0645
The Vine	H320
The Wait	M225
Reese, John.	
Rainmaker	H505
Reeves, Rosser.	
$E = MC^2$	M240
Effigy	M240
Infinity	M235
Reines, Donald F.	
Interplantary Copyright	G805
Reinsberg, Mark.	
Introduction [to The Green Hills of Earth]	H475
Repp, Ed Earl.	
Kleon of the Golden Sun	F700
Repton, Humphrey.	
From a Private Mad-House	D430
Reynolds, Mack.	
The Adventure of the Ball of Nostradamus [August Derleth]	S420
The Adventure of the Extra-Terrestrial	A555
The Adventure of the Snitch in Time [A. Derleth]	D310 S420
And Thou Beside Me	C805
The Business, as Usual	A835 D455 K700
Compounded Interest	M600
D.P. from Tomorrow	D440

AUTHOR–TITLE	ANTHOLOGY
Reynolds, Mack [Cont'd]	
Dark Interlude [Fredric Brown] . . B575 D320	G140
The Discord Makers	C780
Earthlings Go Home!	M630
Freedom	M625
Genus Traitor	A550
Good Indian	A540
Isolationist	C760
The Man in the Moon	L640
The Martians and the Coys	B880
Pacifist	M640
Science Fiction Carnival [Joint Editor]	B880
Rice, Allison.	
The Loolies Are Here	O640
Rice, Jane.	
The Idol of the Flies	T290
The Rainbow Gold	M235
The Willow Tree	M230
Richardson, Robert S. [Pseud. of Philip Latham]	
Kid Anderson	C810
Space Fix	G805
To Explain Mrs. Thompson	P760
Richmond, Leigh.	
Poppa Needs Shorts [Walt Richmond]	M635
Prologue to an Analogue	A535
Richter, Conrad.	
Doctor Hanray's Second Chance	S250
Sinister Journey	S250
Ridenour, Louis N.	
Pilot Lights of the Apocalypse	C810
Riley, Frank.	
The Cyber and Justice Holmes	B595
Roberts, Frank.	
It Could Be You	M640
Roberts, Keith.	
Boulter's Canaries	N540
The Deeps	O640
The Inner Wheel	N555
Manscarer	C306

AUTHOR–TITLE		ANTHOLOGY
Roberts, Keith [Cont'd]		
Sub-Lim		C303
Synth		N565
Robertson, Morgan.		
The Battle of the Monsters		D425
Robin, Ralph.		
Budding Explorer		M195
Pleasant Dreams.		C785
Robinson, Frank M.		
Dream Street		B595
The Fire and the Sword		B645
The Girls from Earth	B580	S645
The Hunting Season		Y395
The Oceans Are Wide		Y405
One Thousand Miles Up		B590
The Reluctant Heroes	D575 . D590	G140
The Santa Claus Planet		B570
Two Weeks in August		A835
The Wreck of the Ship John B.		H320
Robles, Edward G., jr.		
See?		A835
Rocklynne, Ross.		
At the Center of Gravity		M925
Backfire		C785
Jaywalker		G140
Pressure		B645
Quietus		H430
Winner Take All		D445
Rogers, Joel Townsley.		
Beyond Space and Time		B750
Moment Without Time		S795
No Matter Where You Go		M230
Rogers, Kay.		
Experiment.		M200
Rohrer, Robert.		
Keep Them Happy.		M260
The Man Who Found Proteus		M640

AUTHOR–TITLE	ANTHOLOGY
Rome, David.	
Parky	M625
There's a Starman in Ward 7	M645
Rose, Mark.	
We Would See a Sign	A520
Rosny-Aine, J.H.	
Another World	K700
Rosokhvatsky, I.	
Desert Encounter	M277
Ross, Joseph.	
Best of Amazing [Compiler]	R820
Rostand, Edmund.	
Voyage to the Moon	M930
Rothman, Milton A.	
See also Lee Gregor, pseud.	
Heavyplanet	P760
Ruby, B.F.	
The Thing in the Woods [Fletcher Pratt]	C785
Russ, Joanna.	
The Adventuress	0645
I Gave Her Sack and Sherry	0645
My Dear Emily	M245
Russell, Bertrand.	
Planetary Effulgence	M630
Russell, Eric Frank.	
Allamagoosa	A840 . C775 D655
And Then There Were None	S645 Y395
Appointment at Noon	A835
Basic Right	C765
Boomerang	C830 C835
Dear Devil	C760 . S585 S640
Diabologic	B670
Exposure	C790
Fast Falls the Eventide	B580
The Glass Eye	M575
Hobbyist	A875 C945
I Am Nothing	B580
The Illusionaries	N880
Impulse	C780

AUTHOR–TITLE		ANTHOLOGY
Russell, Eric Frank [Cont'd]		
Into Your Tent I'll Creep.		B605
Jay Score.		H505
Late Night Final		A875
Metamorphosite.	D420	G815
Minor Ingredient		A560
Muten.		B880
Panic Button		C840
A Present from Joe		C930
The Room		P720
Second Genesis.		N570
Still Life		C750
Symbiotica.		H430
Take a Seat		M585
Test Piece	C785	D320
This One's On Me		C805
Ultima Thule.		L640
The Witness		M935
Russell, Ray.		
Put Them All Together, They Spell Monster . .		M600
Russell, William Moy.		
The Three Brothers		O140
Rymer, G.A.		
The Atavists		O140
Chain of Command		C805
Saari, Oliver.		
Sitting Duck		D575
Under the Sand-Seas		D585
Saberhagen, Fred.		
Fortress Ship		M635
The Life Hater		I230
Safronov, Y.		
Thread of Life		M277
Saint Clair, Eric.		
Olsen and the Gull		M255
Saint Clair, Margaret.		
The Age of Prophecy		C805
Child of Void	A865	C780
The Gardener		D455

AUTHOR–TITLE	ANTHOLOGY
Saint Clair, Margaret [Cont'd]	
Horrer Howce.	G155
The Nuse Man	G165
An Old-Fashioned Bird Christmas	G170
The Pillows	C795
Prott .C825	C930
Quis Custodiet..?	C815
Saint John, J. Allen.	
At the Earth's Core [Illustrator].	B970
The Land That Time Forgot	B975
Saki [Pseud. of H.H. Munro]	
The Open Window	T290
The Story-Teller	A360
Tobermory	L885
Samachson, Joseph.	
See also William Morrison, pseud.	
A Feast of Demons	P760
Sambrot, William.	
Creature of the Snows	M620
Island of Fear	S250
Leprechaun	M630
Space Secret	S250
Sanders, Winston P.	
Barnacle Bull.	A535
Industrial Revolution	A545
Pact	M230
Say It with Flowers	A555
Santesson, Hans Stefan.	
The Fantastic Universe Omnibus [Editor] . . .	F215
Saparin, Victor.	
The Magic Shoes	M275
The Trial of Tantalus	P965
Satterfield, Charles.	
With Redfern on Capella XII	G200
Saturday Evening Post [Magazine]	
The Post Reader of Fantasy and Science Fiction	S250
Savchenko, V.	
Professor Bern's Awakening.	D980

AUTHOR–TITLE			ANTHOLOGY
Scott, Jody.			
Go for Baroque			M240
Scott, Martin, pseud.			
See Richard Gehman.			
Scott, Robin S.			
Who Needs Insurance?			N365
Seabright, Idris.			
The Altruists			D440
Brightness Falls from the Air			B575
The Causes			M270
An Egg a Month from All Over	A835	C410	M585
The Hole in the Moon			M195
The Listening Child			M190
The Man Who Sold Rope to the Gnoles			M575
New Ritual			M200
Short in the Chest		C790	C845
The Wines of Earth			M220
Sell, William.			
Other Tracks			C800
Sellings, Arthur.			
Blank Form			G155
Gifts of the Gods			N570
The Mission			O140
Senarens, Luis P.			
Frank Reade, Jr.'s Air Wonder			M940
Frank Reade, Jr.'s Strange Adventures with His New Air Ship			M930
Lost in a Comet's Tail, or, Frank Reade, Jr's Strange Adventures with His New Air Ship			M930
Serling, Rod.			
The Avenging Ghost			S490
Back There			S490
The Curse of Seven Towers			S490
Dead Man's Chest			S490
Death's Masquerade			S490
The Ghost of Ticonderoga			S490
The Ghost-Town Ghost			S490
The House on the Square			S490

AUTHOR–TITLE ANTHOLOGY

AUTHOR–TITLE		ANTHOLOGY
Sheckley, Robert [Cont'd]		
The Last Weapon		P770
The Leech		C825
Love, Incorporated		P720
Meeting of the Minds		W750
The Minimum Man		G155
The Monsters		C950
The Odor of Thought		P775
Operating Instructions		M580
Paradise II		D445
The Perfect Woman		A835
Pilgrimage to Earth		A510
Potential		D440
The Prize of Peril	D655	M610
Protection		G150
Something for Nothing		C410
Specialist		G145
Spy Story		P720
Warm		G145
We Are Alone		H850
Sheldon, Walt.		
Chore for a Spaceman		N390
The Hunters		A835
I, the Unspeakable		G140
Shelley, Mary.		
Frankenstein, or the Modern Prometheus		B890
The Last Man		M940
The Mortal Immortal		M930
Shelton, Jerry.		
Culture		C760
Shelton, William Roy.		
Moon Crazy		S250
Shepley, John.		
Gorilla Suit		M225
Three for Carnival		M265
Sherred, T.L.		
E for Effort	A875 . C760	K695
Eye for Iniquity	D440	K710

AUTHOR–TITLE ANTHOLOGY

Shiel, M.P.
The Place of Pain M930
Shiras, Wilmar H.
Children of the Atom [Selection] T290
In Hiding . . . . C310 L530 . S645 T290
Opening Doors B565
Shore, Wilma.
A Bulletin from the Trustees M255 S595
Silverberg, Robert.
Absolutely Inflexible S595
Alaree S585
The Artifact Business C640
Certainty S590
Collecting Team S590
Double Dare G160 S590
Earthmen and Strangers S585
Hawksbill Station H320
A Man of Talent B665
A Mind for Business S590
Misfit S590
New Men for Mars S590
The Old Man S590
The Overlord's Thumb S590
Ozymandias S590
Point of Focus W750
Road to Nightfall F215
Sound Decision [Randall Garrett] A560
To Worlds Beyond S590
Voyagers in Time S595
Silverstein, Shel.
The Distortion M620
Simak, Clifford D.
Aesop S605
All the Traps of Earth S600
The Answers S610 S645
The Asteroid of Gold W865
The Beachhead D420 S610
The Big Front Yard A840 S615

AUTHOR–TITLE			ANTHOLOGY
Simak, Clifford D. [Cont'd]			
Carbon Copy			S615
Census			S605
City			S605
Civilization Game			G200
Condition of Employment			S600
Contraption		P770	S610
Courtesy			S640
Crying Jag			S600
A Death in the House			M615
Death Scene			S615
Desertion	C760	K690	S605
Drop Dead			S600
Dusty Zebra			S615
Earth for Inspiration			M910
Eternity Lost		A875	B565
The Fence			S610
Final Gentlemen			C855
Founding Father			S615
Gleaners			F945
The Golden Bugs			C840
Good Night, Mr. James	D435	G140	S600
Green Thumb		C950	S615
Hobbies			S605
Honorable Opponent		G150	S615
How-2	B590	D580	G190
Huddling Place		M935	S605
Idiot's Crusade			S615
Immigrant			S610
Installment Plan			S600
Jackpot			S615
Junkyard			G145
Kindergarten		D440	S610
Limiting Factor		A510	C795
Lulu			S615
Mirage			S610
Neighbor			S615
New Folk's Home			A545

AUTHOR–TITLE			ANTHOLOGY
Simak, Clifford D. [Cont'd]			
No Life of Their Own		A865	S600
Operation Stinky			S615
Over the River and Through the Woods			W895
Paradise			S605
Project Mastodon			S600
Retrograde Evolution			S610
Second Childhood		G140	S645
Shadow Show		C410	S610
Shotgun Cure			M240
Simple Way			S 605
The Sitters			S600
Skirmish	C830	C835	S610
Strangers in the Universe			S610
Target Generation			S610
The World That Couldn't Be			G220
The Worlds of Clifford Simak			S615
Worrywart		C790	C935
Simonds, Bruce.			
The Search			M640
Singer, Isaac Bashevis.			
Yachid and Yechida			M640
Sladek, John T.			
1937 A.D.!			H320
Slesar, Henry.			
After			P720
Before the Talent Dies			F220
Chief			M620
Examination Day			P720
The Invisible Man Murder Case			D245
My Father, the Cat			F215
Sloane, William Milligan.			
The Edge of Running Water			S635
Let Nothing You Dismay			S645
The Rim of Morning			S635
Space, Space, Space [Editor]			S640
Stories for Tomorrow [Editor]			S645
To Walk the Night			S635

AUTHOR–TITLE	ANTHOLOGY
Smith, Clark Ashton.	
The Great God Awto	S650
The Immortals of Mercury	S650
The Maker of Gargoyles	S650
The Master of the Asteroid	S650
The Metamorphosis of Earth	D420
Morthylla	S650
Mother of Toads	S650
Murder in the Fourth Dimension	S650
Phoenix	D445
The Plutonian Drug	D435
The Root of Ampoi	S650
Schizoid Creator	S650
Seed from the Sepulcher	S650
Seedling of Mars	S650
Symposium of the Gorgon	S650
Tales of Science and Sorcery	S650
The Theft of the Thirty-Nine Girdles	S650
The Tomb-Spawn	S650
Voyage to Sfanomoe	D425
Smith, Cordwainer.	
Alpha Ralpha Boulevard	M240
The Crime and the Glory of Commander Suzdal	C843
Drunkboat	M635
The Game of Rat and Dragon	B595 C940 G150
The Lady Who Saided the Soul	G200
No, No, Not Rogov!	M615
On the Gen Planet	G170
A Planet Named Shayol	A525
Scanners Live in Vain	F700
When the People Fell	G160
Smith, Edward E.	
Atlantis	G815
The Vortex Blasters	M935
Smith, Evelyn E.	
Baxbr Daxbr	C945 D445 L885 W730
The Hardest Bargain	G200
The Last of the Spode	C845

AUTHOR–TITLE **ANTHOLOGY**

AUTHOR–TITLE		ANTHOLOGY
Stringer, David.		
Acclimatization		N550
High Eight		C303
Strugatsky, Arkady.		
Six Matches [Boris Strugatsky]		P965
Spontaneous Reflex [Boris Strugatsky]		D980
Struther, Jan.		
Ugly Sister		M195
Stuart, Don A.		
Forgetfulness	H430	K705
Twilight		K690
Who Goes There?		H430
Stuart, William W.		
A Husband for My Wife		G165
Inside John Barth		G160
Sturgeon, Theodore [Pseud. of Edward Hamilton Waldo]		
Affair with a Green Monkey		S945
And My Fear Is Great		S950
And Now the News	C410. D655 . J330	M215
Baby Is Three	S940	T290
Bianca's Hands		S935
Bulkhead		S950
Cellmate		S935
The Chromium Helmet		L530
The Clinic		P775
The Comedian's Children	F220	M610
Completely Automatic		C795
A Crime for Llewellyn		S945
Die, Maestro, Die!		S935
E Pluribus Unicorn		S935
The Education of Drusilla Strange		C790
The Fabulous Idiot		S940
Farewell to Eden		D435
Fear Is a Business		M270
Fluffy		S935
The Girl Had Guts		S945
The Golden Egg	C830	C835
Granny Won't Knit	G195	G800

AUTHOR–TITLE		ANTHOLOGY
Sturgeon, Theodore [Cont'd]		
The Hurkle Is a Happy Beast	B565 . C815	S950
Hurricane Trio		S950
Introduction [to Beyond the Barriers of Space]		M580
It		K710
It Opens the Sky		S945
It Wasn't Syzygy		S935
Killdozer!		A520
The Love of Heaven		C805
The Man Who Lost the Sea	M230	M615
The Martian and the Moron		D455
Maturity		C850
Memorial		C825
Memory		C960
Mewhu's Jet	C760	S950
Microcosmic God	C765	M935
Minority Report	D425	S950
Mr. Costello, Hero	B670 . P750	S945
Morality		S940
More Than Human		S940
The Music		S935
The Nail and the Oracle		P720
Never Underestimate	C785	C845
The Other Celia		S945
The Other Man		M600
The Perfect Host		M575
The Pod in the Barrier		S945
The Professor's Teddy-Bear		S935
Rule of Three		G140
A Saucer of Loneliness	G145 . M655	S935
Scars		S935
The Sex Opposite		S935
Shottle Bop		D245
The Silken Swift		S935
Special Aptitude		S950
The Stars Are the Styx		G140
Talent		A835
That Low		K850

AUTHOR–TITLE		ANTHOLOGY
Sturgeon, Theodore [Cont'd]		
Thunder and Roses	A875	S950
Tiny and the Monster	C780	S950
To Here and the Easel		P785
To Marry Medusa		G215
A Touch of Strange		S945
The Touch of Your Hand		S945
The Ultimate Egoist		M585
Unite and Conquer	G815	S950
The Wages of Synergy		S795
A Way Home		S950
A Way of Thinking		S935
What Dead Men Tell		B645
When You're Smiling		C935
The [Widget], The [Wadget], and Boff		B750
The World Well Lost		S935
Yesterday Was Monday		C800
Styron, William.		
Pie in the Sky		C410
Sutherland, Herb.		
The Blond Kid		O140
Sutton, Lee.		
Soul Mate		M230
Swift, Jonathan.		
Laputa		D425
Szilard, Leo.		
Calling All Stars		S995
Grand Central Terminal		C810
The Mark Gable Foundation	P760	S995
My Trial as a War Criminal	M625	S995
Nightmare for Future Reference [Poem]		S995
Report on "Grand Central Terminal"		S995
The Voice of the Dolphins		S995
Taine, J.		
Before the Dawn		W880
Teichner, Albert.		
The Junkmakers		G210

AUTHOR–TITLE	ANTHOLOGY
Temple, William F.	
A Date to Remember	C780
Forget-Me-Not	B570
The Two Shadows	B575 C305
A Way of Escape	C800
Tenn, William [Pseud. of Philip Klass]	
Alexander the Bait	C785
Bernie the Faust	C303 M635 P720
Betelgeuse Bridge	G140 H505
Brooklyn Project	C845 S595
Children of Wonder	T290
Child's Play	A875 P910
Coco-Talk	C306
Counter-Transference	B580
The Custodian	J330 T300
The Deserter	P770
Down Among the Dead Men	D320 T300
Eastward Ho!	M230
Errand Boy	T290
Everybody Loves Irving Bommer	T300
Firewater	Y400
Flirgleflip	T300
Generation of Noah	B575
The House Dutiful	M575
The Ionian Cycle	G830
The Jester	C830 C835
The Liberation of Earth	T300
Me, Myself and I	T300
Null-P	A510 D455
Of All Possible Worlds	T300
Project Hush	A835
The Servant Problem	C840
She Only Goes Out at Night	F215
The Sickness	W745
The Tenants	T300
Time Waits for Winthrop	G215
Venus and the Seven Sexes	B880
Venus Is a Man's World	C765 G140

AUTHOR–TITLE		ANTHOLOGY
Tenn, William [Cont'd]		
"Will You Walk a Little Faster?"		C780
Winthrop Was Stubborn		W740
Tevis, Walter S., jr.		
Far from Home		M230
The IFTH of OOFTH.		G165
Thayer, Frank D., jr.		
Family Tree		D450
Thomas, Gilbert.		
Luana		M265
Thomas, Theodore L.		
Day of Succession		K700
December 28th..		P720
The Doctor		0645
The Far Look	A530	M600
The Lonely Man		G175
Satellite Passage		M610
Test		M245
The Weather Man	A540	C640
Thompson, Will.		
No One Believed Me		M580
Thorne, Roger.		
Take a Deep Breath		M600
Thurber, James.		
Interview with a Lemming		H320
Tilley, Robert J.		
Something Else	M260	M645
Townes, Robert Sherman.		
Problem of Emmy	C830	C835
Tremaine, F. Orlin.		
True Confession		M910
Tschirgi, Robert D.		
A Singular Case of Extreme Electrolyte Balance Associated with Folie a Deux		M645
Tsiolkovsky, Konstantin.		
On the Moon		M275
Tubb, E.C.		
Fresh Guy		M610
Home Is the Hero		C295

AUTHOR–TITLE	ANTHOLOGY
Tubb, E.C. [Cont'd]	
J Is for Jeanne	M645
The Last Day of Summer	M595
The Ming Vase	M635
The Seekers	N555
Unfortunate Passage	C290
Tucker, Wilson [Full Name: Arthur Wilson Tucker]	
Able to Zebra	T895
Exit	M920 T895
Gentlemen—the Queen	T895
Home Is Where the Wrec Is	T895
The Job Is Ended	T895
MCMLV	T895
The Mountaineer	T895
My Brother's Wife	T895
Science-Fiction Subtreasury	T895
The Street Walker	T895
The Tourist Trade	B575 H505
The Wayfairing Strangers	T895
Twain, Mark [Pseud of S.L. Clemens]	
A Connecticut Yankee [Selections]	G225
Selection from the London Times	K700
Van Doren, Mark.	
The Strange Girl	M655
Van Dresser, Peter.	
By Virtue of Circumference	D360
Plum Duff	D360
Rocket to the Sun	D360
Van Vogt, Alfred Elton	
Asylum	H430
Automation	C960
Black Destroyer	H430
A Can of Paint	V185
The Chronicler	G810
Cooperate—or Else	D435
Dear Pen Pal	D430 V185
Defense	V185
Destination: Universe	V185

AUTHOR–TITLE	ANTHOLOGY
Van Vogt, A.E. [Cont'd]	
Dormant	C930 . S795 V185
The Enchanted Village	C795 . M935 V185
Far Centaurus	C775 . G820 V185
Final Command	G825
The First Martians	D585
Fulfillment	H435
The Great Judge	A835
Juggernaut	C870
The Monster	V185
Not Only Dead Men	C780
Process	B570
Recruiting Station	C785
Resurrection	A515
Rogue Ship	M330
The Rulers	V185
The Rull	G830
The Search	V185
The Seesaw	D425 K690
The Silkie	I230
Slan	V190
The Sound	V185
Triad	V190
Vault of the Beast	A875
Voyage of the Space Beagle	V190
The Weapons Shops of Isher	B750 H430
The World of A	V190
Vance, Jack.	
The Devil on Salvation Bluff	P780
The Gift of Gab	C940 W725
Green Magic	M250
Hardluck Diggings	C795
I'll Build Your Dream Castle	C775
The King of Thieves	L640
The Last Castle	N365
Men of the Ten Books	B575 W720
Noise	S795
The Potters of Firsk	C640

AUTHOR–TITLE		ANTHOLOGY
Vance, Jack [Cont'd]		
The Sub-Standard Sardines		N885
Winner Lose All		C785
Varshavsky, Ilya.		
In Man's Own Image		M277
Vasilyev, Mikhail.		
Flying Flowers		M275
Vaughn, Frank E.		
Teen-Age Super Science Stories [Illustrator]		E380
Veillot, Claude.		
The First Days of May		K700
Verne, Jules.		
Around the World in Eighty Days		V530
The Begum's Fortune		M940
The Blockade Runners		V530
Dr. Ox's Experiment		D425
Eternal Adam		M930
From the Earth to the Moon and a Trip Around It		V530
Gil Braltar		M225
In the Year 2889		C760
A Journey to the Center of the Earth	B890	L885
The Omnibus Jules Verne		V530
Round the Moon		K950
Twenty Thousand Leagues Under the Sea	K700	V530
Vidal, Gore.		
Visit to a Small Planet [Play]		L885
Vincent, Harl.		
Prowler of the Wastelands		M940
Rex		M910
Vinge, Vernor.		
Apartness		W895
Voisunsky, Yevgeny.		
Formula for the Impossible [Isai Lukodyanov]		M277
Vonnegut, Kurt, jr.		
The Big Trip Up Yonder		P750
Harrison Bergeron		M240
The Report on the Barnhouse Effect	H505	L885
Tomorrow and Tomorrow and Tomorrow		B670

AUTHOR–TITLE		ANTHOLOGY
Vonnegut, Kurt [Cont'd]		
Unready to Wear		G145
Wakefield, H. Russell.		
Death of a Bumblebee		D450
Walde, A.A.		
Bircher		W900
Waldo, Edward Hamilton.		
See Theodore Sturgeon, pseud.		
Wallace, F.L.		
Accidental Flight		G215
Bolden's Pets		C770
Delay in Transit.		G190
End as a World		G150
Growing Season.		F945
The Impossible Voyage Home		C805
Mezzerow Loves Company		G220
Student Body	A53	G145
Tangle Hold		G195
Wallace, Robert.		
A Living Doll.		M640
Walpole, Horace.		
Saturnian Celia		M270
Walsh, Buthram.		
The Case of Omega Smith		O140
Walter, Arnold & Lorraine.		
Science and Sorcery [Illustrators]		F700
Walter, W. Grey.		
The Singers.		P760
Walton, Harry.		
Episode on Dhee Minor		G830
Schedule.		G820
Wandrei, Donald.		
The Blinding Shadows		D420
Colossus		D425
The Crater		D450
Finality Unlimited		D435
Infinity Zero		D430
Strange Harvest		D455

AUTHOR–TITLE	ANTHOLOGY
Webb, Leland.	
A Man for the Moon	P720
Webb, Ron.	
The Girl with the Hundred Proof Eyes	M255
Weinbaum, Stanley G.	
The Ideal [Selections]	K700
The Lotus Eaters	D425 . M930 W875
The Mad Moon	M925
Parasite Planet	W870
Wellen, Edward.	
Deadly Game	M630
Excerpts from the Encyclopedia of Galactic Culture.	G800
IOU	G210
Welles, Orson.	
Introduction [to S-F: The Years Greatest SF]	M595
Wellman, Manly Wade.	
The Desrick on Yandro	M195
Island in the Sky	M330
The Little Black Train	M205
Men Against the Stars	D575 G820
Vandy, Vandy	M200
Walk Like a Mountain	M270
Wells, Herbert George.	
Aepyornis Island	L885 W450 . W455 . W475
The Apple	W450 W455
The Argonauts of the Air	W455 W475
The Beautiful Suit	W455
Best Science Fiction Stories	W450
Catastrophe	W455
The Chronic Argonauts	M940
The Complete Short Stories of H.G. Wells	W455
The Cone	W455
The Country of the Blind	M930 . W455 W475
The Crystal Egg	K700 W450 W455 . W475 W485
A Deal in Ostriches	W455
The Diamond Maker	W450 W455
The Door in the Wall	W455

Wells, H.G. [Cont'd]

A Dream of Armageddon . . . . W450 . W455 W475
The Empire of the Ants W455 W475
Filmer . . . . W450 . W455 W475
The First Men in the Moon W460 W880
The Flowering of the Strange Orchid W455
The Flying Man. W455
The Food of the Gods W460 W480
The Grisly Folk. W455
The Hammerpond Park Burglary W455
In the Abyss . . . . W450 . W455 . W475 W485
In the Avu Observatory . W450 . W455 . W475 W485
In the Days of the Comet. W460 W480
In the Modern Vein: an Unsympathetic Love Story W455
The Inexperienced Ghost. W455
The Invasion from Mars [Abridged] K950
The Invisible Man . . . . K695 . W450 W460
The Island of Dr. Moreau W460
The Jilting of Jane W455
Jimmy Goggles the God W455
The Land Ironclads W455 W475
The Late Mr. Elvesham W475
Little Mother Up the Morderberg W455
Lord of the Dynamos. W450 W455
The Lost Inheritance. W455
The Magic Shop W455 W475
The Man Who Could Work Miracles W450. W455 W475
Men Like Gods W475
Miss Winchelsea's Heart W455
Mr. Brisher's Treasure W455
Mr. Ledbetter's Vacation W455
Mr. Skelmersdale in Fairyland W455
The Moth W455
My First Aeroplane W455
The New Accelerator D2 45
D425. J330. . W450 . W455 W475
The Pearl of Love W455
The Plattner Story . . . . W450 . W455 W475

AUTHOR–TITLE	ANTHOLOGY
Wells, H.G. [Cont'd]	
Pollock and the Porroh Man	W455
The Purple Pileus	W450 W455
The Reconciliation	W455
The Red Room	W455 W485
The Remarkable Case of Davidson's Eyes	W455 W475
The Sad Story of a Dramatic Critic	W455
The Sea Raiders	W450 W455 W475
Seven Science Fiction Novels of H.G. Wells	W460
A Slip Under the Microscope	W455
The Star	B890 D655 K950 W450 W455 W475
Star Begotten	W475
The Stolen Bacillus	W455 W475
The Stolen Body	W455 W475
The Story of Davidson's Eyes	W450
A Story of the Days to Come	W455 W465 W475
The Story of the Last Trump	W455
The Story of the Late Mr. Elvesham	K710 W455 W485
A Story of the Stone Age	W455 W475
The Strange Orchid	W450 W475
The Temptation of Harringay	M585 W455
Three Prophetic Novels	W465
Through a Window	W455
The Time Machine	K950 W455 W460 W465 W470 W485
The Time Machine [Selections]	K700 S595
The Treasure in the Forest	W455
The Triumphs of a Taxidermist	W455
The Truth about Pyecraft	W455 W475 W485
Twenty-Eight Science Fiction Stories	W475
Under the Knife	W455 W475
An Unsympathetic Love Story	W455
The Valley of Spiders	W455 W475 W485
A Vision of Judgment	W455
The War in the Air	W480
The War of the Worlds	B890 W460 W470 W485
When the Sleeper Wakes	W465

AUTHOR–TITLE ANTHOLOGY

AUTHOR–TITLE **ANTHOLOGY**

Wilcox, Don.
- The Smallest Moon B970
- The Voyage That Lasted Six Hundred Years . . L640

Wilde, Niall.
- A Divvil with the Women M235

Wilhelm, Kate.
- Baby, You Were Great 0645
- The Man Without a Planet M245
- The Mile-Long Spaceship B605 K690
- Staras Flonderans O640

Willey, Robert, pseud.
- See Willy Ley.

Williams, Eric.
- Sunout N550

Williams, Jay.
- The Asa Rule M215
- Somebody to Play With M240

Williams, Ralph.
- Business as Usual, During Alterations A560
- Emergency Landing A835 C760
- The Head Hunters C785 S645
- Pax Galactica N885

Williams, Robert Moore.
- Castaway C780
- The Red Death of Mars D360 G820
- Refuge for Tonight B565
- Robot's Return G825 H430
- The Seekers W870
- The Sound of Bugles D585

Williams-Ellis, Amabel.
- Changeling W735
- Out of This World 1-7 [Mably Owen] W720 W725 W730 W735 W740 W745 W750
- Worlds Apart [Mably Owen] W755

Williamson, Ian.
- Chemical Plant C305 W720

Williamson, Jack.
- Breakdown G815
- The Cold Green Eye K850

AUTHOR–TITLE			ANTHOLOGY
Williamson, Jack [Cont'd]			
The Cosmic Express			M940
The Crucible of Power			G810
Guinevere for Everybody			P780
The Happiest Creature		P765	P775
Hindsight			A875
In the Scarlet Star			W865
The Man from Outside			L640
The Metal Man			R820
The Moon Era			L540
Nonstop to Mars			D585
The Peddler's Nose			P750
The Sun Maker			M330
With Folded Hands	C870	M915	M935
Wilson, Angus.			
Introduction [to A.D. 2500]			O140
Mummy to the Rescue			A360
Wilson, Grahan.			
Cartoon Illustrations		M260	M265
Wilson, Richard.			
Back to Julie			P750
The Carson Effect			M640
The Eight Billion			M260
Friend of the Family			P775
Honor			D320
If You Were the Only—			G185
Kill Me with Kindness			G155
Love			D320
The Watchers in the Glade			G180
Winter, J.A., M.D.			
Expedition Mercy			C770
Expedition Polychrome			N890
Winterbotham, R.R.			
The Fourth Dynasty			C785
Wolf, M.			
Homeland			S645
Wolfe, Bernard.			
The Dot and Dash Bird			P720

AUTHOR–TITLE		ANTHOLOGY
Wolfe, Bernard [Cont'd]		
The Never Ending Penny	M620	P720
Self Portrait	G145	G825
Wolfe, Gene		
Trip, Trap		0645
Wollheim, Donald A.		
Disguise		S645
The End of the World [Editor]		W860
Everyboy's Book of Science Fiction		W865
Flight into Space [Compiler]		W870
The Hidden Planet [Editor].		W875
Planet Passage	G225	W870
The Portable Novels of Science [Editor] . . .		W880
Storm Warning		C780
Swordsmen in the Sky		W885
World's Best Science Fiction 1965–1967 . . .		W890
[Terry Carr]	W895	W900
Wood, Edward W.		
Load of Trouble.		B970
Wood, Margaret.		
The Knitting		O140
Worthington, Will.		
Plenitude		M615
Who Dreams of Ivy		M235
Wright, Gary.		
Mirror of Ice		H320
Wright, Lan.		
Operation Exodus		C290
Wright, Sewell Peaslee.		
Infra-Medians		W865
Wright, Sydney Fowler.		
Automata I, II, and III.		C830
The Better Choice.		C805
Brain		H430
Obviously Suicide		A835
The Rat		K950
Wylie, Philip.		
The Answer		S250
Wyndham, John [Pseud of John Beynon Harris]		
Adaptation.		M935

AUTHOR–TITLE **ANTHOLOGY**

Youd, Christopher S.
  See also John Christopher, pseud.
  Christmas Tree G830
Young, Peter.
  Man Manifold O140
Young, Robert F.
  Added Inducement Y750
  The Courts of Jamshyd Y750
  The Dandelion Girl M625 Y750
  A Drink of Darkness Y750
  Emily and the Bards Sublime Y750
  Flying Pan Y750
  The Garden in the Forest C790
  The Girl Who Made Time Stop Y750
  Goddess in Granite M220 Y750
  Hopsoil Y750
  Juke Doll N785
  Jungle Doctor B595
  Little Red School House Y750
  Nikita Eisenhower Jones M235
  Not to Be Opened B570
  Production Problem Y750
  Promised Planet Y750
  Romance in a Twenty-First Century Used Car Lot Y750
  The Stars Are Calling, Mr. Keats Y750
  To Fell a Tree M270
  When Time Was New I230
  The Worlds of Robert F. Young Y750
  Written in the Stars Y750
  You Ghost Will Walk Y750
Young, Roger Flint.
  Suburban Frontiers C800
Young, Wayland.
  See Hilton-Young, W.
Zelazny, Roger.
  Devil Car G185
  The Doors of His Face, the Lamps of His Mouth M260
  N360

AUTHOR–TITLE		ANTHOLOGY
Zelazny, Roger [Cont'd]		
For a Breath I Tarry		W900
He Who Shapes		N360
The Keys to December		W900
The Moment of the Storm		M265
The Monster and the Maiden		G180
A Rose for Ecclesiastes	M255	M275
Zelikovich, E.		
A Dangerous Invention		M275
Zhuraveleva, Valentina.		
The Astronaut	M275	W735
Stone from the Stars		P965
Storm		M277
Zirul, Arthur.		
The Beautiful Things		M610

BIBLIOGRAPHY OF INDEXED ANTHOLOGIES

The anthologies covered by this index are listed in order on the following pages. The index or code number of the book is shown in the first column, an explanatory symbol indicating source or availability is shown in the second column, and the book itself is shown in the last column. Bibliographic information is given as follows: each entry lists the author or editor, the book's title (underlined), the place of publication, publisher, and date of publication. Note: Publishers of in-print editions may vary from those listed below (as in change from hardbound to paperback).

Explanation of symbols used in Bibliography:

$ Indicates that the book is in print, as determined from Books in Print (1970), British Books in Print (1969), or Paperback Books in Print (July 1970).

F Indicates that the work has been listed in the adult Fiction Catalog, published by the H.W. Wilson Company.

H Indicates that the work has been listed in the Senior High School Catalog, published by the H.W. Wilson Company.

J Indicates that the book has been listed in the Junior High School Catalog, published by the H.W. Wilson Company.

[] Indicates that indexing information has been taken from publisher's communication, library analytical entries, etc., and is presumed but not guaranteed to be accurate.

CODE	REFERENCE		ANTHOLOGY
A360			Aldiss, Brian W., ed. Best Fantasy Stories, Edited with an Introduction by Brian W. Aldiss. London: Faber & Faber [c1962] 208pp.
A370	$		Aldiss, Brian W., ed. Introducing S.F. London: Faber & Faber, 1964. 224pp.
A375		F	Aldiss, Brian W. Who Can Replace a Man? The Best Science Fiction Stories of Brian W. Aldiss. NY: Harcourt, Brace and World [c1965] 253pp.
A510	$	F	Amis, Kingsley, and Robert Conquest, eds. Spectrum; a Science Fiction Anthology. NY: Harcourt, Brace & World [c1961] 304pp.
A515	$	F	Amis, Kingsley, and Robert Conquest, eds. Spectrum II; a Science Fiction Anthology. NY: Harcourt, Brace and World [c1962] 271pp.
A520	$	F	Amis, Kingsley, and Robert Conquest, eds. Spectrum III; a Third Science Fiction Anthology. NY: Harcourt, Brace and World [c1963] 272pp.
A525	$	F	Amis, Kingsley, and Robert Conquest, eds. Spectrum IV; a Science Fiction Anthology. NY: Harcourt, Brace and World [c1965] 320pp.
A530	$	F	Amis, Kingsley, and Robert Conquest, eds. Spectrum V; a Science Fiction Anthology. NY: Harcourt, Brace and World [c1966] 272pp.

CODE	REFERENCE	ANTHOLOGY
A535	F	[Analog Science Fact and Science Fiction] Analog I, Edited by John W. Campbell. NY: Doubleday, 1963. 219pp.
A540	F	[Analog Science Fact and Science Fiction] Analog 2, Edited by John W. Campbell. NY: Doubleday, 1964. 275pp.
A545	F	[Analog Science Fact and Science Fiction] Analog 3, Edited by John W. Campbell. NY: Doubleday, 1965. 269pp.
A550	F	[Analog Science Fact and Science Fiction] Analog 4, Edited by John W. Campbell. NY: Doubleday, 1966. 224pp.
A555	F	[Analog Science Fact and Science Fiction] Analog 5, Edited by John W. Campbell. NY: Doubleday, 1967. 242pp.
A560	F	[Analog Science Fact and Science Fiction] Prologue to Analog, Edited by John W. Campbell. NY: Doubleday, 1962. 308pp.
A565	$	Anderson, Poul, and Gordon R. Dickson. Earthman's Burden. NY: Gnome Press [c1957] 185pp.
A570	$	Anderson, Poul. Flandry of Terra. NY: Chilton [1965] 225pp.
A575	$ F	Anderson, Poul. Time and Stars. Garden City, NY: Doubleday [c1964] 249pp.
A580	F	Anderson, Poul. Trader to the Stars. NY: Doubleday, 1964. 176pp.

CODE	REFERENCE	ANTHOLOGY
A585	F	Anderson, Poul. The Trouble Twisters. Garden City, NY: Doubleday, 1966. 189pp.
A830	$ F	Asimov, Isaac. Earth Is Room Enough; Science Fiction Tales of Our Own Planet. NY: Doubleday [c1957] 192pp.
A835	$	Asimov, Isaac. Fifty Short Science Fiction Tales. Edited and with Introductions by Isaac Asimov and Groff Conklin. NY: Collier Books [c1963] 287 pp. Paper.
A840	F	Asimov, Isaac, ed. The Hugo Winners. Garden City, NY: Doubleday, 1962. 318pp.
A845	$ F H J	Asimov, Isaac. I, Robot. Garden City, NY: Doubleday [c1950] 218pp.
A850	$	Asimov, Isaac. The Martian Way, and Other Stories. Garden City, NY: Doubleday [1955] 222pp.
A855	$ F H	Asimov, Isaac. Nine Tomorrows; Tales of the Near Future. Garden City, NY: Doubleday [c1959] 236pp.
A860	$ F H	Asimov, Isaac. The Rest of the Robots. Garden City, NY: Doubleday, 1964. 556pp.
A865	$ J	Asimov, Isaac, ed. Tomorrow's Children; 18 Tales of Fantasy and Science Fiction. Illustrated by Emanuel Schongut. Garden City, NY: Doubleday [c1966] 431 pp.

CODE	REFERENCE	ANTHOLOGY
A870	F	Asimov, Isaac. *Triangle*. Garden City, NY: Doubleday [1965] 516pp.
A875		Astounding Science Fiction Magazine. *The Astounding Science Fiction Anthology*. Selected and with an Introduction by John W. Campbell jr. NY: Simon and Schuster [c1951] 585pp.
B185	$	Ballard, J.G. *The Drowned World and The Wind from Nowhere*. Garden City, NY: Doubleday, 1965. 316pp.
B190		Ballard, J.G. *Terminal Beach*. [NY] Berkley Publishing Corp. [c1964] 160pp. Paper.
B565	F	*The Best Science Fiction Stories: 1950*. Edited by Everett F. Bleiler and T.E. Dikty, with a Guest Introduction by Vincent Starrett. NY: Frederick Fell [c1950] 247pp.
B570	F	*The Best Science Fiction Stories: 1951*. Edited by Everett F. Bleiler and T.E. Dikty. NY: Frederick Fell [c1951]
B575	F	*The Best Science Fiction Stories: 1952*. Edited and with an Introduction by Everett F. Bleiler and T.E. Dikty. NY: Frederick Fell [c1952] 288pp.
B580	F	*The Best Science Fiction Stories: 1953*. Edited by Everett F. Bleiler and T.E. Dikty with a Guest Introduction by Alfred Bester. NY: Frederick Fell [c1953] 279pp.

CODE	REFERENCE	ANTHOLOGY
B590	F	The Best Science Fiction Stories and Novels: 1955. Edited by T.E. Dikty, with the Science-Fiction Year, by T.E. Dikty and The Science Fiction Book Index by Earl Kemp. NY: Frederick Fell [c1955] 544pp.
B595	F	The Best Science Fiction Stories and Novels: 1956. Edited by T.E. Dikty, with The Science Fiction Year, by T.E. Dikty, and the Science Fiction Book Index, by Earl Kemp. NY: Frederick Fell [c1956] 250pp.
B605	F	The Best Science Fiction Stories and Novels, Ninth Series. Edited by T.E. Dikty, with the Science Fiction Year, by T.E. Dikty, and The Science Fiction Book Index, by Earl Kemp. Chicago: [Advent Publishers] 1958. 258pp.
B645	F	Bleiler, Everett F. and T.E. Dikty, Eds. Imagination Unlimited; Science Fiction and Science. NY: Farrar, Strauss and Young [c1952] 430pp. Another Edition: Ibid. Men of Space and Time [London?] Lane, 1953.
[B660]	$	Blish, James. Best Science Fiction Stories. London: Faber and Faber, 1965.

CODE	REFERENCE	ANTHOLOGY
B665		Blish, James, ed. New Dreams This Morning. [A Science Fiction Anthology about the Future of the Arts] Edited, and with an Introduction by James Blish. NY: Ballantine Books [c1966] 190pp. Paper.
B670	$	Boardman, Tom V. Connoisseur's Science Fiction; an Anthology Edited by Tom Boardman. Baltimore, Md: Penguin Books [c1964] 234pp. Paper.
B750	$F H	Boucher, Anthony, pseud., ed. A Treasury of Great Science Fiction, Volume I. Garden City, NY: Doubleday [c1959] 525pp.
B755	$F H	Boucher, Anthony, pseud, ed. A Treasury of Great Science Fiction, Volume II. Garden City, NY: Doubleday [c1959] 522pp.
B790	$J	Boy's Life [Magazine] The Boy's Life Book of Outer Space Stories, Selected by the Editors of Boy's Life. NY: Random House [c1964] 182pp.
B800	$	Bradbury, Ray. The Day It Rained Forever. London: Hart-Davis, 1962. 254pp.
B805	$	Bradbury, Ray. The Golden Apples of the Sun. Drawings by Joe Mugnaini. Garden City, NY: Doubleday, 1953. 250pp.

CODE	REFERENCE	ANTHOLOGY
B810	$F	Bradbury, Ray. The Illustrated Man. Garden City, NY: Doubleday, 1958. 252pp.
B815	$	Bradbury, Ray. The Machineries of Joy; Short Stories by Ray Bradbury. NY: Simon & Schuster, 1964. 255pp.
B820	$F H J	Bradbury, Ray. The Martian Chronicles. Prefatory Note by Clifton Fadiman. Garden City, NY: Doubleday [c1958, c1946] 222pp.
B825	$	Bradbury, Ray. A Medicine for Melancholy. Garden City, NY: Doubleday, 1959 [c1948] 240pp.
B830	$ H	Bradbury, Ray. R Is for Rocket. NY: Bantam Books [1966, c1962] 184pp.
B835	$ J	Bradbury, Ray. S Is for Space. Garden City, NY: Doubleday, 1966. 238pp.
B840	$ F H	Bradbury, Ray. Twice Twenty-Two; the Golden Apples of the Sun [and] A Medicine for Melancholy. Garden City, NY: Doubleday, 1966. 406pp.
B875		Brown, Fredric. Angels and Spaceships. NY: E.P. Dutton [c1954] 186pp.
[B880]		Brown, Fredric, and Mac Reynolds. Science Fiction Carnival; Fun in Science Fiction. Edited, and with Introductions by Fredric Brown and Mack Reynolds. Chicago: Shasta Publishers [1953] 315pp.

CODE	REFERENCE	ANTHOLOGY
B885		Brown, Fredric. Space on My Hands. Chicago: Shasta Publishers [c1951] 224pp.
B890	$	Brown, J.G., ed. From Frankenstein to Andromeda; an Anthology of Science Fiction, Selected and Introduced by J.G. Brown. London: MacMillan, 1966.
B895		Brunner, John. No Future in It. Garden City, NY: Doubleday, 1964. 181pp.
B970	$	Burroughs, Edgar. At the Earth's Core... Three Science Fiction Novels by Edgar Rice Burroughs, with Illustrations by J. Allen St. John and Paul F. Berdanier. NY: Dover Publications [1963, c1922, 23, 30] 433pp. Paper.
B975	$	Burroughs, Edgar. The Land That Time Forgot and The Moon Maid; Two Science Fiction Novels by Edgar Rice Burroughs; Illustrated by J.Allen St. John. NY: Dover Publications [1963, 1924, 1926] 552pp.
B980	$	Burroughs, Edgar. The Pirates of Venus and Lost on Venus; Two Venus Novels by Edgar Rice Burroughs. Illustrated by Fortunino Matania. NY: Dover Publications [1963, 1932-33] 340pp.
B985	$	Burroughs, Edgar. A Princess of Mars and A Fighting Man of Mars; Two Martian Novels by Edgar Rice Burroughs. NY: Dover [1964, c1912, 1930-31] 356pp.

CODE	REFERENCE	ANTHOLOGY
B990		Burroughs, Edgar. Tales of Three Planets. Illustrated by Roy G. Krenkel. NY: Canaveral Press [Affiliate of Biblo & Tannen, 1964] 282pp.
B995	$	Burroughs, Edgar. Three Martian Novels; Thuvia, Maid of Mars; The Chessmen of Mars; The Master Mind of Mars. NY: Dover [c1962, 1920, 1922, 1928] 499pp.
[C290]		Carnell, John, ed. Gateway to the Stars. [London] Museum Press, 1954. 191pp.
[C295]	$	Carnell, John, ed. Gateway to Tomorrow. [London] Museum Press, 1954. 192pp.
[C305]		Carnell, John, ed. No Place Like Earth. [London] T.V. Boardman, 1952. 255pp.
C310	$ F	Carr, Terry, ed. Science Fiction for People Who Hate Science Fiction. NY: Doubleday, 1966. 190pp.
C410	$	Cerf, Christopher, ed. The Vintage Anthology of Science Fantasy. NY: Vintage Books [1966] 310pp.
C590	$ F H	Clarke, Arthur C. Across the Sea of Stars; an Omnibus Containing the Complete Novels Childhood's End and Earthlight and Eighteen Short Stories. Introduction by Clifton Fadiman. NY: Harcourt, Brace, & World [c1959] 584pp.
C595	$	Clarke, Arthur C. An Arthur C. Clarke Omnibus. London: Sidgwick & Jackson [Toronto: Ambassador Books, c1965]

CODE	REFERENCE	ANTHOLOGY
C600	$F	Clarke, Arthur C. Childhood's End. NY: Ballantine Books [1953] 214pp.
C605	$F	Clarke, Arthur C. Expedition to Earth; Eleven Science Fiction Stories. NY: Ballantine Books [1965, c1953] 167pp.
C610	$	Clarke, Arthur C. From the Ocean, from the Stars; an Omnibus Containing the Complete Novels The Deep Range and The City and the Stars and Twenty-Four Short Stories by Arthur C. Clarke. NY: Harcourt, Brace & World [c1953] 515pp.
C615	$F	Clarke, Arthur C. The Nine Billion Names of God; the Best Short Stories of Arthur C. Clarke. NY: Harcourt, Brace & World [c1967] 277pp.
C620	$F H J	Clarke, Arthur C. The Other Side of the Sky. NY: Harcourt, Brace & World [c1958] 245pp.
C625	$F	Clarke, Arthur C. Prelude to Mars; An Omnibus Containing the Complete Novels Prelude to Space and The Sands of Mars and Sixteen Short Stories. NY: Harcourt, Brace & World [c1957, 1965] 497pp.
C630	$	Clarke, Arthur C. Reach for Tomorrow. NY: Ballantine Books [c1956] 166pp.
C635	$F	Clarke, Arthur C. Tales of Ten Worlds. NY: Harcourt, Brace & World [c1962] 245pp.

CODE	REFERENCE	ANTHOLOGY
C640	$F	Clarke, Arthur C. Time Probe: The Sciences in ScienceFiction; Collected and with an Introduction by Arthur C. Clarke. NY: Delacorte Press [c1966] 242pp.
C750		Conklin, Groff, ed. Another Part of the Galaxy. Greenwich, Connecticut: Fawcett [c1966] Paper.
C760		Conklin, Groff, ed. Big Book of Science Fiction. Edited with an Introduction by Groff Conklin. NY: Crown Publishers [c1950] 545pp.
C765	$F	Conklin, Groff, ed. Giants Unleashed. NY: Grosset & Dunlap [c1965] 248pp.
C770	$	Conklin, Groff, ed. Great Science Fiction about Doctors. Edited with an Introduction and Story Prefaces by Groff Conklin and Noah D. Fabricant, M.D. NY: Collier Books [1963] 412pp.
C775	$	Conklin, Groff, ed. Great Stories of Space Travel. NY: Grosset & Dunlap [c1963] 256pp.
C780	$ F H	Conklin, Groff, ed. Invaders of Earth. Edited by Groff Conklin.... NY: The Vanguard Press [c1952] 333pp.
C785	F	Conklin, Groff, ed. Omnibus of Science Fiction, Edited with an Introduction by Groff Conklin. NY: Crown Publishers [c1952] 562pp.

CODE	REFERENCE	ANTHOLOGY
[C790]		Conklin, Groff, ed. Operation Future. NY: Permabooks [Dist. by Pocket Books 1955] 356pp.
[C795]	$F	Conklin, Groff, ed. Possible Worlds of Science Fiction. NY: Vanguard Press [1951] 372pp.
C800	$ F	Conklin, Groff, ed. Science-Fiction Adventures in Dimension. NY: The Vanguard Press [c1953] 354pp.
C805		Conklin, Groff, ed. Science-Fiction Adventures in Mutation. NY: Vanguard Press [1955] 316pp.
C810	$	Conklin, Groff, ed. Science Fiction by Scientists. Edited with an Introduction and Story Prefaces by Groff Conklin. NY: Collier Books [1962] 313pp.
[C815]		Conklin, Groff, ed. The Science Fiction Galaxy. NY: Permabooks [1950] 242pp.
C820		Conklin, Groff, ed. Science Fiction Oddities. [NY] Berkley Publishing Corporation [c1966] 256pp. Paper.
C825	$	Conklin, Groff, ed. Science Fiction Terror Tales [by] Isaac Asimov [and Others] NY: Gnome Press [1955] 262pp.
C830	$F	Conklin, Groff, ed. Science Fiction Thinking Machines: Robots, Androids, Computers. NY: The Vanguard Press [c1954] 367pp.

CODE	REFERENCE	ANTHOLOGY
C835		Conklin, Groff, ed. Selections from Science Fiction Thinking Machines, Edited by Groff Conklin. NY: Bantam Books [1964] 201pp. Paper.
C840		Conklin, Groff, ed. Seven Come Infinity. Greenwich, Conn: Fawcett Publications [c1966] 288pp. Paper.
C843		Conklin, Groff, ed. Seven Trips Through Time and Space. Greenwich, Conn: Fawcett Publications [c1968] 256pp.
[C845]	$	Conklin, Groff, ed. 17 x Infinity. NY: Dell Publishing Co. [1963] 272pp.
[C850]		Conklin, Groff, ed. 6 Great Short Novels of Science Fiction. [First Ed.] NY: Dell Publishing Company [1954] 384pp.
[C855]		Conklin, Groff, ed. Six Great Short Science Fiction Novels. [NY] Dell Publishing Co. [1960] 350pp.
C870	F	Conklin, Groff, ed. A Treasury of Science Fiction, Edited by Groff Conklin. [NY] Berkley Publishing Corporation. [1965, 1948] 192pp. Paper.
C930	$	Crispin, Edmund, pseud., ed. Best SF Science Fiction Stories, Edited and with an Introduction by Edmund Crispin. London: Faber & Faber [1962, 1955] 368pp.

CODE	REFERENCE	ANTHOLOGY
C935	$	Crispin, Edmund, pseud., ed. *Best SF Two Science Fiction Stories,* Edited with an Introduction by Edmund Crispin. London: Faber & Faber [1956] 296pp.
C940	$	Crispin, Edmund, pseud, ed. *Best SF Three Science Fiction Stories,* Edited with an Introduction by Edmund Crispin. London: Faber [1958] 224pp.
C945	$	Crispin, Edmund, pseud., ed. *Best SF Four Science Fiction Stories,* Edited by Edmund Crispin. London: Faber and Faber [1961] 224pp.
C950	$	Crispin, Edmund, pseud, ed. *Best SF Five Science Fiction Stories,* Edited by Edmund Crispin. London: Faber and Faber [1963] 256pp.
C960		Crossen, Kendell Foster, ed. *Adventures in Tomorrow.* NY: Greenberg Publisher [c1951] 278pp.
C965		Crossen, Kendell Foster, ed. *Future Tense.* New and Old Tales of Science Fiction. NY: Greenberg Publishers [c1952] 364pp.
D245		Davenport, Basil, ed. *Invisible Men,* Edited by Basil Davenport. NY: Ballantine Books [1966, c1960] 158pp. Paper.
D290		De Camp, Lyon Sprague. *The Continent Makers, and Other Tales of the Viagens.* NY: Twayne Publishers [c1953] 272pp.

CODE	REFERENCE	ANTHOLOGY
D300	F	De Camp, Lyon Sprague. A Gun for Dinosaur, and Other Imaginative Tales. Garden City, NY: Doubleday, 1963. 359pp.
D310	$	De Ford, Miriam Allen, ed. Space, Time, and Crime. NY: Paperback Library, Inc. [1968, 1964] 174pp. Paper.
D320	$	De Graeff, Allen, ed. Human and Other Beings. With an Introduction by Groff Conklin, General Editor, Collier Science Fiction. NY: Collier Books [c1963] 319pp.
D360		Del Rey, Lester. The Year after Tomorrow. An Anthology of Science Fiction Stories Selected by Lester Del Rey [et al] Illustrated by Mel Hunter. Philadelphia: John C. Winston [c1954] 339pp.
D420		Derleth, August, ed. Beachheads in Space. London: Weidenfeld & Nicholson [c1952] 224pp.
D425	F	Derleth, August, ed. Beyond Time and Space. NY: Pellegrini & Cudahy, 1950. 643pp.
D430		Derleth, August, ed. Far Boundaries; 20 Science Fiction Stories Selected by August Derleth. NY: Pellegrini and Cudahy [c1951] 292pp.
D435		Derleth, August, ed. The Outer Reaches; Favorite Science Fiction Tales Chosen by Their Authors. [NY] Pellegrini & Cudahy [c1951] 342pp.

CODE	REFERENCE	ANTHOLOGY
D440		Derleth, August, ed. Portals of Tomorrow; the Best Tales of Science Fiction and Other Fantasy. NY: Rinehart [1954] 371pp.
D445	$	Derleth, August. Time to Come: Science-Fiction Stories of Tomorrow. NY: Farrar, Strauss & Young [c1954] 311pp.
D450		Derleth, August, ed. Travelers by Night. Sauk City, Wis: Arkham House, 1967.
D455	F	Derleth, August, ed. Worlds of Tomorrow; Science Fiction with a Difference, Selected and with a Foreword by August Derleth. [NY] Pellegrini and Cudahy, 1953. 351pp.
[D575]		Dikty, T.E., ed. Every Boy's Book of Outer Space Stories. NY: Frederick Fell [1960] 283pp.
D580		Dikty, T.E., ed. Five Tales from Tomorrow; Selected from the Best Science Fiction Stories: 1955. Greenwich, Conn: Fawcett Publications [c1957] 176pp. Paper.
D585	$	Dikty, T.E., ed. Great Science Fiction Stories about Mars. NY: Frederick Fell [c1966] 187pp.
D590	$	Dikty, T.E., ed. Great Science Fiction Stories about the Moon, Edited by T. E. Dikty. NY: Fell [1967] 221pp.

CODE	REFERENCE	ANTHOLOGY
D655	$	Doherty, G.D., ed. Second Orbit; a New Science Fiction Anthology for Schools, Compiled by G.D. Doherty, B.A. London: John Murray [c1965] 218pp.
D755	$	Doyle, Arthur Conan. The Poison Belt. Illustrated by William Pene du Bois; Introduction by John Dickson Carr; Epilogue by Dr. Harlow Shapley. NY: Macmillan [c1964, c1913] 158pp.
D980	$	Dutt, Violet L., Translator. Soviet Science Fiction. With a New Introduction by Isaac Asimov. NY: Collier Books [c1962] 189pp.
E375	$	Elam, Richard M., jr. Teen-Age Science Fiction Stories. Introduction by Capt. Burr W. Leyson. Illustrated by Charles H. Geer. NY: Lantern Press [c1952] 254pp.
E380	$	Elam, Richard M., jr. Teen-Age Super Science Stories.... Illustrated by Frank E. Vaughn. NY: Lantern Press [c1957] 253pp.
E460		Ellison, Harlan. From the Land of Fear. NY: Belmont Books [c1967] 176pp.
F215		Fantastic Universe. The Fantastic Universe Omnibus, Edited by Hans Stefan Santesson. Introduction by Lester Del Rey. Englewood Cliffs, N.J: Prentice-Hall [c1960] 270pp.

CODE	REFERENCE	ANTHOLOGY
F220	$	Ferman, Joseph, ed. *No Limits,* Edited by Joseph W. Ferman. NY: Ballantine Books [1964, 1958] 192pp. Paper.
F225		Finney, Jack. *The Third Level.* NY: Rinehart & Co. [c1957] 188pp.
[F700]		Ford, Garrett. *Science and Sorcery;* Illustrated by Arnold and Lorraine Walter. Los Angeles: Fantasy Publishing Co. [1953] 327pp.
F945	$	*The Frozen Planet and Other Stories.* [NY] Macfadden-Bartell [1966] 160pp.
[G140]		Galaxy Science Fiction Magazine. *The [First] Galaxy Reader of Science Fiction.* NY: Crown Publishers [1952] 566 pp.
G145		Galaxy Science Fiction Magazine. *The Second Galaxy Reader of Science Fiction.* Edited and with an Introduction by H.L.Gold.... NY: Crown Publishers [c1954] 504pp.
G150		Galaxy Science Fiction Magazine. *The Third Galaxy Reader.* Edited by H.L. Gold. Garden City, NY: Doubleday [c1958] 262pp.
G155	F	Galaxy Science Fiction Magazine. *The Fourth Galaxy Reader.* Edited by H.L. Gold. Garden City, NY: Doubleday [c1959] 264pp.

CODE	REFERENCE	ANTHOLOGY
G160		Galaxy Science Fiction Magazine. The Fifth Galaxy Reader. Edited by H.L. Gold. Garden City, NY: Doubleday, 1961. 260pp.
G165	F	Galaxy Science Fiction Magazine. The Sixth Galaxy Reader. Edited by H.L. Gold. Garden City, NY: Doubleday, 1962. 240pp.
G170	F	Galaxy Science Fiction Magazine. The Seventh Galaxy Reader. Edited by Frederik Pohl. Garden City, NY: Doubleday, 1964. 247pp.
G175	F	Galaxy Science Fiction Magazine. The Eighth Galaxy Reader. Edited by Frederik Pohl. Garden City, NY: Doubleday, 1965. 248pp.
G180	F	Galaxy Science Fiction Magazine. The Ninth Galaxy Reader. Edited by Frederik Pohl. Garden City, NY: Doubleday, 1966. 203pp.
G185	F	Galaxy Science Fiction Magazine. The Tenth Galaxy Reader. Edited by Frederik Pohl. Garden City, NY: Doubleday, 1967. 232pp.
G190		Galaxy Science Fiction Magazine. Bodyguard and Four Other Short Novels from Galaxy. Introduction by Frederik Pohl. Garden City, NY: Doubleday, 1960. 312pp.

CODE	REFERENCE	ANTHOLOGY
G195		Galaxy Science Fiction Magazine. Five Galaxy Short Novels. Edited by H.L. Gold. Garden City, NY: Doubleday, 1958. 287pp.
G200		Galaxy Science Fiction Magazine. Mind Partner and 8 Other Novelets from Galaxy. Edited by H.L. Gold. NY: Pocket Books [c1961] 241pp. Paper.
G210	$	Galaxy Science Fiction Magazine. The Six Fingers of Time and Other Stories. [From Galaxy Magazine] [NY] Macfadden-Bartell [1965] 128pp. paper.
G215		Galaxy Science Fiction Magazine. Time Waits for Winthrop, and Four Other Short Novels from Galaxy, Edited by Frederik Pohl. Garden City, NY: Doubleday, 1962. 336pp.
G220		Galaxy Science Fiction Magazine. The World That Couldn't Be and 8 Other Novelets from Galaxy. Garden City, NY: Doubleday, 1959. 288pp.
[G225]		Gallant, Joseph, ed. Stories of Scientific Imagination. NY: Oxford Book Co., 1954. 152pp.
G800	F	Greenberg, Martin, ed. All About the Future [by] Poul Anderson [and Others] Introductions by Robert A. Heinlein [and] Isaac Asimov. [1st Ed.] NY: Gnome Press [1955] 374pp.

CODE	REFERENCE	ANTHOLOGY
G805		Greenberg, Martin, ed. *Coming Attractions.* Introduction by Dwight Wayne Batteau. NY: Gnome Press [c1957] 254pp.
G810		Greenberg, Martin. *Five Science Fiction Novels* [1st ed] NY: Gnome Press [1952] 382pp.
G815		Greenberg, Martin, Ed. *Journey to Infinity.* Introduced by Fletcher Pratt. NY: Gnome Press [c1951] 381pp.
G820		Greenberg, Martin, ed. *Men Against the Stars.* Introduced by Willy Ley. NY: Gnome Press [1950] 351pp.
G825		Greenberg, Martin, ed. *The Robot and the Man.* NY: Gnome Press [c1953] 251pp.
G830	F	Greenberg, Martin, ed. *Travelers of Space.* Introduced by Willy Ley; Illustrated by Edd Cartier. Special Feature: Science Fiction Dictionary; Introd. by Samuel Anthony Peoples. Special Story for Illustration by David Kyle. [1st Ed.] NY: Gnome Press [c1951] 400pp.
H320	$	Harrison, Harry and Brian W. Aldiss, eds. *Best SF: 1967.* NY: Berkley Publishing Co. [c1968] 256pp. Paper.
H430	$ F	Healy, Raymond J. and Francis McComas, eds. *Famous Science-Fiction Stories.* NY: The Modern Library [c1946, 1957] 997pp.

CODE	REFERENCE	ANTHOLOGY
H435	F	Healy, Raymond J., ed. New Tales of Space and Time. Introduction by Anthony Boucher. NY: Henry Holt & Company [c1951] 294pp.
H440	F	Healy, Raymond J., ed. 9 Tales of Space and Time. [NY: Henry Holt & Company, c1954] 307pp.
H470	$	Heinlein, Robert A. Assignment in Eternity, by Robert A. Heinlein [NY] New American Library [c1953] 192pp.
H475	$ F	Heinlein, Robert A. The Green Hills of Earth; Rhysling and the Adventure of the Entire Solar System. With an Appreciation by Mark Reinsberg. Chicago: Shasta Pubs. [1951] 256pp.
H480	$	Heinlein, Robert A. The Man Who Sold the Moon. [NY] New American Library [1963] 159pp.
H485	$ F	Heinlein, Robert A. The Menance from Earth. NY: New American Library [c1959] 189pp.
H490	$ F	Heinlein, Robert A. The Past Through Tomorrow; "Future History" Stories. NY: G.P. Putnam's Sons [c1967] 667pp.
H500	$ F	Heinlein, Robert A. Three by Heinlein: The Puppet Masters, Waldo, Magic, Inc., by Robert A. Heinlein. Garden City, NY: Doubleday, 1965. 426pp.

CODE	REFERENCE	ANTHOLOGY
H505	F	Heinlein, Robert A. Tomorrow, the Stars; a Science Fiction Anthology Edited and with an Introduction by Robert A. Heinlein. Garden City, NY: Doubleday, 1952. 249pp.
H510	$ F	Heinlein, Robert A. Waldo and Magic, Inc. Two Short Novels by Robert A. Heinlein. NY: Pyramid Books [1963, c1950] 191pp. Paper.
H515	$ F	Henderson, Zenna. The Anything Box. Garden City, NY: Doubleday, 1965. 205pp.
H520	$ F	Henderson, Zenna. The People: No Different Flesh. Garden City, NY: Doubleday, 1967. 236pp.
H850		Howard, Ivan, ed. Escape to Earth. NY: Belmont Books [1963, c1952-7] 173pp.
H855		Howard, Robert E. The Coming of Conan. NY: The Gnome Press [c1953] 224pp.
H857	$	Howard, Robert E., and L. Sprague de Camp. Conan the Adventurer. NY: Lancer Books [c1966] 224pp. Paper.
H859	$	Howard, Robert E., and L. Sprague de Camp. Conan the Warrior. NY: Lancer Books [c1967] 222pp. Paper.
H860		Howard, Robert E., and L. Sprague de Camp. Tales of Conan. NY: Gnome Press [c1955]

CODE	REFERENCE	ANTHOLOGY
H865	$	Howard, Robert E. Wolfshead. Edited by Glenn Lord. NY: Lancer Books [c1968] 190pp. Paper.
H870	$	Hoyle, Fred. Element 79. [NY] New American Library [c1967] 180pp.
I230	$ F	If [Magazine] The If Reader of Science Fiction. Edited by Frederik Pohl. Garden City, NY: Doubleday, 1966. 252 pp.
J310		Jameson, Malcolm. Bullard of the Space Patrol. Edited by Andre Norton. Cleveland & NY: World Publishing Co. [c 1951] 255pp.
J330	$	Janifer, Laurence M., ed. Master's Choice: the Best Science-Fiction Stories of All Time Chosen by the Masters of Science Fiction. NY: Simon & Schuster [c1966] 350pp.
K690	$ F	Knight, Damon, ed. Beyond Tomorrow; Ten Science Fiction Adventures. NY: Harper and Row [c1965] 333pp.
K695	$ F	Knight, Damon, ed. A Century of Great Short Science Fiction Novels. Edited by Damon Knight. NY: Delacorte Press [c1964] 379pp.
K700	F	Knight, Damon, ed. A Century of Science Fiction. Edited, with an Introduction and Notes, by Damon Knight. NY: Simon & Schuster, 1962. 352pp.

CODE	REFERENCE	ANTHOLOGY
K705	$ F	Knight, Damon, ed. Cities of Wonder. Garden City, NY: Doubleday, 1966. 252pp.
K710		Knight, Damon, ed. The Dark Side. Garden City, NY: Doubleday, 1965. 240pp.
K715		Knight, Damon. Far Out; 13 Science Fiction Stories by Damon Knight. NY: Simon and Schuster, 1961. 282pp. In print: British edition.
K720	F	Knight, Damon. Three Novels: Rule Golden, Natural State, The Dying Man. Garden City, NY: Doubleday, 1967. 189pp.
K725	$	Knight, Damon. Turning on; Thirteen Stories. Garden City, NY: Doubleday, 1966. 180pp.
K730	$	Knight, Damon, ed. Worlds to Come; Nine Science Fiction Adventures, Edited by Damon Knight. NY: Harper and Row [c1967] 335pp.
K840		Kornbluth, C.M. The Explorers; Short Stories. NY: Ballantine Books [1963, c1954] 147pp. Paper.
K845	$	Kornbluth, C.M. A Mile Beyond the Moon. Garden City, NY: Doubleday, 1958. 239pp.

CODE	REFERENCE	ANTHOLOGY
K850	F	Kornbluth, Mary, ed. Science Fiction Showcase; an Anthology Edited by Mary Kornbluth. Garden City, NY: Doubleday [c1959] 264pp.
K950	F	Kuebler, Harold W., Ed. The Treasury of Science Fiction Classics. Garden City, NY: Hanover House [1954] 694pp.
K970		Kuttner, Henry. Ahead of Time; Ten Stories of Science Fiction and Fantasy. NY: Ballantine Books [c1953] 177pp.
L375		Laumer, Keith. Galactic Diplomat; Nine Incidents of the Corps Diplomatique Terrestrienne. Garden City, NY: Doubleday, 1965. 227pp.
L380	$ F	Laumer, Keith. Nine by Laumer. Garden City, NY: Doubleday, 1967. 222pp.
L530	F	Leinster, Murray, Ed. Great Stories of Science Fiction. Introduction by Clifton Fadiman. NY: Random House [c1951] 321pp.
L535		Leinster, Murray. Sidewise in Time, and Other Scientific Adventures. Chicago: Shasta Publishers, 1950. 211pp.
L540		Leinster, Murray, et.al. Three Stories. by Murray Leinster, Jack Williamson, and John Wyndham. With an Introduction by Sam Moskowitz. Garden City, NY: Doubleday, 1967. 184pp.

CODE	REFERENCE	ANTHOLOGY
L640		Lesser, Milton, Ed. Looking Forward; an Anthology of Science Fiction. NY: The Beechhurst Press [c1953] 400pp.
L885		Loughlin, Richard L., and Lilian M. Popp, Eds. Journeys in Science Fiction. NY: Globe Book Co. [c1961] 655pp.
M190	F	The Magazine of Fantasy and Science Fiction. The Best from Fantasy and Science Fiction, Edited by Anthony Boucher and J. Francis McComas. Boston: Little, Brown [c1952] 214pp.
M195	$	The Magazine of Fantasy and Science Fiction. The Best from Fantasy and Science Fiction, Second Series, Edited by Anthony Boucher and J.Francis McComas. Boston: Little, Brown [c1953] 270pp.
M200	$	The Magazine of Fantasy and Science Fiction. The Best from Fantasy and Science Fiction, 3rd Series. Edited by Anthony Boucher and J.Francas McComas. Garden City, NY: Doubleday [c1954]
M205		The Magazine of Fantasy and Science Fiction. The Best from Fantasy and Science Fiction, Fourth Series. Edited by Anthony Boucher. Garden City, NY: Doubleday [c1955] 250pp.
M210	$	The Magazine of Fantasy and Science Fiction. The Best from Fantasy and Science Fiction, 5th Series. Edited by Anthony Boucher. Garden City, NY: Doubleday, 1956. 256pp.

CODE	REFERENCE	ANTHOLOGY
M215	$	The Magazine of Fantasy and Science Fiction. The Best from Fantasy and Science Fiction, Sixth Series. Edited by Anthony Boucher. Garden City, NY: Doubleday [c1957] 255pp.
M220		The Magazine of Fantasy and Science Fiction. The Best from Fantasy and Science Fiction, Seventh Series. Edited by Anthony Boucher. NY: Doubleday [c1956-58] 264pp.
M225		The Magazine of Fantasy and Science Fiction. The Best from Fantasy and Science Fiction, Eighth Series. Edited by Anthony Boucher. Garden City, NY: Doubleday [c1957-59] 240pp.
M230		The Magazine of Fantasy and Science Fiction. The Best from Fantasy and Science Fiction, 9th Series. Edited by Robert P. Mills. Garden City, NY: Doubleday, 1960. 264pp.
M235		The Magazine of Fantasy and Science Fiction.The Best from Fantasy and Science Fiction, Tenth Series. Edited by Robert P. Mills. Garden City, NY: Doubleday, 1961. 262pp.
M240	$	The Magazine of Fantasy and Science Fiction. The Best from Fantasy and Science Fiction, Eleventh Series. Edited by Robert P. Mills. Garden City, NY: Doubleday, 1962. 258pp.

CODE	REFERENCE	ANTHOLOGY
M245	$	The Magazine of Fantasy and Science Fiction. The Best from Fantasy and Science Fiction, 12th Series. Edited by Avram Davidson. Garden City, NY: Doubleday, 1963. 225pp.
M250	$	The Magazine of Fantasy and Science Fiction. The Best from Fantasy and Science Fiction, Thirteenth Series. Edited by Avram Davidson. Garden City, NY: Doubleday, 1964. 255pp. In print: British edition.
M255	$ H	The Magazine of Fantasy and Science Fiction. The Best from Fantasy and Science Fiction, 14th Series. Edited by Avram Davidson. Garden City, NY: Doubleday, 1965. 251pp. In print: British edition.
M260	H	The Magazine of Fantasy and Science Fiction. The Best from Fantasy and Science Fiction, 15th Series. Edited by Edward L. Ferman. Garden City, NY: Doubleday, 1966. 248pp.
M265		The Magazine of Fantasy and Science Fiction. The Best from Fantasy and Science Fiction, 16th Series. Edited by Edward L. Ferman. Garden City, NY: Doubleday, 1967. 264pp.
M270		The Magazine of Fantasy and Science Fiction. A Decade of Fantasy and Science Fiction. Selected by Robert P. Mills. Garden City, NY: Doubleday [c1958] 406pp.

CODE	REFERENCE	ANTHOLOGY
M275	$	Magidoff, Robert, Comp. *Russian Science Fiction,* an Anthology. Compiled and Edited with an Introduction by Robert Magidoff. Translated by Doris Johnson. [NY] New York University Press [1964] 272pp.
M277	$	Magidoff, Robert, Comp. *Russian Science Fiction 1968;* an Anthology Compiled and Edited with an Introduction by Robert Magidoff. Translated by Helen Jacobson. NY: New York University Press, 1968. 211pp.
M280		Malec, Alexander. *Extrapolasis;* Stories by Alexander Malec. Garden City, N Y: Doubleday, 1967. 192pp.
M330		Margulies, Leo, and Oscar J. Friend, Eds. *The Giant Anthology of Science Fiction;* 10 Complete Short Novels. NY: Merlin Press [c1954] 580pp.
M455	F	Maurois, Andre. *The Weigher of Souls and The Earth Dwellers;* Autobiographical Introduction; Epilogue by Jacques Choron. Tr. by Hamis Miles; Illus. by by Leonard Everett Fisher. NY: Macmillan, 1963. 187pp.
M570	$	Merril, Judith, Comp. *Best of the Best* NY: Dell, 1967.
M575	F	Merril, Judith, Ed. *Beyond Human Ken;* Twenty-one Startling Stories of Science Fiction and Fantasy. With an Introduction by Fletcher Pratt. NY: Random House [c1952] 334pp.

CODE	REFERENCE	ANTHOLOGY
M580	F	Merril, Judith, Ed. Beyond the Barriers of Space and Time. With an Introduction by Theodore Sturgeon. NY: Random House [1954] 294pp.
[M585]		Merril, Judith, Ed. Human? NY: Lion Books by Arrangement with Postal Publications [1954] 190pp.
M595	F	Merril, Judith, Ed. S-F: the Year's Greatest Science Fiction and Fantasy; with an Introduction by Orson Welles. NY: Gnome Press [1956] 342pp.
M600	F	Merril, Judith, Ed. SF: '57; the Year's Greatest Science Fiction and Fantasy. NY: The Gnome Press [c1957] 320pp.
M605		Merril, Judith, Ed. SF: '58; the Year's Greatest Science Fiction and Fantasy. Hicksville, NY: The Gnome Press [c1958] 255pp.
M610		Merril, Judith, Ed. SF: '59; the Year's Greatest Science Fiction and Fantasy. Hicksville, NY: The Gnome Press [c1959] 256pp.
M615		Merril, Judith, Ed. The 5th Annual of the Year's Best S-F. NY: Simon and Schuster, 1960. 320pp.
M620	$ F	Merril, Judith, Ed. The Year's Best S-F; the 6th Annual. NY: Simon and Schuster, 1961. 381pp.

CODE	REFERENCE	ANTHOLOGY
M625		Merril, Judith, ed. The 7th Annual of the Year's Best S-F. NY: Simon & Schuster, 1962. 399pp.
M630	F	Merril, Judith, Ed. The 8th Annual of the Year's Best S-F. NY: Simon and Schuster, 1963. 382pp.
M635	F	Merril, Judith, Ed. The 9th Annual of the Year's Best S-F. NY: Simon and Schuster, 1964. 384pp.
M640	F	Merril, Judith, Ed. The Year's Best SF; 10th Annual Edition. NY: Delacorte [c1965] 400pp.
M645	F	Merril, Judith, Ed. The Year's Best S-F; 11th Annual Edition. NY: Delacorte Press [c1966] 384pp.
M655	$	Mills, Robert P., Ed. The Worlds of Science Fiction, Edited and with an Introduction by Robert P. Mills. NY: Dial Press, 1963. 349pp.
M910	$	Moskowitz, Sam, Ed. The Coming of the Robots; Edited and with an Introduction by Sam Moskowitz. NY: Collier Books [c1963] 254pp.

CODE	REFERENCE	ANTHOLOGY
M915	$	Moskowitz, Sam, Ed. Doorway into Time and Other Stories from Modern Masterpieces of Science Fiction, Edited by Sam Moskowitz. [NY] Macfadden-Bartell [c1965] 144pp. Paper.
M920		Moskowitz, Sam, Comp. Editor's Choice in Science Fiction. NY: The McBride Company [c1954] 285pp.
M925	$	Moskowitz, Sam, Ed. Exploring Other Worlds. Edited and with an Introduction by Sam Moskowitz. NY: Collier Books [c1963] 256pp.
M930	$ F	Moskowitz, Sam, Ed. Masterpieces of Science Fiction. NY: World Publishing Co. [c1966] 552pp.
M935	F	Moskowitz, Sam, Ed. Modern Masterpieces of Science Fiction. NY: World Publishing Co. [c1965] 518pp.
M940		Moskowitz, Sam, and Roger Elwood, Eds. Strange Signposts; an Anthology of the Fantastic. NY: Holt, Rinehart and Winston [c1966] 319pp.
N360	$ F	Nebula Award Stories, 1965. Edited by Damon Knight. Garden City, NY: Doubleday, 1966. 299pp.
N365	$	Nebula Award Stories: Two. Edited by Brian W. Aldiss and Harry Harrison. Garden City, NY: Doubleday, 1967 254pp.

CODE	REFERENCE	ANTHOLOGY
N530	$	New Writings in SF-1. Edited by John Carnell. London: Dennis Dobson [c1964]
N535	$	New Writings in SF-2. Edited by John Carnell. [NY: Bantam Books, c1964] 150pp.
N540	$	New Writings in SF-3. Edited by John Carnell. London: Dennis Dobson [c1965]
N545	$	New Writings in SF-4. Edited by John Carnell. NY: Bantam Books [c1965] 154pp.
N550	$	New Writings in SF-5. Edited by John Carnell. London: Dennis Dobson [c1965]
N555	$	New Writings in SF-6. Edited by John Carnell. London: Dennis Dobson [c1965]
N560	$	New Writings in SF-7. Edited by John Carnell. London: Dennis Dobson [c1966] 190pp.
N565	$	New Writings in SF-8. Edited by John Carnell. London: Dennis Dobson [c1966]
N570	$	New Writings in SF-9. Edited by John Carnell. London: Dennis Dobson [c1966]

CODE	REFERENCE	ANTHOLOGY
N785	$	Nolan, William F. The Pseudo-People; Androids in Science Fiction. Edited by William F. Nolan. With an Introduction by A.E. Van Vogt. Los Angeles: Sherbourne Press [1965] 238pp.
N880		Norton, Andre, Ed. Space Pioneers. Edited with an Introduction and Notes by Andre Norton. NY: World Publishing Company [c1954] 294pp.
N885		Norton, Andre, Ed. Space Police. Edited with an Introduction and Notes by Andre Norton. NY: World Publishing Company [c1956] 255pp.
N890		Norton, Andre, Ed. Space Service, Edited, with an Introduction and Notes by Andre Norton. Cleveland: World Publishing Co. [1953] 277pp.
N930	$	Nourse, Alan E. The Counterfeit Man; More Science Fiction Stories. NY: David McKay Co. [c1952] 185pp.
N935	$ J	Nourse, Alan E. Tiger by the Tail, and Other Science Fiction Stories. NY: David McKay [c1961] 184pp.
[O140]		The Observer [London] A.D. 2500; The Observer Prize Stories, 1954. With an Introduction by Angus Wilson. London: Heineman [1955] 241pp.
O640	$ F	Orbit I; a Science Fiction Anthology. Edited by Damon Knight. NY: G.P. Putnam's Sons [c1966] 192pp.

CODE	REFERENCE	ANTHOLOGY
0645		Knight, Damon, ed. Damon Knight's Orbit 2; the Best New Science Fiction of the Year. NY: G. P. Putnam's [c1967] 255pp.
P125		Padgett, Lewis. A Gnome There Was, and Other Tales of Science Fiction and Fantasy. NY: Simon and Schuster, 1950. 276pp.
P130		Padgett, Lewis. Robots Have No Tails. NY: Gnome Press [c1952] 224pp.
P495		The Petrified Planet. With an Introduction by John D. Clark. NY: Twayne Publishers, 1952. 263pp.
P720	$ F	Playboy Magazine. The Playboy Book of Science Fiction and Fantasy, Selected by the Editors of Playboy. [Chicago] Playboy Press [c1966] 402pp.
P750	F	Pohl, Frederik, Ed. Assignment in Tomorrow; an Anthology Edited and with an Introduction by Frederik Pohl. Garden City, NY: Hanover House [c1954] 317pp.
P757	$	Pohl, Frederik. Digits and Dastards [Science Fiction (and Fact)] NY: Ballantine Books [c1966] 192pp. Paper.
P760		Pohl, Frederik, Ed. The Expert Dreamers. Garden City, NY: Doubleday, 1962. 248pp.
P765	F	Pohl, Frederik, Ed. Star of Stars. Garden City, NY: Doubleday [c1960]240pp.

CODE	REFERENCE	ANTHOLOGY
P770	F	Pohl, Frederik, Ed. Star Science Fiction Stories. NY: Ballantine Books [c1953] 205pp.
P775	F	Pohl, Frederik, Ed. Star Science Fiction Number 2. NY:Ballantine Books[c1953]
P780	F	Pohl, Frederik, Ed. Star Science Fiction Stories Number 3. NY: Ballantine Books [c1954] 186pp.
P785		Pohl, Frederik, Ed. Star Short Novels. NY: Ballantine Books [c1954] 168pp.
P910	F	Pratt, Fletcher, Ed. World of Wonder; an Introduction to Imaginative Literature. Foreword by Edith Mirrieless. NY: Twayne Publishers [c1951] 445pp.
P965	$	Prokofieva, R., Translator. More Soviet Science Fiction. With an Introduction by Isaac Asimov. NY: Collier Books [1962] 190pp. Paper.
R820	$	Ross, Joseph, Comp. Best of Amazing. Selected by Joseph Ross. Garden City, NY: Doubleday, 1967. 222pp.
S250	F	The Saturday Evening Post [Periodical] The Post Reader of Fantasy and Science Fiction, Selected by the Editors of The Saturday Evening Post. Garden City, NY: Doubleday, 1964. 311pp.
S355		Schmitz, James H. Agent of Vega. Hicksville, NY: The Gnome Press [c1960] 191pp.

CODE	REFERENCE	ANTHOLOGY
S360		Schmitz, James H. A Nice Day for Screaming, and Other Tales of the Hub. NY: Chilton Books [c1965] 157pp.
S420		The Science-Fictional Sherlock Holmes. 2845 South Gilpin Street, Denver, Colorado; The Council of Four, 1960 [c1960 by Robert C. Peterson] 137pp.
S485		Serling, Rod. New Stories from the Twilight Zone. NY: Bantam Books [c1962] 122pp. Paper.
S490	$	Serling, Rod. Rod Serling's The Twilight Zone. Adapted by Walter B. Gibson; Illustrated by Earl E. Mayan. NY: Grosset & Dunlap [c1963] 207pp.
S585	$ F	Silverberg, Robert. Earthmen and Strangers; Nine Stories of Science Fiction. NY: Duell, Sloan & Pearce [c1966] 240pp.
S590		Silverberg, Robert. To Worlds Beyond; Stories of Science Fiction by Robert Silverberg [with a Foreword by Isaac Asimov] NY: Chilton [c1965] 170pp.
S595	$	Silverberg, Robert, Ed. Voyagers in Time; Twelve Tales of Science Fiction. NY: Meredith Press [1967] 243pp.
S600	$ F	Simak, Clifford D. All the Traps of Earth, and Other Stories. Garden City, NY: Doubleday, 1962. 287pp.

CODE	REFERENCE	ANTHOLOGY
S605	$ F	Simak, Clifford D. City. [NY] The Gnome Press [1952] 244pp.
S610		Simak, Clifford D. Strangers in the Universe; Science Fiction Stories by Clifford Simak. NY: Simon and Schuster [c1966] 281pp.
S615	F	Simak, Clifford D. The Worlds of Clifford Simak. NY: Simon and Schuster, 1960. 378pp.
S635	$ F	Sloane, William Milligan. The Rim of Morning; Including The Edge of Running Water [and] To Walk the Night NY: Dodd, Mead & Co. [1964, c1955] 295, 306pp.
S640	J	Sloane, William Milligan, Ed. Space, Space, Space. Stories about the Time when Men Will Be Adventuring to the Stars; Selected, Introduction and Commentaries by William Sloane. NY: Grosset & Dunlap [c1953] 288pp.
S645	F	Sloane, William Milligan, Ed. Stories for Tomorrow; an Anthology of Modern Science Fiction [by] Bradbury [and Others] NY: Funk & Wagnalls, 1954. 628pp.
S650	$	Smith, Clark Ashton. Tales of Science and Sorcery. Sauk City, Wis. Arkham House, 1964. 256pp.

CODE	REFERENCE	ANTHOLOGY
S790	F	Stapledon, Olaf. To the End of Time; the Best of Olaf Stapledon. Selection and Introduction by Basil Davenport. NY: Funk & Wagnalls [1953] 775pp
S795		Startling Stories. The Best from Startling Stories, Compiled by Samuel Mines, with an Introduction by Robert A. Heinlein. NY: Henry Holt & Co. [1953] 301pp.
S935	$	Sturgeon, Theodore, pseud. E Pluribus Unicorn; a Collection of Short Stories of Theodore Sturgeon. NY: Abelard Press [c1953] 276pp.
S940	$	Sturgeon, Theodore. More than Human. NY: Ballantine Books [c1953] 188pp.
S945	$	Sturgeon, Theodore. A Touch of Strange. Garden City, NY: Doubleday, 1958. 262pp.
S950	$ F	Sturgeon, Theodore. A Way Home; Stories of Science Fiction and Fantasy, Selected and with an Introduction by Groff Conklin. NY: Funk & Wagnalls, 1955. 333pp.
S995	$ F	Szilard, Leo. The Voice of the Dolphins, and Other Stories. NY: Simon and Schuster, 1961. 122pp.
T290		Tenn, William, pseud., Ed. Children of Wonder; 21 Remarkable and Fantastic Tales Edited and with an Introduction by William Tenn. NY: Simon and Schuster [c1953] 336pp.

CODE	REFERENCE	ANTHOLOGY
T300	$	Tenn, William. Of All Possible Worlds. Stories by William Tenn. NY: Ballantine Books [c1955] 161pp.
T895		Tucker, [Arthur] Wilson. Science Fiction Subtreasury. NY: Rinehart [c1954] 240pp.
V185	$ F	Van Vogt, A.E. Destination: Universe! NY: Pellegrini & Cudahy [c1952] 295pp.
V190		Van Vogt, A.E. Triad; Three Complete Science Fiction Novels. NY: Simon and Schuster [c1951] 527pp.
V530	$	Verne, Jules. The Omnibus Jules Verne. NY: Lippincott, n.d. 822pp.
W450	$	Wells, Herbert George. Best Science Fiction Stories. NY: Dover Publications [1966] 303pp.
W455	$	Wells, Herbert George. The Complete Short Stories of H.G. Wells. London: Ernest Benn; Hackensack, NJ: Wehman Bros [1965] 1038pp.
W460	$ H J	Wells, Herbert George. Seven Science Fiction Novels of H.G. Wells. NY: Dover Publications, 1950. 1015pp.
W465	$	Wells, Herbert George. Three Prophetic Novels. Selected and with an Introduction by E.F. Bleiler. NY: Dover Publications [1960] 335pp.

CODE	REFERENCE	ANTHOLOGY
W470	$ F H	Wells, Herbert George. The Time Machine [and] The War of the Worlds. Illustrated by Joe Mugnaini. NY: The Heritage Press [c1964] 98, 188pp.
W475	$ F H	Wells, Herbert George. 28 Science Fiction Stories of H.G. Wells. [NY] Dover Publications [c1952] 915pp.
W480	$	Wells, Herbert George. The War in the Air; In the Days of the Comet; The Food of the Gods; Three Science Fiction Novels by H.G. Wells. NY: Dover Publications [c1963, 1908, 1904, 1906] 645pp.
W485	$ F H J	Wells, Herbert George. The War of the Worlds, The Time Machine, and Selected Short Stories; Special Foreword by Kingsley Amis. Complete and Unabridged. [NY] Platt, 1963. 514pp.
W720	$	Williams-Ellis, Amabell, and Mably Owen, Eds. Out of This World I. London: Blackie and Son [c1960]
W725	$	Williams-Ellis, Amabell, and Mably Owen, Eds. Out of This World 2. London: Blackie and Son [c1961]
W730	$	Williams-Ellis, Amabell, and Mably Owen, Eds. Out of This World 3. London: Blackie and Son [c1961]
W735	$	Williams-Ellis, Amabell, and Mably Owen, Eds. Out of This World 4. London: Blackie and Son [c1964]

CODE	REFERENCE	ANTHOLOGY
W740	$	Williams-Ellis, Amabell, and Mably Owen, Eds. Out of This World 5. London: Blackie and Son [c1965]
W745	$	Williams-Ellis, Amabell, and Mably Owen, Eds. Out of This World 6. London: Blackie and Son [c1967]
W750	$	Williams-Ellis, Amabell, and Mably Owen, Eds. Out of This World 7. London: Blackie and Son [c1968]
W755	$	Williams-Ellis, Amabell, and Mably Owen, Eds. Worlds Apart. London: Blackie and Son [c1966]
W860		Wollheim, Donald A., Ed. The End of the World [Stories] NY: Ace Books [1956] 159pp. Paper.
[W865]		Wollheim, Donald A., Ed. Everyboy's Book of Science Fiction. NY: Fell [1951] 254pp.
W870		Wollheim, Donald A., Ed. Flight into Space; Great Science Fiction Stories of Interplanetary Travel. NY: Fell [1950] 251pp.
W875		Wollheim, Donald A., Ed. The Hidden Planet; Science-Fiction Adventures on Venus. NY: Ace Books [c1959] 190pp.
W880	F	Wollheim, Donald A., Ed. The Portable Novels of Science; Selected and with Introductions by Donald A. Wollheim. NY: Viking, 1945. 737pp.

CODE	REFERENCE	ANTHOLOGY
W885	$	Wollheim, Donald A., Ed. Swordsmen in the Sky. NY: Ace Books [c1964] 192pp. Paper.
W890		Wollheim, Donald A., and Terry Carr, Eds. World's Best Science Fiction:1965. NY: Ace Books [c1965] 288pp. Paper.
W895		Wollheim, Donald A., and Terry Carr, Eds. World's Best Science Fiction: 1966. NY: Ace Books [c1966] 287pp. Paper.
W900		Wollheim, Donald A., and Terry Carr, Eds. World's Best Science Fiction:1967. NY: Ace Books [c1967]
W985	$	Wyndham, John. Consider Her Ways and Others. London: Michael Joseph [1961] 223pp.
W990	$	Wyndham, John. The John Wyndham Omnibus. NY: Simon & Schuster [c1964, c1951-55] 532 pp.
W995	$	Wyndham, John. The Seeds of Time. London: Michael Joseph [1960, 1956] 253pp.
Y395	F	Year's Best Science Fiction Novels, 1952; Edited and with an Introduction by Everett F. Bleiler and T.E. Dikty. [NY] Fell, 1952. 352pp.
Y400		Year's Best Science Fiction Novels, 1953. Edited, and with an Introduction by Everett F. Bleiler and T.E. Dikty. NY: Frederick Fell [c1953] 315pp.

CODE	REFERENCE	ANTHOLOGY
Y405		Year's Best Science Fiction Novels, 1954. Edited and with an Introduction by Everett F. Bleiler and T.E. Dikty. NY: Frederick Fell [c1954] 317pp. Note: This series was absorbed by The Best Science-Fiction Stories (q.v.) and continued as The Best Science-Fiction Stories and Novels.
Y750	F	Young, Robert F. The Worlds of Robert F. Young; Sixteen Stories of Science Fiction and Fantasy. NY: Simon and Schuster [c1965] 223pp.

TITLE-AUTHOR AND ANTHOLOGY-CODE INDEX

TITLE	AUTHOR
Aepyornis Island	Wells, H.G.
Aesop	Simak, C.D.
Affair with a Green Monkey	Sturgeon, T.
After	Slesar, H.
Afterthought	Fyfe, H.B.
The Age of Invention	Spinrad, N.
The Age of Prophecy	Saint Clair, M.
Agent of Vega	Schmitz, J.
Agent 38	Hoyle, F.
Ahead	Aldiss, B.
Ahead of Time	Kuttner, H.
Ajax of Ajax	Pearson, M.
Alaree	Silverberg, R.
Alas, All Thinking!	Bates, H.
Alexander the Bait	Tenn, W.
Alien	Del Rey, L.
The Aliens	Leinster, M.
All About the Future	G800
All About the "Thing"	Garrett, R.
All Good BEMS	Brown, F.
All Roads	Farnsworth, M.
All Summer in a Day	Bradbury, R.
All That Glitters	Clarke, A.C.
All the Colors of the Rainbow	Brackett, L.
All the Sounds of Fear	Ellison, H.
All the Tea in China	Bretnor, R.
All the Time in the World	Clarke, A.C.
All the Traps of Earth	Simak, C.
All the Troubles of the World	Asimov, I.
All You Zombies	Heinlein, R.
Allamagoosa	Russell, E.
Almost the End of the World	Bradbury, R.
Alpha in Omega	Stones, J.
Alpha Ralpha Boulevard	Smith, C.
The Altar at Midnight	Kornbluth, C.
The Altruists	Seabright, I.
Amateur in Chancery	Smith, G.
The Amazing Mrs. Mimms	Knight, D.C.
The Ambassadors	Boucher, A.

TITLE	AUTHOR
Ambition	Bade, W.
Amen and Out	Aldiss, B.
Among the Dangs	Elliott, George P.
Among the Hairy Earthmen	Lafferty, R.
Anachron	Knight, D.
Analog I-5	A535 A540 A545 A550 A555
The Analogues	Knight, D.
The Anarchist	Fawcett, D.
An Ancient Madness	Knight, D.
And a Little Child	Henderson, Z.
And a Star to Steer By	Correy, L.
And All the Earth a Grave	MacApp, C.
And Be Merry	MacLean, K.
And He Built a Crooked House	Heinlein, R.
And It Comes Out Here	Del Rey, L.
And Lo! the Bird	Bond, N.
And Madly Teach	Biggle, L.
And My Fear Is Great	Sturgeon, T.
And Now the News	Sturgeon, T.
And So Died Riabouchinska	Bradbury, R.
And Someday to Mars	Long, F.
And the Moon Be Still as Bright	Bradbury, R.
And the Rock Cried Out	Bradbury, R.
And the Sailor, Home from the Sea	Bradbury, R.
And the Walls Came Tumbling Down	Wyndham, J.
And Then She Found Him	Budrys, A.
And Then There Were None	Russell, E.
And Thou Beside Me	Reynolds, M.
The Angel Was a Yankee	Benet, S.
Angela's Satyr	Cleeve, B.
The Angelic Angleworm	Brown, F.
Angels and Spaceships	B875
Angel's Egg	Pangborn, E.
Angels in the Jets	Bixby, J.
Angels Unawares	Henderson, Z.
The Animal-Cracker Plot	De Camp, L.
Anniversary	Asimov, I.
The Anomaly of the Empty Man	Boucher, A.
Another Antigone	Morrison, D.

TITLE	AUTHOR
Another Part of the Galaxy	C750
Another Word for Man	Presslie, R.
Another World	Rosny Aine, J.
Answer	Brown, F.
Answer	Clement, H.
The Answer	Wylie, P.
Answering Service	Leiber, F.
The Answers	Simak, C.
The Ant and the Eye	Oliver, C.
The Anthem Sprinters	Bradbury, R.
Any More at Home Like You?	Oliver, C.
The Anything Box	Henderson, Z.
Apartness	Vinge, V.
An Ape about the House	Clarke, A.C.
Apology to Inky	Green, R.
The Appendix and the Spectacles	Breuer, M.
The Apple	Wells, H.G.
Appointment at Noon	Russell, E.
Appointment in Tomorrow	Leiber, F.
The Apprentice	White, J.
Apres Nous	Davidson, A.
The April Witch	Bradbury, R.
Ararat	Henderson, Z.
Arena	Brown, F.
The Argonauts of the Air	Wells, H.G.
Aristotle and the Gun	De Camp, L.
Armageddon	Brown, F.
Armaments Race	Clarke, A.C.
Around the World in 80 Days	Verne, J.
An Arthur C. Clarke Omnibus	C595
The Artifact Business	Silverberg, R.
As Never Was	Miller, P.
The Asa Rule	Williams, J.
Ask Me Anything	Knight, D.
Asleep in Armageddon	Bradbury, R.
The Assassination of John Fitzgerald Kennedy Considered as a Downhill Motor Race	Ballard, J.

TITLE	AUTHOR
Assignment in Eternity	Heinlein, R.
Assignment to Alderbaran	Crossen, K.
Assisted Passage	White, J.
Asteroid of Fear	Gallun, R.
The Asteroid of Gold	Simak, C.
The Astounding Science Fiction Anthology	A875
The Astronaut	Zhuraveleva, V.
Asylum	Van Vogt, A.
At No Extra Cost	Phillips, P.
At the Center of Gravity	Rocklynne, R.
At the Earth's Core	Burroughs, E.
At the End of the Orbit	Clarke, A.C.
The Atavists	Rymer, G.
Atlantis	Plato
Atlantis	Smith, E.
Atrophy	Hill, E.
Attitude	Clement, H.
Attitudes	Farmer, P.
Aunt Millicent at the Races	Guttridge, L.
The Author's Ordeal	Asimov, I.
Auto-Da-Fe	Knight, D.
Automata I, II, and III	Wright, S.
Automatic	Reed, K.
Automatic Tiger	Reed, K.
Automation	Van Vogt, A.
The Available Data on the Worp Reaction	Miller, L.
The Avenging Ghost	Serling, R.
The Awakening	Clarke, A.
The Ax	Hoyle, F.
Axolotl	Abernathy, R.
B+M — Planet 4	Heard, G.
Babel II	Knight, D.
Baby Is Three	Sturgeon, T.
Baby Killers	Elliott, R.
A Baby on Neptune	Harris, C.
Baby, You Were Great	Wilhelm, Kate
Back There	Serling, R.
Back There in the Grass	Morris, G.
Back to Julie	Wilson, R.

TITLE	AUTHOR
Back to the Drawing Boards	Ellison, H.
Backfire	Rocklynne, R.
Backward, O Time	Knight, D.
Backwardness	Anderson, P.
A Bad Day for Sales	Leiber, F.
A Bad Day for Vermin	Laumer, K.
Badinage	Goulart, R.
Badman	Brunner, J.
Bait	Clough, R.
Balaam	Boucher, A.
Balance	Christopher, J.
Balanced Ecology	Schmitz, J.
Ballade of an Artifical Satellite [Poem]	Anderson, P.
Ballad of the Shoshonu	Dickson, G.
The Barbarian	Anderson, P.
A Bargain with Cashel	Kersh, G.
Barnacle Bull	Sanders, W.
Barney	Stanton, W.
Baron Bagge	Lernet-Holenia, A.
Barrier	Boucher, A.
Barrier of Dread	Merril, J.
Basic Right	Russell, E.
Basis for Negotiation	Aldiss, B.
Battle of the Monsters	Robertson, M.
Battle of the S...S	Elliott, B.
Battle of the Unborn	Blish, J.
Battle without Banners	Ellison, H.
Baxbr/Daxbr	Smith, E.
Be of Good Cheer	Leiber, F.
Beach Scene	King, M.
Beachhead	Simak, C.
Beachheads in Space	D420
Beanstalk	Blish, J.
The Beat Cluster	Leiber, F.
Beautiful, Beautiful, Beautiful!	Friedman, S.
The Beautiful Suit	Wells, H.G.
The Beautiful Things	Zirul, A.
Becalmed in Hell	Niven, L.

TITLE	AUTHOR
Bedside Manner	Morrison, W.
Beep	Blish, J.
The Bees from Borneo	Gray, W.
Before Eden	Clarke, A.
Before the Curtain	Boucher, A.
Before the Dawn	Taine, J.
Before the Talent Dies	Slesar, H.
The Beggar on the O'Connell Bridge	Bradbury, R.
The Begum's Fortune	Verne, J.
Behind the News	Finney, J.
Behold It Was a Dream	Broughton, R.
Behold the Man	Moorcock, M.
Belief	Asimov, I.
A Benefactor of Humanity	Farrell, J.
Bernie the Faust	Tenn, W.
Berom	Berryman, J.
Best Fantasy Stories [Brian W. Aldiss]	A 360
Best Friend	Lightner, A.
Best from Fantasy and Science Fiction 1-16th Series	M190. M195 M200 M205 M210 M215 M220 M225 M230. M235 M240 M245 M250 M255 M260 M265.
The Best from Startling Stories	S795
The Best of All Possible Worlds	Bradbury, R.
Best of Amazing	R820.
The Best Policy	Garrett, R.
Best SF: 1967	H320
Best SF Science Fiction Stories 1-5	C930 C935 C940 C945 C950
Best Science Fiction Stories [of H.G. Wells]	W450
The Best Science Fiction Stories & Novels:1955	B590
The Best Science Fiction Stories & Novels:1956	B595
The Best Science Fiction Stories & Novels:9th	B605
The Best Science Fiction Stories: 1950	B565
The Best Science Fiction Stories: 1951	B570
The Best Science Fiction Stories: 1952	B575
The Best Science Fiction Stories: 1953	B580
Betelgeuse Bridge	Tenn, W.
The Better Bet	Brode, A.

TITLE	AUTHOR
The Better Choice	Wright, S.
A Better Mousetrap	Brunner, J.
Better than Ever	Kirs, A.
Bettyann	Neville, K.
Between the Thunder and the Sun . . .	Oliver, C.
Beyond Bedlam	Guin, W.
Beyond Human Ken	M575.
Beyond Space and Time	Rogers, J.
Beyond the Barriers of Space and Time	M580.
Beyond the Black River	Howard, R.
Beyond the Farthest Star	Burroughs, E.
Beyond Time and Space	D425.
Beyond Tomorrow	K690.
Bianca's Hands	Sturgeon, T.
The Big Black and White Game	Bradbury, R.
Big Book of Science Fiction	C760.
The Big Contest	MacDonald, J.
The Big Engine	Leiber, F.
The Big Front Yard.	Simak, C.
Big Game Hunt	Clarke, A.
A Big Man with the Girls.	MacCreigh, J.
The Big Pat Boom	Knight, D.
The Big Stink	Cogswell, T.
Big Sword	Ash, P.
The Big Trek	Leiber, F.
The Big Trip Up Yonder.	Vonnegut, K.
The Big Wheel.	McMorrow, F.
Billenium	Ballard, J.
The Biography Project	Dell, D.
Bircher	Walde, A.
Birds Can't Count	Clingerman, M.
The Birthmark	Hawthorne, N.
The Bitterest Pill.	Pohl, F.
The Black Ball.	De Camp, L.
Black Charlie	Dickson, G.
The Black Cloud.	Hoyle, F.
Black Destroyer	Van Vogt, A.
Black Eyes and the Daily Grind	Lesser, M.

TITLE	AUTHOR
The Black Ferris	Bradbury, R.
Black Pits of Luna	Heinlein, R.
The Black Stone	Howard, R.
Blackmail	Hoyle, F.
Blacksword	Offutt, A.
Blank Form	Sellings, A.
The Blast	Cloete, S.
The Blight	Cox, A.
Blind Alley	Asimov, I.
Blind Alley	Jameson, M.
Blind Lightning	Ellison, H.
Blind Man's Buff	Jameson, M.
Blind Man's Lantern	Lang, A.
Blind Man's World	Bellamy, E.
The Blind Pilot	Henneberg, C.
The Blinding Shadows	Wandrei, D.
The Blindness	Latham, P.
The Bliss of Solitude	McIntosh, J.
Blockade Runner	Jameson, M.
The Blockade Runners	Verne, J.
The Blond Kid	Sutherland, H.
Blood Bank	Miller, W.
Blood Brother	Beaumont, C.
The Blood-Stained God	Howard, R.
Blood's a Rover	Oliver, C.
Blowup Blues	Cogswell, T.
Blowups Happen	Heinlein, R.
The Blue Giraffe	De Camp, L.
Blueprint for Tomorrow	Mines, S.
The Blurring of the Lines	Doyle, A.
Bodyguard	Grimm, C.
Bodyguard and Four Other Short Novels	G190.
Bolden's Pets	Wallace, F.
The Bomb in the Bathtub	Scortia, T.
Books	Boucher, A.
Boomerang	Russell, E.
Born of Man and Woman	Matheson, R.
Botany Bay	Hubbard, P.

TITLE	AUTHOR
Bottomless Pit	High, P.
Boulter's Canaries	Roberts, K.
The Bounty Hunter	Davidson, A.
The Box	Blish, J.
The Boy Next Door	Oliver, C.
The Boy's Life Book of Outer Space Stories	B790.
Boys! Raise Giant Mushrooms in Your Cellar	Bradbury, R.
The Brain	Wiener, N.
Brain	Wright, S.
Brain Wave	Anderson, P.
The Brass God	Laumer, K.
Brave New Word	McComas, J.
Brave New World	Huxley, A.
Breakdown	Williamson, J.
Breaking Strain	Clarke, A.
Breeds There a Man?	Asimov, I.
The Brick Moon	Hale, E.
Bridge	Blish, J.
Bridle and Saddle	Asimov, I.
Bright Illusion	Moore, C.
Brightness Falls from the Air	Seabright, I.
Brightside Crossing	Nourse, A.
Brimstone Bill	Jameson, M.
Brooklyn Project	Tenn, W.
The Brotherhood of Keepers	McLaughlin, D.
The Brothers	Dance, C.
Brothers Beyond the Void	Fairman, P.
Budding Explorer	Robin, R.
Build-Up	Ballard, J.
Built Down Logically	Schoenfeld, H.
Built Up Logically	Schoenfeld, H.
Bulkhead	Sturgeon, T.
Bullard of the Space Patrol	Jameson, M.
Bullard Reflects	Jameson, M.
Bulletin	Jackson, S.
A Bulletin from the Trustees	Shore, W.
Bumberboom	Davidson, A.
Bureau of Slick Tricks	Fyfe, H.

TITLE	AUTHOR
The Bureaucrat	Jameson, W.
Burning Bright	Browning, J.
The Business, as Usual	Reynolds, M.
Business as Usual, During Alterations	Williams, R.
Business of Killing	Leiber, F.
But Who Can Replace a Man?	Aldiss, B.
But Without Horns	Page, N.
Butch	Anderson, P.
Buy Jupiter!	Asimov, I.
By His Bootstraps.	Heinlein, R.
By His Bootstraps.	MacDonald, A.
By Jupiter	Elam, R.
By the Waters of Babylon	Benet, S.
By These Presents	Kuttner, H.
By Virtue of Circumference	Van Dresser, P.
The C Chute	Asimov, I.
Cabin Boy	Knight, D.
The Cage	Chandler, B.
The Cairn on the Headland	Howard, R.
Call Him Lord	Dickson, G.
Call Me Adam.	Marks, W.
Call Me Joe	Anderson, P.
The Call of the Stars	Clarke, A.
Callahan and the Wheelies	Barr, S.
Calling All Stars	Szilard, L.
Calling Dr. Clockwork	Goulart, R.
Camouflage	Kuttner, H.
A Can of Paint	Van Vogt, A.
The Canal Builders	Abernathy, R.
A Canticle for Leibowitz	Miller, W.
The Canvas Bag	Nourse, A.
Captain Honario Harpplayer, R.N.	Harrison, H.
Captive Audience	Griffith, A.
Captivity	Finney, C.
Captivity	Henderson, Z.
Carbon Copy	Simak, C.
Careless Love	Friborg, A.
Caretaker,	Schmitz, J.

TITLE	AUTHOR
The Carson Effect	Wilson, R.
The Case	Redgrove, P.
A Case of Conscience	Blish, J.
A Case of Identity	Garrett, R.
The Case of Omega Smith	Walsh, B.
Casey Agonistes	McKenna, R.
Castaway	Chandler, A.
Castaway	Clarke, A.
Castaway	Williams, R.
The Castle of Light	Laumer, K.
Catastrophe	Wells, H.G.
Catch That Martian	Knight, D.
Catch That Rabbit	Asimov, I.
Category Phoenix	Ellanby, B.
Cato the Martian	Fast, H.
Cattle Trucks	Hoyle, F.
The Causes	Seabright, I.
The Cave of Night	Gunn, J.
The Caves of Steel	Asimov, I.
Cease Fire	Herbert, F.
The Cellars	Campbell, J.
Cellmate	Sturgeon, T.
Census	Simak, C.
The Census Takers	Pohl, F.
A Century of Great Short Science Fiction Novels	K695.
A Century of Science Fiction	K700.
The Cerebrative Psittacoid	Nearing, H.
Certainty	Silverberg, R.
The Certificate	Davidson, A.
Chain of Command	Rynas, S.
Chain Reaction	Ellanby, B.
Chain Reaction	Budrys, A.
Change of Heart	Whitley, G.
Changeling	Williams-Ellis, A.
Changelling	Bradbury, R.
The Cheery Soul	Bowen, E.
Chemical Plant	Williamson, I.
The Chessmen of Mars	Burroughs, E.

TITLE	AUTHOR
The Chessplayers	Harness, C.
The Chicken or the Egghead	Fenton, F.
Chief	Slesar, H.
Child by Chronos	Harness, C.
A Child Is Crying	MacDonald, J.
Child of Void	Saint Clair, M.
Childhood's End	Clarke, A.
The Children of Night	Pohl, F.
Children of the Atom	Shiras, W.
Children of Wonder	Tenn, W.
The Children's Hour	Kuttner, H.
Child's Play	Schnirring, M.
Child's Play	Tenn, W.
The Choice	Hilton-Young, W.
Chore for a Spaceman	Sheldon, W.
Christmas on Ganymede	Asimov, I.
Christmas Treason	White, J.
Christmas Tree	Youd, C.
Christmas Trombone	Banks, R.
The Chromium Helmet	Sturgeon, T.
The Chronic Argonauts	Wells, H.G.
The Chronicler	Van Vogt, A.
The Chronoclasm	Wyndham, J.
The Chronokinesis of Jonathan Hull	Boucher, A.
Chronopolis	Ballard, J.
The Chrysalids	Wyndham, J.
Chrysalis	Bradbury, R.
The Cicerones	Aickman, R.
Cinderella Story	Lang, A.
Circe Underseas	MacBeth, G.
The Circuit Riders	FitzPatrick, R.
The Circular Ruins	Borges, J.
Circus	Hawkins, P.
Circus	Nourse, A.
Cities of Wonder	K705.
The City	Bradbury, R.
City	S605.
The City and the Stars	Clarke, A.

TITLE	AUTHOR
The City of Force	Galouye, D.
City of the Sun	Campanella, G.
The Civilization Game	Simak, C.
Civilized	Clifton, M.
Clark Ashton Smith: a Memoir	Price, E.
Clash by Night	O'Donnell, L.
Clerical Error	Clifton, M.
The Clinic	Sturgeon, T.
The Closed Door	Crossen, K.
C/O Mr. Makepeace	Phillips, P.
Coco-Talk	Temple, W.
Cocoon	Laumer, K.
The Coffin Cure	Nourse, A.
Coincidence Day	Brunner, J.
The Cold, Cold Box	Fast, H.
The Cold Equations	Godwin, T.
Cold Front	Clement, H.
The Cold Green Eye	Williamson, J.
Cold War	Clarke, A.
Cold War	Kuttner, H.
Cold War	Neville, K.
Collecting Team	Silverberg, R.
The Collector	Heard, H.
Collector's Item	Knight, D.
Colonial	Christopher, J.
The Color Out of Space	Lovecraft, H.
Colossus	Wandrei, D.
Columbus Was a Dope	Heinlein, R.
Columbus Was a Dope	Monroe, L.
Come and Go Mad	Brown, F.
Come into My Cellar	Bradbury, R.
Come on, Wagon!	Henderson, Z.
The Comedian's Children	Sturgeon, T.
Comic Inferno	Aldiss, B.
Coming Attractions	Leiber, F.
Coming Attractions	G805.
Coming-of-Age-Day	Jorgensson, A.
The Coming of Conan	H855.

TITLE	AUTHOR
The Coming of the Robots	M910.
The Command	De Camp, L.
Command	Kahn, B.
Command Performance	Miller, W.
Commencement Night	Ashby, R.
Common Demoninator	MacDonald, J.
Common Time	Blish, J.
Compassion Circuit	Wyndham, J.
Competition	Hull, E.
The Competitors	Lawson, J.
The Compleat Consummators.	Nourse, A.
The Compleat Werewolf	Boucher, A.
The Complete Short Stories of H.G. Wells	W455.
Completely Automatic	Sturgeon, T.
Compliments of the Author	Padgett, L.
Compound B	Fink, D.
Compounded Interest	Reynolds, M.
Computers Don't Argue	Dickson, G.
Computer's Mate	Rackham, J.
Conan the Adventurer	H857.
Conan the Warror	H859.
The Concrete Mixer	Bradbury, R.
Condition of Employment	Simak, C.
Conditionally Human	Miller, W.
The Cone	Wells, H.G.
Cones	Long, F.
Confessions of the First Number	Owsley, C.
The Congruent People	Budrys, A.
A Connecticut Yankee	Twain, M.
Connoisseur's Science Fiction	B670.
The Conqueror	Clifton, M.
Conqueror's Isle	Bond, N.
Conquest	Boucher, A.
The Conquest of Two Worlds	Hamilton, E.
Consider Her Ways	Wyndham, J.
Conspiracy	Christopher, J.
The Conspirators	White, J.
Contact, Incorporated	Osborne, R.

TITLE	AUTHOR
The Crime and the Glory of Commander Suzdal	Smith, C.
A Crime for Llewellyn	Sturgeon, T.
Crime Machine	Bloch, R.
Criminal Negligence	McComas, J.
Crisis	Grendon, E.
Crisis in Utopia	Knight, N.
Crisis, 1999	Brown, F.
Critical Factor	Clement, H.
Critical Mass	Clarke, A.
Critical Mass	Pohl, F.
Critique of Impure Reason	Anderson, P.
The Critters	Long, F.
The Crooked Man	Beaumont, C.
A Cross of Centuries	Kuttner, H.
The Crucible of Power	Williamson, J.
Crucifixus Etiam	Miller, W.
Crying Jag	Simak, C.
The Crystal Egg	Wells, H.G.
Culture	Shelton, J.
The Cure	Padgett, L.
Cure for a Ylith	Leinster, M.
The Curious Case of Benjamin Button	Fitzgerald, F.
The Currents of Space	Asimov, I.
The Curse	Clarke, A.
The Curse of Seven Towers	Serling, R.
The Custodian	Tenn, W.
The Cyber and Justice Holmes	Riley, F.
Cyclops	Heard, H.
D.P. from Tomorrow	Reynolds, M.
Daedalus	Bulfinch, T.
Dagon	Davidson, A.
Daisies	Brown, F.
The Damned Thing	Bierce, A.
The Damnedest Thing	Kanin, G.
Damon Knight's Orbit 2	0645
Dance of a New World	MacDonald, J.
Dance of the Dead	Matheson, R.
The Dancing Partner	Jerome, J.
The Dandelion Girl	Young, R.
A Dangerous Invention	Zelikovich, E.

TITLE	AUTHOR
The Darfsteller	Miller, W.
Dark Conception	Adams, L.
The Dark Door	Nourse, A.
Dark Interlude	Brown, F.
The Dark Night of the Soul	Blish, J.
Dark Nuptial	Locke, R.
The Dark Side	K710.
Dark They Were and Golden Eyed	Bradbury, R.
A Dash of Spring	Finney, J.
A Date to Remember	Temple, W.
Daughters of Earth	Merril, J.
David's Daddy	Brown, R.
Dawningsburgh	West, W.
Day at the Beach	Emshwiller, C.
The Day Before Never	Presslie, R.
A Day in the Life of Kelvin Throop	Phillips, R.
Day Is Done	Del Rey, L.
The Day It Rained Forever	Bradbury, R.
Day Million	Pohl, F.
Day of Succession	Thomas, T.
The Day of the Triffids	Wyndham, J.
A Day on Death Highway	Elliott, C.
The Day Rembrandt Went Public	Auerbach, A.
The Day the Flag Fell	Elam, R.
The Day They Got Boston	Gold, H.
The Day We Celebrate	Bond, N.
Daybroke	Bloch, R.
Daymare	Brown, F.
De Profundis	Kuttner, H.
De Profundis	Leinster, M.
Dead Center	Merril, J.
Dead End	MacFarlane, W.
Dead Man's Chest	Serling, R.
The Dead Past	Asimov, I.
The Dead Planet	Hamilton, E.
Dead Ringer	Del Rey, L.
The Dead World	Doyle, A.
Deadlock	Kuttner, H.

TITLE	AUTHOR
Deadlock	Padgett, L.
Deadly Game	Wellen, E.
A Deal in Ostriches	Wells, H.G.
Dear Devil	Russell, E.
Dear Pen Pal	Van Vogt, A.
Death and the Maiden	Bradbury, R.
Death and the Senator	Clarke, A.
The Death Dust	Harvey, F.
Death from the Stars	Hilliard, A.
A Death in the House	Simak, C.
Death of a Bumblebee	Wakefield, H.
Death of a Sensitive	Bates, H.
The Death of the Moon	Phillips, A.
The Death of the Sea	Gironella, J.
Death Scene	Simak, C.
Death Sentence	Asimov, I.
Death's Masquerade	Serling, R.
A Decade of Fantasy and Science Fiction	M270.
Decadence	Gary, R.
December 28th	Thomas, T.
The Deep	Asimov, I.
The Deep Down Dragon	Merril, J.
The Deep Range	Clarke, A.
Deep Space	Abernathy, R.
The Deeps	Roberts, K.
Defense	Van Vogt, A.
Defense Mechanism	King, V.
Defense Mechanism	MacLean, K.
Delay in Transit	Wallace, F.
Delilah and the Space-Rigger	Heinlein, R.
Deluge	Henderson, Z.
Demobilization	Cowie, G.
The Demoiselle D'Ys	Chambers, R.
Denkirch	Drake, D.
Derelict	Gallun, R.
The Derelict	Hodgson, W.
Descending	Disch, T.
A Descent into the Maelstrom	Poe, E.

TITLE	AUTHOR
Dog Star	Clarke, A.
Dominions Beyond	Moore, W.
Dominoes	Kornbluth, C.
Don Jones	Anderson, P.
Don't Live in the Past	Knight, D.
Don't Look Now	Kuttner, H.
Doodad	Bradbury, R.
The Doom of the Great City	Fawcett, D.
Doomsday Deferred	Jenkins, W.
Doomsday's Color-Press	Jones, R.
The Door in the Wall	Wells, H.
Door to Anywhere	Anderson, P.
The Doorbell	Keller, D.
The Doors of His Face, the Lamps of His Mouth	Zelazny, R.
Doorstep	Laumer, K.
The Doorstop	Bretnor, R.
Doorway into Time	Moore, C.
Doorway into Time	M195.
Dormant	Van Vogt, A.
The Dot and Dash Bird	Wolfe, B.
Double Dome	Banks, R.
Double, Double, Toil and Trouble	Cantine, H.
The Double Dyed Villains	Anderson, P.
Double Standard	Brown, F.
Double Take	Finney, J.
Double Take	Marks, W.
Doubledare	Silverberg, R.
Down Among the Dead Men	Tenn, W.
D.P. from Tomorrow	Reynolds, M.
The Dragon	Bradbury, R.
A Dream of Armageddon	Wells, H.
Dream Street	Robinson, F.
The Dreamer	Coppel, A.
Dreaming Is a Private Thing	Asimov, I.
Dreams Are Sacred	Phillips, P.
Dream's End	Kuttner, H.
The Dreamsman	Dickson, G.
Dreamworld	Asimov, I.

TITLE	AUTHOR
Dress of White Silk	Matheson, R.
A Drink of Darkness	Young, R.
The Drop	Christopher, J.
Drop Dead	Simak, C.
The Drowned Giant	Ballard, J.
The Drowned World	Ballard, J.
The Drummer Boy of Shiloh	Bradbury, R.
Drums of Tombalku	Howard, R.
Drunkboat	Smith, C.
Dumb Martian	Wyndham, J.
Dumb Show	Aldiss, B.
Dumb Waiter	Miller, W.
Dune Roller	May, J.
The Dusty Death	Kippax, J.
Dusty Zebra	Simak, C.
A Dweller in Two Worlds	Gor, G.
Dwellers in Silence	Bradbury, R.
The Dwindling Sphere	Hawkins, W.
The Dying Man	Knight, D.
The Dying Night	Asimov, I.
$E=MC^2$	Reeves, R.
E for Effort	Sherred, T.
E Pluribus Unicorn	S935.
Each an Explorer	Asimov, I.
The Earlier Service	Irwin, M.
The Earth and the Overlords	Clarke, A.
The Earth Dwellers	Maurois, A.
Earth Eighteen	Pohl, F.
Earth for Inspiration	Simak, C.
Earth Is Room Enough	A830.
The Earth Men	Bradbury, R.
Earthlight	Clarke, A.
Earthlings Go Home!	Reynolds, M.
Earthman's Burden	Anderson, P.
Earthmen and Strangers	S585.
Earthmen Bearing Gifts	Brown, F.
Earth's Natural Satellite	Dikty, T.
Easter Eggs	Carr, S.

TITLE	AUTHOR
Eastward Ho!	Tenn, W.
Easy as A.B.C.	Kipling, R.
Ed Lear Wasn't So Crazy!	Schenck, H.
The Edge of Running Water	Sloane, W.
The Edge of the Sea	Budrys, A.
Editor's Choice in Science Fiction	M920.
The Education of Drusilla Strange	Sturgeon, T.
The Education of Tigress Macardle	Kornbluth, C.
The Eel	De Ford, M.
An Eel by the Tail	Lang, A.
Effigy	Reeves, R.
The Egg	De Camp, L.
An Egg a Month from All Over	Seabright, I.
The Ego Machine	Kuttner, H.
The Eight Billion	Wilson, R.
Eight O'Clock in the Morning	Nelson, R.
The Eighth Annual of the Year's Best S-F	M630.
The Eighth Galaxy Reader.	G175.
El Dia de Muerte	Bradbury, R.
Elected Silence	Brunner, J.
Element 79	Hoyle, F.
An Elephant for the Prinkip	Stecher, L.
Elsewhen	Heinlein, R.
Embroidery	Bradbury, R.
Emergency Landing	Williams, R.
Emergency Operation	Porges, A.
Emergency Working	James, E.
Emily and the Bards Sublime.	Young, R.
The Empire of the Ants	Wells, H.
Employment	De Camp, L.
Emreth.	Morgan, D.
En La Noche	Bradbury, R.
The Enchanted Forest.	Leiber, F.
Enchanted Village	Van Vogt, A.
Enchantment	Emmett, E.
Enchantress of Venus	Brackett, L.
Encounter at Dawn.	Clarke, A.

TITLE	AUTHOR
End as a Hero	Laumer, K.
End as a World	Wallace, F.
End Game	Ballard, J.
The End of the Beginning	Bradbury, R.
The End of the Line	Schmitz, J.
The End of the Party	Greene, G.
The End of the Race	Bermel, A.
The End of the World	W860.
Endowment Policy	Padgett, L.
Enemies in Space	Grunert, K.
The Enemy	Knight, D.
The Enormous Room	Gold, H.
Environment	Geier, C.
Epilogue	Anderson, P.
Epilogue [to The Weigher of Souls]	Choron, J.
Episode on Dhee Minor	Walton, H.
Epithalamium	Buck, D.
Eripmav	Knight, D.
Errand Boy	Tenn, W.
Escape!	Asimov, I.
Escape from Orbit	Anderson, P.
Escape into Yesterday	Burks, A.
Escape to Earth	Banister, M.
Escape to Earth	H850.
Essay on Sturgeon	Conklin, G.
Etaoin Shrdlu	Brown, F.
Eternal Adam	Verne, J.
The Eternal Machines	Spencer, W.
Eternity Lost	Simak, C.
The Ethical Equations	Leinster, M.
Ethical Quotient	Phillifent, J.
The Ethicators	Marsh, W.
Eve Times Four	Anderson, P.
Evening Primrose	Collier, J.
The Events Leading Down to the Tragedy	Kornbluth, C.
Every Boy's Book of Outer Space Stories	D575.
Everybody Knows Joe	Kornbluth, C.

TITLE	AUTHOR
Everybody Loves Irving Bommer	Tenn, W.
Everyboy's Book of Science Fiction	W865.
Evidence	Asimov, I.
The Evitable Conflict	Asimov, I.
Evolution's End	Arthur, R.
Ex Machina	Padgett, L.
The Exalted	De Camp, L.
Examination Day	Slesar, H.
Excerpts from the Encyclopedia	Wellen, E.
The Executioner	Budrys, A.
Exile	Cole, E.
Exile	Coppel, A.
Exile	Hamilton, E.
Exile from Space	Merril, J.
Exile of the Eons	Clarke, A.
Exiled from Earth	Merwin, S.
The Exiles	Bradbury, R.
Exiles on Asperus	Wyndham, J.
Exit	Tucker, W.
Exit Line	Merwin, S.
Exit the Professor	Padgett, L.
The Expanding Man	Mackelworth, R.
Expedition	Brown, F.
Expedition Mercy	Winter, J.
Expedition Pluto	Elam, R.
Expedition Polychrome	Winter, J.
Expedition to Earth	Clarke, A.
Expendable	Dick, P.
Experiment	Rogers, K.
Experiment in Autobiography	Goulart, R.
Experiment Station	Neville, K.
The Expert Dreamers	P760.
The Expert Touch	Nourse, A.
Exploration Team	Leinster, M.
The Explorers	K840.
Exploring Other Worlds	M925.
Exposure	Russell, E.

TITLE	AUTHOR
Extempore	Knight, D.
Extending the Holdings	Grinnell, D.
Extra Sensory Perfection	Gernsback, H.
Extrapolasis	Malec, A.
An Eye for a What?	Knight, D.
Eye for Iniquity	Sherred, T.
Eye of Night	Budrys, A.
The Eyes	Hasse, H.
Eyes Do More Than See	Asimov, I.
The Eyes Have It	McKimmey, J.
FYI	Blish, J.
The Fabulous Idiot	Sturgeon, T.
The Face in the Photo	Finney, J.
The Faces Outside	McAllister, B.
Facts in the Case of M. Valdemar	Poe, E.
Fair	Brunner, J.
Fall of Knight	Chandler, A.
Fallout Island	Murphy, R.
False Dawn	Chandler, A.
Family Portrait	Kent, M.
Family Resemblance	Nourse, A.
Family Tree	Thayer, F.
Famous Science Fiction Stories	H430.
The Fantastic Universe Omnibus	F215.
Faq'	Elliott, G.
Far Below	Johnson, R.
Far Boundaries	D430.
Far Centaurus	Van Vogt, A.
Far from Home	Tevis, W.
The Far Look	Thomas, T.
Far Out; 13 Science Fiction Stories	K715.
Farewell to Eden	Sturgeon, T.
Farewell to the Master	Bates, H.
The Farthest Horizon	Jones, R.
The Fascinating Stranger	Fessier, M.
Fast Falls the Eventide	Russell, E.
Fast Trip	White, J.
The Fasterfaster Affair	Anmar, F.
The Fastest Gun Dead	Grow, J.
Father of the Stars	Pohl, F.

TITLE	AUTHOR
The Father-Thing	Dick, P.
Fear Is a Business	Sturgeon, T.
The Fear Planet	Bloch, R.
Fearsome Fable	Elliott, B.
A Feast of Demons	Morrison, W.
Feathered Friend	Clarke, A.
The Feeling of Power	Asimov, I.
The Fellow Who Married the Maxill Girl	Moore, W.
The Felony	Causey, J.
The Fence	Simak, C.
Fessenden's Worlds	Hamilton, E.
Fever Dream	Bradbury, R.
A Few Kindred Spirits	Christopher, J.
The Fiction Machines	Okhotnikov, V.
Fiddler's Green	McKenna, R.
Field Expedient	Oliver, C.
Field Study	Phillips, P.
The Fiend	Pohl, F.
Fifteen Mules	Bova, B.
The Fifth Annual of the Year's Best S-F	M615.
The Fifth Galaxy Reader	G160.
Fifty Short Science Fiction Tales	A835.
Fighting Division	Garrett, R.
A Fighting Man of Mars	Burroughs, E.
The Figure	Grendon, E.
A Filbert Is a Nut	Raphael, R.
Filmer	Wells, H.
Final Clearance	Maddux, R.
Final Command	Van Vogt, A.
Final Encounter	Harrison, H.
Final Gentleman	Simak, C.
The Final Solution	Mackelworth, R.
Finality Unlimited	Wandrei, D.
The Finest Story in the World	Kipling, R.
Finished	De Camp, L.
A Finishing Touch	Chandler, A.
The Fire and the Sword	Robinson, F.
The Fire Balloons	Bradbury, R.
The Fire of Asshurbanipal	Howard, R.

TITLE	AUTHOR
The Fires of Night	Etchison, D.
The Fires Within	Clarke, A.
Firewater	Tenn, W.
First Contact	Leinster, M.
The First Days of May	Veillot, C.
First Lady	McIntosh, J.
First Law	Asimov, I.
First Lesson	Clingerman, M.
The First Man into Space	Elam, R.
The First Martians	Van Vogt, A.
The First Men	Fast, H.
The First Men in the Moon	Wells, H.
The First Night of Lent	Bradbury, R.
The Fittest	MacLean, K.
Five Eggs	Disch, T.
Five Galaxy Short Novels	G195.
The Five Hells of Orion	Pohl, F.
5, 271, 009	Bester, A.
Five Science Fiction Novels	G810.
Five Tales from Tomorrow	D580.
Five Years in the Marmalade	Krepps, R.
The Flame Knife	Howard, R.
The Flames	Stapledon, O.
Flandry of Terra	Anderson, P.
A Flask of Fine Arcturan	MacApp, C.
Flatlander	Niven, L.
Flaw	MacDonald, J.
Flies	Asimov, I.
Flight into Darkness	Marlowe, W.
Flight into Space	W870.
A Flight of Ravens	Bradbury, R.
Flight of the Centaurus	Elam, R.
The Flight That Failed	Hull, E.
Flight to Forever	Anderson, P.
Flirgleflip	Tenn, W.
Flower Arrangement	Brown, R.
The Flowering of the Strange Orchid	Wells, H.
Flowers for Algernon	Keyes, D.
Fluffy	Sturgeon, T.

TITLE	AUTHOR
Flux	Moorcock, M.
The Fly	Langelaan, G.
The Fly	Porges, A.
Flying Dutchman	Moore, W.
Flying Flowers	Vasilyev, M.
Flying High	Ionesco, E.
The Flying Machine	Bradbury, R.
The Flying Man	Wells, H.
The Flying Men	Stapledon, O.
Flying Pan	Young, R.
The Fog Horn	Bradbury, R.
Folly to Be Wise	Mason, D.
Fondly Fahrenheit	Bester, A.
The Food Farm	Reed, K.
The Food of the Gods	Wells, H.
Food to All Flesh	Henderson, Z.
A Foot in the Door	Friedman, B.
Footprints	Gilbert, R.
For a Breath I Tarry	Zelazny, R.
For I Am a Jealous People	Del Rey, L.
For Love	Budrys, A.
For the Public	Kahn, B.
The Forest of Zil	Neville, K.
Forever and the Earth	Bradbury, R.
Forget-Me-Not	Temple, W.
Forgetfulness	Stuart, D.
The Forgiveness of Tenchu Taen	Kummer, F.
The Forgotten Enemy	Clarke, A.
Forgotten World	Hamilton, E.
Formula for the Impossible	Voisunsky, Y.
Fortress Ship	Saberhagen, F.
Foster, You're Dead	Dick, P.
The Foundation of Science Fiction Success	Asimov, I.
Founding Father	Simak, C.
The Founding of Civilization	Yarov, R.
The Four-Dimensional-Roller-Press	Olsen, B.
Four Ghosts in Hamlet	Leiber, F.
Four in One	Knight, D.
The Fourth Dimensional Demonstration	Leinster, M.

TITLE	AUTHOR
The Fourth Dynasty	Winterbotham, R.
The Fourth Galaxy Reader	G155.
The Fox in the Forest	Bradbury, R.
The Foxholes of Mars	Leiber, F.
Frances Harkins	Goggin, R.
Franchise	Neville, K.
Franchise	Asimov, I.
Frank Reade, jr.'s Air Wonder	Senarens, L.
Frank Reade, jr.'s Strange Adventure	Senarens, L.
Frankenstein, or the Modern Prometheus	Shelley, M.
Frankenstein—Unlimited	Highstone, H.
Fred One	Ransom, J.
Freedom	Reynolds, M.
Freedom of Space	Clarke, A.
Fresh Guy	Tubb, E.
Friday	Kippax, J.
Friend of the Family	Wilson, R.
A Friend to Man	Ellison, H.
Friend to Man	Kornbluth, C.
The Friendly Demon	Defoe, D.
The Frightened Tree	Budrys, A.
From a Private Mad-House	Repton, H.
From Beyond	Lovecraft, H.
From Frankenstein to Andromeda	B890.
From the Earth to the Moon	Verne, J.
From the Land of Fear	Ellison, H.
From the Ocean, From the Stars	C610.
From Two Universes [Poem]	Buck, D.
Frost and Fire	Bradbury, R.
The Frost Giant's Daughter	Howard, R.
Frozen Planet	F945.
The Frozen Planet	Laumer, K.
The Fruit at the Bottom of the Bowl	Bradbury, R.
Fuel for the Future	Hatcher, J.
Fulfillment	Van Vogt, A.
Full Sun	Aldiss, B.
The Fun They Had	Asimov, I.
Future Tense	C965.
The Gadget Had a Ghost	Leinster, M.
Gadget vs. Trend	Anvil, C.

TITLE	AUTHOR
The Galactic Calabash	Edmondson, C.
Galactic Diplomat	L375.
The Galaxy Reader of Science Fiction	G140.
Gallegher Plus	Padgett, L.
Galley Slave	Asimov, I.
The Galton Whistle	De Camp, L.
Game	Barthelme, D.
Game for Blondes	MacDonald, J.
The Game of Glory	Anderson, P.
The Game of Rat and Dragon	Smith, C.
Game Preserve	Phillips, R.
Games	MacLean, K.
Gandolphus	Boucher, A.
The Garbage Collector	Bradbury, R.
The Garden in the Forest	Young, R.
Garden in the Void	Anderson, P.
The Garden of Time	Ballard, J.
The Gardener	Saint Clair, M.
Gas Mask	Houston, J.
Gateway to Darkness	Brown, F.
Gateway to the Stars	C290.
Gateway to Tomorrow	C295.
Gavagan's Bar	De Camp, L.
Geever's Flight	Fritch, C.
Generation of Noah	Tenn, W.
Genius	Anderson, P.
The Genius Heap	Blish, J.
Genius of the Species	Bretnor, R.
The Gentle Vultures	Asimov, I.
The Gentleman Is an EPWA	Jacobi, C.
Gentlemen, Be Seated	Heinlein, R.
Gentlemen, the Queen	Tucker, W.
The Gentlest Unpeople	Pohl, F.
Genus Traitor	Reynolds, M.
Geography for Time Travelers	Ley, W.
George	West, J.
Ghost	Kuttner, H.

TITLE	AUTHOR
The Ghost of Me	Boucher, A.
The Ghost of Ticonderoga.	Serling, R.
The Ghost Ship of Space	Elam, R.
The Ghost-Town Ghost	Serling, R.
Ghosts	Marquis, D.
The Giant Anthology of Science Fiction	M330.
Giant Killer	Chandler, A.
Giants Unleashed	C765.
The Gift	Bradbury, R.
The Gift of Gab.	Vance, J.
Gifts of the Gods	Sellings, A.
Gil Braltar	Verne, J.
Gilead.	Henderson, Z.
Gimmicks Three	Asimov, I.
The Girl Had Guts.	Sturgeon, T.
The Girl in the Golden Atom	Cummings, R.
The Girl Who Drew the Gods	Jacobs, H.
The Girl Who Made Time Stop.	Young, R.
The Girl With the Hundred Proof Eyes .	Webb, R.
The Girls from Earth	Robinson, F.
Git Along!	De Camp, L.
The Glass Eye.	Russel, E.
Gleaners	Simak, C.
A Gleeb for Earth	Schafhauser, C.
Glimpses of the Moon	West, W.
The Gnarly Man.	De Camp, L.
A Gnome There Was	Padgett, L.
The Gnurrs Come from the Voodvork Out	Bretnor, R.
Go for Baroque	Scott, J.
The God in the Bowl	Howard, R.
Goddess in Granite	Young, R.
Going Up!	Driscoll, D.
The Gold Makers	Haldane, J.
The Golden Age.	Clarke, A.
The Golden Apples of the Sun	Bradbury, R.
The Golden Brick	Hubbard, P.
The Golden Bugs	Simak, C.
The Golden Egg.	Sturgeon, T.
The Golden Horn	Pangborn, E.

TITLE	AUTHOR
The Golden Kite, The Silver Wind	Bradbury, R.
The Golden Man	Dick, P.
The Golden Pyramid	Moscowitz, S.
Goldfish Bowl	Heinlein, R.
The Golem	Davidson, A.
Gomez	Kornbluth, C.
Good-bye Ilha!	Manning, L.
Good Indian	Reynolds, M.
Good Night, Mr. James	Simak, C.
The Good Provider	Gross, M.
The Goodly Creatures	Kornbluth, C.
Gorilla Suit	Shepley, J.
The Gostak and the Doshes	Breuer, M.
Grand Central Terminal	Szilard, L.
Grandma's Lie Soap	Abernathy, R.
Grandpa	Schmitz, J.
Granny Won't Knit	Sturgeon, T.
The Grantha Sighting	Davidson, A.
Gratitude	De Camp, L.
Gratitude Guaranteed	Bretnor, R.
The Gravity Professor	Cummings, R.
The Great Automatic Grammatisator	Dahl, R.
The Great Awakening	Doyle, A.
The Great Cold	Long, F.
The Great Collision of Monday Last	Bradbury, R.
The Great Devon Mystery	Healy, R.
The Great Fire	Bradbury, R.
The Great Fog	Heard, H.
The Great God Awto	Smith, C.
The Great Judge	Van Vogt, A.
The Great Keinplatz Experiment	Doyle, A.
The Great Nebraska Sea	Danzig, A.
Great Science Fiction about Doctors	C770.
Great Science Fiction by Scientists	C810.
Great Science Fiction Stories about Mars	D585.
Great Science Fiction Stories about the Moon	D590.
Great Stories of Science Fiction	L530.
Great Stories of Space Travel	C775.

TITLE	AUTHOR
The Great Wide World Over There . .	Bradbury, R.
The Greatest Tertian	Boucher, A.
The Green Cat	Cartmill, C.
Green Fingers	Clarke, A.
The Green Hills of Earth	Heinlein, R.
Green Magic	Vance, J.
The Green Morning	Bradbury, R.
Green Thumb	Simak, C.
Grenville's Planet	Shaara, M.
The Grisly Folk	Wells, H.
Growing Season	Wallace, F.
The Grunder	Henderson, Z.
Guardian Angel	Page, G.
The Guided Man	De Camp, L.
Guilty as Charged	Porges, A.
Guinevere for Everybody	Williamson, J.
Gulf	Heinlein, R.
The Gumdrop King	Stanton, W.
A Gun for Dinosaur	De Camp, L.
The Gun without a Bang	O'Donnevan, F.
Gypsy	Anderson, P.
Haggard Honeymoon	Green, J.
Hail and Farewell	Bradbury, R.
Half a Hoka-Poul Anderson	Dickson, G.
Hall of Mirrors	Brown, F.
Hallucination Orbit	McIntosh, J.
The Hammerpond Park Burglary	Wells, H.
A Handful of Silver	Counselman, M.
The Handler	Knight, D.
The Hands	Baxter, J.
Hands Across the Deep	Elam, R.
Hang Head, Vandal!	Clifton, M.
Hans Phaall—a Tale	Poe, E.
Hans Schnap's Spy-Glass	Erckmann, E.
The Happiest Creature	Williamson, J.
Happy Ending	Kuttner, H.
Hard Bargain	Nourse, A.
The Hardest Bargain	Smith, E.

TITLE	AUTHOR
Hardluck Diggings	Vance, J.
Harrison Bergeron	Vonnegut, K.
The Hat Trick	Brown, F.
The Hatchery	Huxley, A.
Hate	Clarke, A.
The Hated	Flehr, P.
The Haunted Corpse	Pohl, F.
The Haunted Space Suit	Clarke, A.
The Haunted Village	Dickson, G.
Hawks over Shem	Howard, R.
Hawksbill Station	Silverberg, R.
He Walked Around the Horses	Piper, H.
He Who Shapes	Zelazny, R.
He Who Shrank	Hasse, H.
The Head Hunters	Williams, R.
The Headpiece	Bradbury, R.
The Heart of Blackness	Ray, R.
The Heart of the Serpent [Cor Serpentis]	Yefremov, I.
The Heart on the Other Side	Gamow, G.
Heavyplanet	Rothman, M.
Heirs Apparent	Abernathy, R.
Helen O'Loy	Del Rey, L.
The Hell-Bound Train	Bloch, R.
Hell-Fire	Asimov, I.
Hell-Planet	Rackham, J.
Help! I Am Dr. Morris Goldpepper	Davidson, A.
The Helping Hand	Anderson, P.
Hemingway in Space	Amis, K.
Here There Be Tygers	Bradbury, R.
Heresies of the Huge God	Aldiss, B.
Heritage	Abernathy, R.
Hermit of Saturn's Ring	Jones, N.
Hermit on Bikini	Langdon, J.
The Heroic Feat	Dnieprov, A.
Hickory, Dickory, Kerouac	Gehman, R.
The Hidden Planet	W875.
Hide and Seek	Clarke, A.
Hiding Place	Anderson, P.
High Barbarry	Durrell, L.

TITLE	AUTHOR
High Eight	Stringer, D.
High Threshold	Nourse, A.
The Highway	Bradbury, R.
Highway	Lowndes, R.
Hilda	Hickey, H.
Hilifter	Dickson, G.
Hindsight	Williamson, J.
Historical Note	Leinster, M.
History Lesson	Clarke, A.
The History of Doctor Frost	Hodgins, R.
Hitch-Hike to Paradise	Whybrow, G.
Hobbies	Simak, C.
Hobbyist	Russell, E.
Hobo God	Jameson, M.
Hobson's Choice	Bester, A.
Hog-Belly Honey	Lafferty, R.
Hoity-Toity	Belayev, A.
Hold Back Tomorrow	Neville, K.
Holdout	Sheckley, R.
The Hole in the Moon	Seabright, I.
Hole in the Sky	Cox, I.
The Hole on the Corner	Lafferty, R.
The Holes Around Mars	Bixby, J.
Holiday	Bradbury, R.
Home from the Shore	Dickson, G.
Home Is the Hero	Tubb, E.
Home Is the Hunter	Kuttner, H.
Home Is Where the Wrec Is	Tucker, W.
Home There's No Returning	Kuttner, H.
Homeland	Wolf, M.
The Homing Instinct of Joe Vargo	Barr, S.
Homo Sol	Asimov, I.
Honeymoon in Hell	Brown, F.
Honor	Wilson, R.
Honorable Opponent	Simak, C.
The Hoofer	Miller, W.
Hop-Friend	Carr, T.
Hopsoil	Young, R.
Horizontal Man	Spencer, W.

TITLE	AUTHOR
Hormone	Pratt, F.
Horrer Howce	Saint Clair, M.
The Horror from the Middle Span	Lovecraft, H.
The Horror from the Mound	Howard, R.
Hostess	Asimov, I.
Hot Argument	Garrett, R.
Hot Planet	Clement, H.
Hothouse	Aldiss, B.
The Hour of Letdown	White, E.
The House by the Crab Apple Tree	Johnson, S.
The House Dutiful	Tenn, W.
The House of Arabu	Howard, R.
The House on the Square	Serling, R.
The House the Blakeneys Built	Davidson, A.
Houyhnhnms & Company	Crossen, K.
How Beautiful with Banners	Blish, J.
How High the Ladder?	Paige, L.
How Near Is the Moon?	Merril, J.
How the Old World Died	Harrison, H.
How to Count on Your Fingers	Pohl, F.
How to Learn Martian	Hockett, C.
How to Think a Science Fiction Story	Stine, G.
How to Write Science Fiction	Gold, H.
How-2	Simak, C.
The Hub	MacDonald, P.
Huddling Place	Simak, C.
Huge Beast	Cartmill, C.
The Hugo Winners	A840.
Human?	M585.
Human and Other Beings	D320.
Humanity on Venus	Stapledon, O.
Humpty Dumpty Had a Great Fall	Long, F.
The Hunch	Anvil, C.
Hunger Over Sweetwaters	Kapp, C.
The Hungry Guinea Pig	Breuer, M.
Hunter, Come Home	McKenna, R.
The Hunters	Sheldon, W.
Hunting Machine	Emshwiller, C.

TITLE	AUTHOR
The Hunting Season	Robinson, F.
The Hurkle Is a Happy Beast	Sturgeon, T.
Hurricane Trio	Sturgeon, T.
A Husband for My Wife	Stuart, W.
Hush!	Henderson, Z.
The Hyborian Age	Howard, R.
Hybrid	Laumer, K.
Hyperpilosity	De Camp, L.
The Hyperspherical Basketball	Nearing, H.
The Hypnoglyph	Anthony, J.
IBM	Genberg, M.
The IFTH of OOFTH	Tevis, W.
IOU	Wellen, E.
I Am a Nucleus	Barr, S.
I Am Nothing	Russell, E.
I Do Not Love Thee, Doctor Fell	Bloch, R.
I Don't Mind	Smith, R.
I Gave Her Sack and Sherry	Russ, J.
I Kill Myself	Kawaleck, J.
I Never Ast No Favors	Kornbluth, C.
I Remember Babylon	Clarke, A.
I, Robot	Asimov, I.
I, Robot	Binder, E.
I See You Never	Bradbury, R.
I, the Unspeakable	Sheldon, W.
Icarus Montgolfier Wright	Bradbury, R.
The Ideal	Weinbaum, S.
Idealist	Del Rey, L.
The Idealists	Campbell, J.
Ideas Die Hard	Asimov, I.
Idiot Stick	Knight, D.
Idiot's Crusade	Simak, C.
Idol of the Flies	Rice, J.
If I Forget Thee, Oh Earth	Clarke, A.
The If Reader of Science Fiction	1230.
If the Court Pleases	Loomis, N.
If There Were No Benny Cemoli	Dick, P.
If This Goes On	Heinlein, R.
If You Was a Maklin	Leinster, M.

TITLE	AUTHOR
In the Imagicon	Smith, G.
In the Modern Vein	Wells, H.
In the Ruins	Dahl, R.
In the Scarlet Star	Williamson, J.
In the World's Dusk	Hamilton, E.
In the Year 2889	Verne, J.
In This Sign	Bradbury, R.
In Value Deceived	Fyfe, H.
Inanimate Objection	Elliott, H.
Incident on a Lake	Collier, J.
Incommunicado	MacLean, K.
Incubation	MacDonald, J.
Industrial Revolution	Sanders, W.
The Inexperienced Ghost	Wells, H.
Infinity	Reeves, R.
Infinity Zero	Wandrei, D.
An Informal Biography of Conan the Cimmerian	Howard, R.
Infra Draconis	Gurevich, G.
Infra-Medians	Wright, S.
Inheritance	Clarke, A.
The Inner Wheel	Roberts, K.
The Inner Worlds	Morrison, W.
The Innocent Arrival	Anderson, P.
An Inquiry Concerning the Curvature	Price, R.
The Insane Ones	Ballard, J.
Inside Earth	Anderson, P.
Inside John Barth	Stuart, W.
Inside the Comet	Clarke, A.
Insidekick	Bone, J.
Inspector's Teeth	De Camp, L.
Installment Plan	Simak, C.
Instinct	Del Rey, L.
Intangibles, Inc.	Aldiss, B.
Interbalance	MacLean, K.
Interim	Bradbury, R.
Interloper	Anderson, P.
Internal Combustion	De Camp, L.
Interplanetary Copyright	Reines, D.

TITLE	AUTHOR
It's a Great Big Wonder Universe	Aandahl, V.
It's Great to Be Back	Heinlein, R.
It's Such a Beautiful Day	Asimov, I.
Izzard and the Membrane	Miller, W.
J.G.	Price, R.
J Is for Jeanne	Tubb, E.
Jackpot	Simak, C.
Jackson Wong's Story	Bolsover, J.
Jay Score	Russell, E.
Jaywalker	Rocklynne, R.
The Jazz Machine	Matheson, R.
Jerry Was a Man	Heinlein, R.
The Jester	Tenn, W.
Jesting Pilot	Kuttner, H.
Jesting Pilot	Padgett, L.
The Jet-Propelled Couch	Lindner, R.
The Jewbird	Malamud, B.
Jewels of Gwahlur	Howard, R.
Jezebel	Leinster, M.
The Jilting of Jane	Wells, H.
Jimmy Goggles the God	Wells, H.
Jizzle	Wyndham, J.
The Job Is Ended	Tucker, W.
John Grant's Little Angel	Grove, W.
John Sze's Future	Pierce, J.
John the Revelator	La Farge, O.
John Thoma's Cube	Leimert, J.
The John Wyndham Omnibus	W990.
John's Other Practice	Marks, W.
Join Our Gang?	Lanier, S.
Jokester	Asimov, I.
Jon's World	Dick, P.
Jordan	Henderson, Z.
The Journey	Leinster, M.
Journey to Infinity	G815.
A Journey to the Centre of the Earth	Verne, J.
Journey's End	Anderson, P.
Journeys in Science Fiction	L885.

TITLE	AUTHOR
The Joy of Living	Nolan, W.
Judas Ram	Merwin, S.
Judgment Day	De Camp, L.
Judgment Night	Serling, R.
The Judgment of Aphrodite	Hoyle, F.
Juggernaut	Van Vogt, A.
Juke Doll	Young, R.
Jungle Doctor	Young, R.
Jungle Substitute	Aldiss, B.
Junior	Abernathy, R.
Junior Achievement	Lee, W.
Jungle Journey	Wylie, P.
The Junkmakers	Teichner, A.
Junkyard	Simak, C.
Jupiter Five	Clarke, A.
A Jury of Five	Hoyle, F.
Kaldar, World of Antares	Hamilton, E.
Kaleidoscope	Bradbury, R.
Kangaroo Court	Kidd, V.
Kazam Collects	Kornbluth, C.
Keep Out	Brown, F.
Keep Them Happy	Rohrer, R.
Keeper of the Dream	Beaumont, C.
The Key	Asimov, I.
Key to Chaos	Mackin, E.
Keyhole	Leinster, M.
The Keys to December	Zelazny, R.
Kid Anderson	Richardson, R.
Kid Stuff	Asimov, I.
Kill Me with Kindness	Wilson, R.
Killdozer!	Sturgeon, T.
The Killer in the TV Set	Friedman, B.
A Kind of Artistry	Aldiss, B.
Kindergarten	Simak, C.
Kindness	Del Rey, L.
The King and the Oak	Howard, R.
The King of the Beasts	Farmer, P.
The King of the City	Laumer, K.

TITLE	AUTHOR
King of the Grey Spaces	Bradbury, R.
The King of Thieves	Vance, J.
King's Evil	Davidson, A.
Kings Who Die	Anderson, P.
Kleon of the Golden Sun	Repp, E.
Knights of the Paper Space Ship	Aldiss, B.
The Knitting	Wood, M.
Knock	Brown, F.
The Kraken Wakes	Wyndham, J.
The Lady Who Saided the Soul	Smith, C.
The Lagging Profession	Lockhard, J.
Lament by a Maker	De Camp, L.
The Land Ironclads	Wells, H.
The Land of No Shadow	Claudy, C.
The Land That Time Forgot	Burroughs, E.
Landmark	Malec, A.
Landscape with Sphinxes	Anderson, K.
Language for Time Travelers	De Camp, L.
The Laocoon Complex	Furnas, J.
Laputa	Swift, J.
The Large Ant	Fast, H.
The Last American	Mitchell, J.
The Last and First Men	Stapledon, O.
The Last Castle	Vance, J.
The Last Command	Laumer, K.
The Last Day of Summer	Tubb, E.
Last Enemy	Piper, H.
The Last Generation	Clarke, A.
The Last Letter	Leiber, F.
The Last Lonely Man	Brunner, J.
The Last Man	Shelley, M.
The Last Man Left in the Bar	Kornbluth, C.
The Last Martian	Brown, F.
The Last Monster	Anderson, P.
The Last Night of Summer	Coppel, A.
The Last Night of the World	Bradbury, R.
The Last of the Spode	Smith, E.
The Last Present	Stanton, W.

TITLE	AUTHOR
The Last Prophet	Clingerman, M.
The Last Question	Asimov, I.
Last Rites	Beaumont, C.
The Last Seance	Christie, A.
The Last Secret Weapon of the Third Reich	Nesvadba, J.
The Last Shall Be First	Mills, R.
The Last Step	Henderson, Z.
The Last Terrestrials	Stapledon, O.
The Last Trump	Asimov, I.
The Last Victory	Godwin, T.
The Last Weapon	Sheckley, R.
The Last Word	Knight, D.
The Last Word	Oliver, C.
The Last World of Mr. Goddard	Ballard, J.
Last Year's Grave Undug	Davis, C.
The Late Mr. Elvesham	Wells, H.
Late Night Final	Russell, E.
Later Than You Think	Leiber, F.
Learning Theory	McConnell, J.
The Leech	Sheckley, R.
The Left-Hand Way	Chandler, A.
The Legend of Joe Lee	MacDonald, J.
Lenny	Asimov, I.
Leprechaun	Sambrot, W.
Let Me Live in a House	Oliver, C.
Let Nothing You Dismay	Sloane, W.
Let There Be Light	Clarke, A.
Let There Be Light	Heinlein, R.
Let's Be Frank	Aldiss, B.
Let's Get Together	Asimov, I.
Let's Have Fun	De Camp, L.
Letter of the Law	Nourse, A.
Letter to a Phoenix	Brown, F.
Letter to a Tyrant King [Poem]	Butler, B.
Letter to Donald Wollheim	Lovecraft, H.
Letter to Ellen	Davis, C.
Letter to P. Schuyler Miller	Howard, R.
Letter to the Martians	Ley, W.

TITLE	AUTHOR
Little Red School House	Young, R.
The Little Terror	Leinster, M.
The Littlest People.	Banks, R.
The Live Coward	Anderson, P.
A Living Doll	Wallace, R.
The Living Galaxy.	Manning, L.
The Living Machine	Keller, D.
Living Space	Asimov, I.
Load of Trouble	Wood, E.
Locked Out	Fyfe, H.
The Locusts	Bradbury, R.
A Logic Named Joe	Leinster, M.
Logic of Empire	Heinlein, R.
A Loint of Paw	Asimov, I.
The Lonely Man	Thomas, T.
The Long Dawn	Loomis, N.
Long Day in Court	Brand, J.
The Long Memory	Spencer, W.
The Long Rain	Bradbury, R.
The Long Remembered Thunder.	Laumer, K.
The Long Remembering	Anderson, P.
A Long Spoon	Wyndham, J.
The Long View	Pratt, F.
Long Watch	Heinlein, R.
The Long Years	Bradbury, R.
The Longest Voyage	Anderson, P.
Looking Backward	Feiffer, J.
Looking Forward	L640.
The Loolies Are Here.	Rice, A.
Loophole	Clarke, A.
The Lord of the Dynamos	Wells, H.
The Los Amigos Fiasco	Doyle, A.
Lost Art	Smith, G.
The Lost Chord	Moskowitz, S.
The Lost Continent.	Household, G.
Lost in a Comet's Tail	Senarens, L.
The Lost Inheritance	Wells, H.
Lost Legacy	Heinlein, R.
The Lost Machine	Wyndham, J.

TITLE	AUTHOR
Lost Memory	Phillips, P.
Lost on Venus	Burroughs, E.
The Lost World	Doyle, A.
The Lost Years	Lewis, O.
Lot	Moore, W.
Lot's Daughter	Moore, W.
Lotus Eaters	Weinbaum, S.
Love	Wilson, R.
Love Called This Thing	Davidson, A.
Love in the Dark	Gold, H.
Love, Incorporated	Sheckley, R.
Love Letter from Mars [Poem]	Ciardi, J.
The Love of Heaven	Sturgeon, T.
Love Story	Monig, C.
Love Thy Vimp	Nourse, A.
Lover When You're Near Me	Matheson, R.
Lover, When You're New	Matheson, R.
Lower Than Angels	Budrys, A.
Luana	Thomas, G.
The Luck of Ignatz	Del Rey, L.
The Luckiest Man in Denv	Kornbluth, C.
Lufe Hutch	Ellison, H.
The Luggage Store	Bradbury, R.
Lulu	Simak, C.
Lulungomeena	Dickson, G.
Lunar Trap	Elam, R.
The Lysenko Maze	Grinnell, D.
MCMLV	Tucker, W.
Ms Fnd in a Lbry	Draper, H.
Ms. Found in a Bus	Baker, R.
Ms. Found in a Chinese Fortune Cookie	Kornbluth, C.
MacDonough's Song	Kipling, R.
Machine	Jakes, J.
Machine Made	McIntosh, J.
The Machine Stops	Forster, E.
The Machine That Was Lonely	Wells, R.
The Machine That Won the War	Asimov, I.
The Machineries of Joy	Bradbury, R.

TITLE	AUTHOR
The Machmen	Schmitz, J.
McIlvaine's Star	Derleth, A.
McNamara's Fish	Goulart, R.
The Mad Moon	Weinbaum, S.
Made in U.S.A.	McIntosh, J.
Made to Measure	Gault, W.
Maelstrom II	Clarke, A.
Magic City	Bond, N.
Magic, Inc.	Heinlein, R.
The Magic Shoes	Saparin, V.
The Magic Shop	Wells, H.
The Magnetosphere	Hoyle, F.
A Magus	Ciardi, J.
Maid to Measure	Knight, D.
Maiden Voyage	Rankine, J.
Make a Prison	Block, L.
Make Mine Mars	Kornbluth, C.
The Maker of Gargoyles	Smith, C.
The Maladjusted Classroom	Nearing, H.
Malice Afe Thought	Grinnel, D.
The Man	Bradbury, R.
A Man for the Moon	Webb, L.
The Man from Outside	Williamson, J.
The Man from When	Plachta, D.
Man in a Quandary	Stecher, L.
Man in His Time	Aldiss, B.
Man in Space	Lang, D.
Man in the Jar	Knight, D.
The Man in the Moon	Reynolds, M.
The Man in the Moon	Norton, H.
The Man in the Moone	Godwin, F.
Man in the Sky	Budrys, A.
Man Manifold	Young, P.
Man of Destiny	Christopher, J.
Man of Distinction	Shaara, M.
Man of Parts	Gold, H.
A Man of Talent	Silverberg, R.
Man of the Stars	Moskowitz, S.

TITLE	AUTHOR
Man on Bridge	Aldiss, B.
Man on Top	Bretnor, R.
Man Overboard	Collier, J.
The Man Who Always Knew	Budrys, A.
The Man Who Ate the World	Pohl, F.
The Man Who Came Early	Anderson, P.
The Man Who Could Work Miracles	Wells, H.
The Man Who Found Proteus	Rohrer, R.
The Man Who Liked Lions	Daley, J.
The Man Who Lost the Sea	Sturgeon, T.
The Man Who Made Friends with Electricty	Leiber, F.
The Man Who Missed the Ferry	Mason, D.
The Man Who Never Grew Young	Leiber, F.
The Man Who Ploughed the Sea	Clarke, A.
The Man Who Rode the Saucer	Holmes, K.
The Man Who Rode the Trains	Carter, P.
The Man Who Saw the Future	Hamilton, E.
The Man Who Sold the Moon	Heinlein, R.
The Man Who Sold Rope to the Gnoles	Seabright, I.
The Man With English	Gold, H.
Man with the Strange Head	Breuer, M.
The Man without a Planet	Wilhelm, K.
The Man Without an Appetite	Breuer, M.
Manipulation	Kingston, J.
Manna	Phillips, P.
Manners of the Age	Fyfe, H.
Manscarer	Roberts, K.
Mantage	Matheson, R.
Manuscript Found in a Vacuum	Hubbard, P.
The Maracot Deep	Doyle, A.
The Marching Morons	Kornbluth, C.
Margin for Error	Padgett, L.
Mariana	Leiber, F.
Marionettes, Inc.	Bradbury, R.
The Mark Gable Foundation	Szilard, L.
The Mark of the Beast	Kipling, R.
Marooned off Vesta	Asimov, I.
The Marriage-Mender	Bradbury, R.

TITLE	AUTHOR
Mars Is Heaven!	Bradbury, R.
Mars Is Ours!	Buchwald, A.
The Martian	Bradbury, R.
The Martian	Kazantsev, A.
A Martian Adventure	Ley, W.
The Martian and the Magician	Smith, E.
The Martian and the Moron	Sturgeon, T.
The Martian Crown Jewels	Anderson, P.
A Martian Glossary	Burroughs, E.
The Martian Shop	Fast, H.
The Martian Star-Gazers	Pohl, F.
The Martian Way	Asimov, I.
The Martians	Hoyle, F.
The Martians	Stapledon, O.
The Martians and the Coys	Reynolds, M.
The Martyr	Anderson, P.
Mary	Knight, D.
The Mary Celeste Move	Herbert, F.
The Master Key	Anderson, P.
The Master Mind of Mars	Burroughs, E.
The Master Minds of Mars	Claudy, C.
A Master of Babylon	Pangborn, E.
Master of the Asteroid	Smith, C.
Master Race	Ashby, R.
Masterpieces of Science Fiction	M930.
Master's Choice	J330.
Matayama	Malec, A.
Mate in Two Moves	Marks, W.
The Mathematical Voodoo	Nearing, H.
The Mathematicians	Feldman, A.
The Mathenauts	Kagan, N.
Matog	Basch, J.
A Matter of Energy	Blish, J.
A Matter of Ethics	Shango, J.
A Matter of Form	Gold, H.
A Matter of Size	Bates, H.
Maturity	Sturgeon, T.
The Maxwell Equations	Dnieprov, A.

TITLE	AUTHOR
Maybe Just a Little One	Bretnor, R.
Me	Schenck, H.
Me, Myself and I	Tenn, W.
The Meadow	Bradbury, R.
Mechanical Answer	MacDonald, J.
The Mechanical Bride	Leiber, F.
Mechanical Mice	Hugi, M.
Med Service	Leinster, M.
The Meddlers	Kornbluth, C.
Medicine Dancer	Brown, B.
A Medicine for Melancholy	Bradbury, R.
Meeting of Relations	Collier, J.
Meeting of the Board	Nourse, A.
Meeting of the Minds	Sheckley, R.
Meihem in Ce Klasrum	Edwards, D.
Mellonta Tauta	Poe, E.
Memento Homo	Miller, W.
Memo to Secretary [Poem]	De Graw, P.
Memorial	Sturgeon, T.
Memory	Sturgeon, T.
Men Against the Stars	G820.
Men Against the Stars	Wellman, M.
Men Are Different	Bloch, A.
Men Like Gods	Wells, H.
Men of Iron	Endore, G.
Men of Space and Time	B645.
Men of the Ten Books	Vance, J.
The Men Who Murdered Mohammed . .	Bester, A.
The Menace from Earth	Heinlein, R.
The Mercurian	Long, F.
Mercy Flight to Luna	Elam, R.
The Message	Asimov, I.
A Message in Secret	Anderson, P.
The Metal Man	Williamson, J.
Metamorphosis	Kafka, F.
The Metamorphosis of Earth	Smith, C.
Metamorphosite	Russell, E.
Meteor.	Powers, W.

TITLE	AUTHOR
Meteor	Wyndham, J.
Methuselah's Children	Heinlein, R.
Mewhu's Jet	Sturgeon, T.
Mex	Harris, L.
Mezzerow Loves Company	Wallace, F.
Mickey Finn [Poem]	Buck, D.
Microcosmic God	Sturgeon, T.
The Microscopic Giants	Ernst, P.
The Midas Plague	Pohl, F.
The Middle of the Week after Next	Leinster, M.
The Midnight Sun	Serling, R.
A Mile Beyond the Moon	K845.
The Mile-Long Spaceship	Wilhelm, K.
The Million-Year Picnic	Bradbury, R.
Mimsy Were the Borogoves	Padgett, L.
Mind Alone	McIntosh, J.
Mind for Business	Silverberg, R.
Mind Partner	Anvil, C.
Mind Partner and 8 Other Novlets	G200.
The Mindworm	Kornbluth, C.
Mine Own Ways	McKenna, R.
The Ming Vase	Tubb, E.
The Miniature	MacDonald, J.
The Minimum Man	Sheckley, R.
Minimum Sentence	Cogswell, T.
Minister Without Portfolio	Clingerman, M.
Ministering Angels	Lewis, C.
Ministry of Disturbance	Piper, H.
Minor Ingredient	Russell, E.
Minority Report	Sturgeon, T.
Minus One	Ballard, J.
A Miracle of Rare Device	Bradbury, R.
The Miracle of the Broom Closet	Wiener, N.
A Miracle Too Many	Smith, P.
Mirage	Simak, C.
Miriam	Capote, T.
Mirror of Ice	Wright, G.
The Mirrors of Tuzun Thune	Howard, R.

TITLE	AUTHOR
Misadventure	Dunsany, E.
Misbegotten Missionary	Asimov, I.
Misfit	Fischer, M.
Misfit	Heinlein, R.
Misfit	Silverberg, R.
The Misogynist	Gunn, J.
Miss Winchelsea's Heart	Wells, H.
Missing One's Coach	Anonymous.
The Mission	Nissenson, H.
The Mission	Sellings, A.
Mission "Red Clash"	Poyer, J.
The Mist	Cartur, P.
Mistake Inside	Blish, J.
Mr. Brisher's Treasure	Wells, H.
Mr. Costello, Hero	Sturgeon, T.
Mr. Kincaid's Pasts	Coupling, J.
Mr. Ledbetter's Vacation	Wells, H.
Mr. Murphy of New York	McMorrow, T.
Mr. Sakrison's Halt	Clingerman, M.
Mr. Skelmersdale in Fairyland	Wells, H.
Mr. Stilwell's Stage	Davidson, A.
Mr. Strenberrry's Tale	Priestly, J.
Mr. Waterman	Redgrove, P.
Mrs. Pigafetta Swims Well	Bretnor, R.
Mrs. Poppledore's Id	Bretnor, R.
The Model of a Judge	Morrison, W.
Modern Masterpieces of Science Fiction	M935.
The Mole Pirate	Leinster, M.
The Moment of the Storm	Zelazny, R.
Moment without Time	Rogers, J.
Monsignor Primo Macinno	Malec, A.
The Monster	Del Rey, L.
The Monster	Van Vogt, A.
The Monster and the Maiden	Zelazny, R.
The Monsters	Sheckley, R.
Monument	Biggle, L.
The Moon	Wyndham, J.
Moon Crazy	Shelton, W.

TITLE	AUTHOR
Moon of Delirium	James, D.
The Moon Era	Williamson, J.
The Moon Is Green	Leiber, F.
The Moon Maid	Burroughs, E.
Moon Prospector	Ellern, W.
The Moon That Vanished	Brackett, L.
Moon Duel	Leiber, F.
Moonwalk	Fyfe, H.
Morality	Sturgeon, T.
More Soviet Science Fiction	P965.
More Than Human	S940.
The Morning of the Day They Did It	White, E.
The Mortal Immortal	Shelley, M.
Morthylla	Smith, C.
The Moth	Wells, H.
Mother	Farmer, P.
Mother Earth	Asimov, I.
Mother of Invention	Godwin, T.
The Mother of Necessity	Oliver, C.
Mother of Toads	Smith, C.
The Mountaineer	Tucker, W.
Mourners for Hire	Ellison, H.
Mourning Song	Beaumont, C.
Mouse	Brown, F.
Mousetrap	Norton, A.
Moving Spirit	Clarke, A.
Moxon's Master	Bierce, A.
Multum in Parvo	Sharkey, J.
Mummy to the Rescue	Wilson, A.
Murder in the Fourth Dimension	Smith, C.
The Murderer	Bradbury, R.
A Murkle for Jesse	Jennings, G.
Museum Piece	Carlson, E.
The Music	Sturgeon, T.
The Music Master of Babylon	Pangborn, E.
The Musicians	Bradbury, R.
The Mute Question	Ackerman, F.
The Muted Horn	Davis, D.

TITLE	AUTHOR
Muten	Russell, E.
Mutiny	Bakhnov, V.
My Boy Friend's Name Is Jello	Davidson, A.
My Brother Paulie	Ellison, H.
My Brother's Wife	Tucker, W.
My Dear Emily	Russ, J.
My Father, the Cat	Slesar, H.
My Friend Bobby	Nourse, A.
My First Aeroplane	Wells, H.
My Lady Green Sleeves	Pohl, F.
My Private World of Science	Bester, A.
My Trial as a War Criminal	Szilard, L.
Mysterious Message	Anderson, P.
Mystery Eyes Over Earth	Elam, R.
The Mystery of Green Crossing	Emtsov, M.
The NRACP	Elliott, G.
Nada	Disch, T.
The Nail and the Oracle	Sturgeon, T.
The Naked Sun	Asimov, I.
Name Your Symptom	Harmon, J.
The Naming of Names	Bradbury, R.
Narapoia	Nelson, A.
Native Intelligence	Laumer, K.
The Native Soil	Nourse, A.
Natural State	Knight, D.
Near Miss	Kuttner, H.
Nebula Award Stories 1 & 2	N360 N365.
Neighbor	Simak, C.
Nellthu	Boucher, A.
Nemesis	Clarke, A.
Nerves	Del Rey, L.
The Neutrino Bomb	Cooper, R.
The Never Ending Penny	Wolfe, B.
Never on Mars	Harris, J.
Never Underestimate	Sturgeon, T.
The New Accelerator	Wells, H.
New Arcadia	De Camp, L.
New Atlantis	Bacon, F.

TITLE	AUTHOR
New Dreams This Morning	B665.
The New Encyclopaedist	Becker, S.
The New Father Christmas	Aldiss, B.
New Folk's Home	Simak, C.
A New Game	Lightner, A.
A New Lo!	Goulart, R.
New Men for Mars	Silverberg, R.
The New Reality	Harness, C.
New Ritual	Seabright, I.
New Stories from the Twilight Zone	S485.
New Tales of Space and Time	H435.
The New Wine	Christopher, J.
New Writings in SF 1-9	Carnell, J.
A New Year's Fairy Tale	Dudintsev, V.
The Next Tenants	Clarke, A.
A Nice Day for Screaming	Schmitz, J.
Night	Campbell, J.
The Night-Flame	Kapp, C.
The Night He Cried	Leiber, F.
Night Meeting	Bradbury, R.
The Night of Lies	Knight, D.
The Night of the Seventh Finger	Presslie, R.
The Night of the Meek	Serling, R.
Night Piece	Anderson, P.
Night Watch	Inglis, J.
Nightfall	Asimov, I.
Nightmare Blues	Herbert, F.
Nightmare Brother	Nourse, A.
Nightmare for Future Reference [Poem]	Szilard, L.
Nightmare for Future Reference [Poem]	Benet, S.
Nightmare in Time	Brown, F.
Nightmare Number Four	Bloch, R.
Nightmare with Zeppelins	Pohl, F.
Nightsound	Budrys, A.
Nikita Eisenhower Jones	Young, R.
Nina Sol	Marti-Ibanez, F.
The Nine Billion Names of God	Clarke, A.
Nine by Laumer	L380.
Nine-Finger Jack	Boucher, A.

TITLE	AUTHOR
Nine Hundred Grandmothers	Lafferty, R.
Nine Tales of Space and Time	H440.
Nine Tomorrows	A855.
1937 A.D!	Sladek, J.
The 9th Annual of the Year's Best SF	M635.
The 9th Galaxy Reader	G180.
No Different Flesh	Henderson, Z.
No Fire Burns	Davidson, A.
No Future in It	Brunner, J.
No Land of Nod	Springer, S.
No Life of Their Own	Simak, C.
No Limits	F220.
No Man Pursueth	Moore, W.
No Matter Where You Go	Rogers, J.
No Moon for Me	Miller, W.
No Morning After	Clarke, A.
No, No, Not Rogov!	Smith, C.
No One Believed Me	Thompson, W.
No Particular Night or Morning	Bradbury, R.
No Place Like Earth	C305.
No Place Like Earth	Wyndham, J.
No-Sided Professor	Gardner, M.
No Truce with Kings	Anderson, P.
No Woman Born	Moore, C.
The Nobel Prize Winners	Gordon, W.
Nobody Bothers Gus	Budrys, A.
Nobody Here But—	Asimov, I.
Nobody Saw the Ship	Leinster, M.
The Noise	Purdy, K.
Noise	Vance, J.
Noise in the Night	Hodgson, W.
Noise Level	Jones, R.
Nonstop to Mars	Williamson J.
Nor Dust Corrupt	McConnell, J.
Not Final!	Asimov, I.
Not Fit for Children	Smith, E.
Not for an Age	Aldiss, B.
Not in the Literature	Anvil, C.

TITLE	AUTHOR
Not Only Dead Men	Van Vogt, A.
Not There	Metcalfe, J.
Not To Be Opened	Young, R.
Not with a Bang	Knight, D.
Note on "Hans Phaall"	Poe, E.
Nothing Happens on the Moon	Ernst, P.
Nothing Sirius	Brown, F.
Novice	Schmitz, J.
Now Is Forever	Disch, T.
Now Let Us Sleep	Davidson, A.
Now Wakes the Sea	Ballard, J.
Null-P	Tenn, W.
Number Nine	Cartmill, C.
The Number of the Beast	Leiber, F.
Number Ten Q Street	McCloy, H.
The Nuse Man	Saint Clair, M.
Obviously Suicide	Wright, S.
The Oceans Are Wide	Robinson, F.
Odd	Wyndham, J.
Odd Boy Out	Etchison, D.
Odd John	Stapledon, O.
Oddy and Id	Bester, A.
The Odor of Thought	Sheckley, R.
Of All Possible Worlds	T300.
Of Course	Oliver, C.
Of Missing Persons	Finney, J.
Of Those Who Came	Langdon, G.
Of Time and Third Avenue	Bester, A.
The Off Season	Bradbury, R.
Official Record	Pratt, F.
Oh, to Be a Blobel!	Dick, P.
Oh, Where, Now, Is Peggy Macrafferty	Wyndham, J.
Okie	Blish, J.
Old Faithful	Gallun, R.
An Old-Fashioned Bird Christmas	Saint Clair, M.
Old Hundredth	Aldiss, B.
The Old Man	Silverberg, R.
Old Man Henderson	Neville, K.

TITLE	AUTHOR
The Old Ones	Bradbury, R.
Old Testament	Bixby, J.
Olsen and the Gull	Saint Clair, M.
O'Mara's Orphan	White, J.
Omega	Long, A.
The Omen	Jackson, S.
The Omnibus Jules Verne	V530.
Omnibus of Science Fiction	C785.
Omnilingual	Piper, H.
On Binary Digits and Human Habits	Pohl, F.
On Camera	Novotny, J.
On Handling the Data	Hirshfield, H.
On Lethal Space Clouds	Shapley, H.
On the Feasibility of Coal-Driven ...	Frisch, O.
On the Fourth Planet	Bone, J.
On the Gen Planet	Smith, C.
On the Moon	Tsiolkovsky, K.
Once a Greech	Smith, E.
Once Was	Malec, A.
$1.98	Porges, A.
One for the Books	Matheson, R.
One Leg Too Many	Alexander, W.
One of Those Days	Nolan, W.
One Ordinary Day, with Peanuts	Jackson, S.
One Reason Why We Lost	Stine, G.
$1000 a Plate	McKenty, J.
One Thousand Miles Up	Robinson, F.
One Way Street	Bixby, J.
One Way to Mars	Bloch, R.
One Who Returns	Berry, J.
The One Who Waits	Bradbury, R.
Oneiromachia	Aiken, C.
Only an Echo	Barclay, A.
The Only Thing We Learn	Kornbluth, C.
Opaxtl	Malec, A.
Open Secret	Padgett, L.
Open, Sesame	Grendon, S.
The Open Window	Saki.
Opening Doors	Shiras, W.

TITLE	AUTHOR
Operating Instructions	Sheckley, R.
Operation Exodus	Wright, L.
Operation Future	C790.
Operation Pumice	Gallun, R.
Operation RSVP	Piper, H.
Operation Stinky	Simak, C.
Opposite Number	Wyndham, J.
Or All the Seas with Oysters	Davidson, A.
Or Else	Kuttner, H.
Or the Grasses Grow	Davidson, A.
Orbit I	O640.
Orbit 2	0645
Ordeal in Space	Heinlein, R.
Orders	Jameson, M.
Origin of the Species	Anderson, K.
The Origin of the Species	MacLean, K.
Oscar	Cartmill, C.
The Other Celia	Sturgeon, T.
The Other Foot	Bradbury, R.
The Other Inauguration	Boucher, A.
The Other Likeness	Schmitz, J.
The Other Man	Sturgeon, T.
The Other Now	Leinster, M.
The Other People	Brackett, L.
The Other Side	Kubilius, W.
The Other Side of the Sky	Clarke, A.
The Other Tiger	Clarke, A.
Other Tracks	Sell, W.
The Other Wife	Finney, J.
The Other World	Leinster, M.
Ottmar Balleau X 2	Bamber, G.
An Ounce of Cure	Nourse, A.
An Ounce of Dissension	Loran, M.
An Ounce of Prevention	Carter, P.
Our Fair City	Heinlein, R.
Out of Order	Brunner, J.
Out of the Cradle, Endlessly Orbiting	Clarke, A.
Out of the Sun	Clarke, A.
Out of This World I-7	Williams-Ellis, M.

TITLE	AUTHOR
The Outer Limit	Doar, G.
The Outer Reaches	D435.
Outside	Aldiss, B.
Over the River and Through the Woods	Simak, C.
Over the Top	Del Rey, L.
The Overlord's Thumb	Silverberg, R.
Overproof	MacKenzie, J.
Overthrow	Cartmill, C.
Overture	Neville, K.
Ozymandias	Silverberg, R.
The Pacifist	Clarke, A.
Pacifist	Reynolds, M.
Pact	Sanders, W.
Page and Player	Bixby, J.
A Pail of Air	Leiber, F.
Pandora's Planet	Anvil, C.
Panic Button	Russell, E.
Paradise	Simak, C.
Paradise II	Sheckley, R.
Paradox Lost	Brown, F.
The Parasite	Clarke, A.
Parasite Planet	Weinbaum, S.
Pardon My Mistake	Pratt, F.
Parking Problem	Morgan, D.
Parky	Rome, D.
A Passage from the Stars	Hurlbut, K.
Passer-by	Clarke, A.
Passion Pills	Kornbluth, C.
The Past and Its Dead People	Bretnor, R.
The Past Through Tomorrow	H490.
Pastoral Affair	Stearns, C.
Patent Pending	Clarke, A.
The Patient	Hull, E.
Pattern	Brown, F.
Pattern for Survival	Matheson, R.
The Pause	Asimov, I.
Pausodyne	Allen, G.
Pawley's Peepholes	Wyndham, J.
Pax Galactica	Williams, R.
Peacebringer	Moore, W.

TITLE	AUTHOR
The Peaceful Martian	Oliver, J.
The Pearl of Love	Wells, H.
Pebble in the Sky	Asimov, I.
A Peculiar People	Curtiss, B.
The Peddler's Nose	Williamson, J.
The Pedestrian	Bradbury, R.
Peggy and Peter Go to the Moon	White, D.
Pellucidar	Burroughs, E.
Pelt	Emshwiller, C.
The Pen and the Dark	Kapp, C.
Pen Pal	Lesser, M.
The People: No Different Flesh	H520.
The People of the Black Circle	Howard, R.
People of the Crater	Norton, A.
The Peoples of the Pit	Merritt, A.
People Soup	Arkin, A.
Perchance to Dream	Bradbury, R.
Perchance to Dream	Joyce, M.
Perfect Answer	Stecher, L.
The Perfect Gentleman	McGregor, R.
The Perfect Host	Sturgeon, T.
Perfect Murder	Gold, H.
The Perfect Woman	Sheckley, R.
Perforce to Dream	Wyndham, J.
Perhaps We Are Going Away	Bradbury, R.
The Peril from Outer Space	Elam, R.
Peril of the Blue World	Abernathy, R.
The Permanent Implosion	McLaughlan, D.
Perpetual Motion	De Camp, L.
Personnel Problem	Gold, H.
Pete Can Fix It	Jones, R.
The Petrified Planet	P945.
Phalanstery of Theleme	Rabelais, F.
The Phantom Setter	Murphy, R.
Philosopher's Stone	Anvil, C.
Phoenix	Smith, C.
Pi in the Sky	Brown, F.
The Pi Man	Bester, A.

TITLE	AUTHOR
Pictures Don't Lie	MacLean, K.
Pie in the Sky	Styron, W.
The Piebald Hippogriff	Anderson, K.
Piggy Bank	Kuttner, H.
Pile of Trouble	Kuttner, H.
Pilgrimage	Bond, N.
Pilgrimage to Earth	Sheckley, R.
Pillar of Fire	Bradbury, R.
Pillar to Post	Wyndham, J.
The Pillows	Saint Clair, M.
The Pilot and the Bushman	Jacobs, S.
Pilot Lights of the Apocalypse	Ridenour, L.
Pipeline to Pluto	Leinster, M.
The Piper's Son	Padgett, L.
The Pirates of Venus	B980.
The Pirokin Effect	Eisenberg, L.
The Place of Pain	Shiel, M.
The Place of the Gods	Benet, S.
The Place of the Tigress	Mayne, I.
The Place Where Chicago Was	Harmon, J.
Placement Test	Laumer, K.
Placet Is a Crazy Place	Brown, F.
Plagiarist	Phillips, P.
The Plague	Keller, T.
Plague	Leinster, M.
The Plague of Masters	Anderson, P.
A Planet Named Shayol	Smith, C.
Planet of Forgetting	Schmitz, J.
Planet Passage	Wollheim, D.
Planetary Effulgence	Russell, B.
The Planetoid of Doom	Colladay, M.
The Plants	Leinster, M.
The Plattner Story	Wells, H.
The Playboy Book of Science Fiction	P720.
The Playground	Bradbury, R.
The Play's the Thing	Hoyle, F.
Pleasant Dreams	Robin, R.
Please Stand By	Goulart, R.

TITLE	AUTHOR
Plenitude	Worthington, W.
The Plot	Herzog, T.
Plum Duff	Van Dresser, P.
The Plutonian Drug	Smith, C.
The Pod in the Barrier	Sturgeon, T.
Point of Focus	Silverberg, R.
The Poison Belt	D755.
Police Operation	Piper, H.
Politeness	Brown, F.
Politics	Leinster, M.
Pollock and the Porroh Man	Wells, H.
The Pool of the Black One	Howard, R.
Poor Little Warrior!	Aldiss, B.
Poor Planet	McIntosh, J.
Poor Superman	Leiber, F.
Poppa Needs Shorts	Richmond, W.
The Portable Novels of Science	W880.
The Portable Phonograph	Clark, W.
Portals of Tomorrow	D440.
The Portobello Road	Spark, M.
Portrait of the Artist	Harrison, H.
Poseidon Project	Rackham, J.
The Possessed	Clarke, A.
The Possible Worlds of Science Fiction	C795.
The Post Reader of Fantasy and Science	S250.
Postpaid to Paradise	Arthur, R.
Potential	Malcolm, D.
Potential	Sheckley, R.
Pottage	Henderson, Z.
The Potters of Firsk	Vance, J.
A Pound of Cure	Del Rey, L.
The Power	Leinster, M.
The Power of Positive Thinking	White, M.
Powerhouse	Bradbury, R.
Prelude to Mars	C625.
Prelude to Space	Clarke, A.
Preposterous	Brown, F.
A Present from Joe	Russell, E.
Pressure	Rocklynne, R.

TITLE	AUTHOR
Pretty Maggie Moneyeyes	Ellison, H.
Pride	Jameson, M.
A Pride of Carrots	Nathan, R.
A Pride of Islands	MacApp, C.
Prima Belladonna	Ballard, J.
The Primitives	Herbert, F.
The Prince and the Pirate	Laumer, K.
A Princess of Mars	Burroughs, E.
The Prisoner	Anvil, C.
Private Eye	Kuttner, H.
Private-Keep Out	MacDonald, P.
A Prize for Edie	Bone, J.
The Prize of Peril	Sheckley, R.
The Pro	Hamilton, E.
PRoblem	Nourse, A.
Problem Child	Porges, A.
Problem for Emmy	Townes, R.
Problem on Balak	Dee, R.
Process	Van Vogt, A.
Production Problem	Young, R.
Production Test	Jones, R.
Profession	Asimov, I.
Professor Bern's Awakening	Savchenko, V.
The Professor Challenger Stories [Bibliography]	Doyle, A.
The Professor's Teddy-Bear	Sturgeon, T.
Project	Padgett, L.
Project Hush	Tenn, W.
Project Inhumane	Malec, A.
Project Mastodon	Simak, C.
Project Nightmare	Heinlein, R.
Project Nursemaid	Merril, J.
Project Ocean Floor	Elam, R.
Prolog	McKnight, J.
Prologue to an Analogue	Richmond, L.
Prologue to Analogue	A560.
Promised Planet	Young, R.
Proof	Clement, H.
Proof Positive	Greene, G.
Proof Positive	Malec, A.

TITLE	AUTHOR
Propagandist	Leinster, M.
Protect Me from My Friends	Brunner, J.
Protected Species	Fyfe, H.
Protection	Sheckley, R.
Protest Note	Laumer, K.
Prott	Saint Clair, M.
The Proud Robot	Padgett, L.
Prowler of the Wastelands.	Vincent, H.
Proxima Centauri	Leinster, M.
Psalm	Del Rey, L.
The Pseudo-People.	N875.
The Psychophonic Nurse	Keller, D.
Psyclops	Aldiss, B.
Public Eye	Boucher, A.
The Public Hating	Allen, S.
Publicity Campaign	Clarke, A.
Punch	Pohl, F.
Punishment without Crime.	Bradbury, R.
The Pupped Masters	Heinlein, R.
Puppet Show	Brown, F.
The Purple Fields	Crane, R.
The Purple Pileus	Wells, H.
Push-Button Passion	Friborg, A.
PushButton War	Martino, J.
Pushover Planet	Pedersen, C.
Put Them All Together, They Spell Monster	Russell, R.
Puzzle for Spacemen	Brunner, J.
Pym Makes His Point	Hoyle, F.
Q.U.R.	Boucher, A.
Quads from Vars	Greer, W.
The Quaker Cannon	Kornbluth, C.
The Quality of Mercy	Keyes, D.
Queen of the Black Coast.	Howard, R.
The Queen's Messenger	McGuire, J.
The Quest for Saint Aquin	Boucher, A.
A Question of Residence	Clarke, A.
Quietus	Rocklynne, R.
Quis Custodiet..?	Saint Clair, M.
Quit Zoomin' Those Hands Through the Air	Finney, J.

TITLE	AUTHOR
R.U.R.	Capek, K.
R Is for Rocket	Bradbury, R.
Rabbits to the Moon	Banks, R.
Race around the Sun	Elam, R.
The Radiant Enemies	Starzl, R.
Radiation Blues	Cogswell, T.
The Rag Thing	Grinnell, D.
The Railways up on Cannis	Kapp, C.
Rain Check	Padgett, L.
Rainbird	Lafferty, R.
The Rainbow Gold	Rice, J.
Rainmaker	Reese, J.
Rake	Goulart, R.
Ralph Wollstonecraft Hedge: a Memoir	Goulart, R.
Random Quest	Wyndham, J.
Random Sample	Caravan, T.
Ransom	Fyfe, H.
The Rape of the Solar System	Stone, L.
Rappaccini's Daughter	Hawthorne, N.
The Rat	Wright, S.
Rat Race	De Courcy, D.
The Rat That Could Speak	Dickens, C.
The Rats	Porges, A.
Reach for Tomorrow	Clarke, A.
Reason	Asimov, I.
Re-Birth	Wyndham, J.
Reconciliation	Brown, F.
The Reconciliation	Wells, H.
Recruiting Station	Van Vogt, A.
The Recurrent Suitor	Goulart, R.
"Red Clash"	Poyer, J.
The Red Death of Mars	Williams, R.
The Red Egg	Gironella, J.
The Red Hills of Summer	Pangborn, E.
Red Nails	Howard, R.
The Red Planet	Dikty, T.
The Red Queen's Race	Asimov, I.
The Red Room	Wells, H.

TITLE	AUTHOR
Red Sands	Elam, R.
Red Storm on Jupiter	Long, F.
The Red White and Blue Rum Collins	Brust, J.
Referent	Bradbury, R.
Refuge for Tonight	Williams, R.
Refugee	Clarke, A.
Rejection Slips	Asimov, I.
The Reluctant Heroes	Robinson, F.
The Reluctant Orchid	Clarke, A.
The Remarkable Case of Davidson's Eyes	Wells, H.
Remember the Alamo!	Fehrenbach, T.
The Remorseful	Kornbluth, C.
Remote Incident	Malec, A.
"Repent, Harlequin," Said the Ticktock Man	Ellison, H.
The Replacement	Murray, R.
Report on "Grand Central Terminal"	Szilard, L.
The Report on the Barnhouse Effect	Vonnegut, K.
Report on the Nature of the Lunar Surface	Brunner, J.
Requiem	Hamilton, E.
Requiem	Heinlein, R.
Rescue	Edmondson, G.
Rescue Party	Clarke, A.
The Rest of the Robots	Asimov, I.
Restricted Clientele	Crossen, K.
Resurrection	Van Vogt, A.
The Resurrection of Jimber-Jaw	Burroughs, E.
Retreat to the Stars	Brackett, L.
Retrograde Evolution	Simak, C.
Return	Henderson, Z.
The Return	Piper, H.
Return Engagement	Del Rey, L.
Return from Oblivion	Serling, R.
Return of a Legend	Gallun, R.
The Return of the Moon Man	Malpass, E.
Reverse Phylogeny	Long, A.
The Revolt of the Pedestrians	Keller, D.
Rex	Vincent, H.
Ribbon in the Sky	Leinster, M.

TITLE	AUTHOR
Richard Adams Locke	Poe, E.
The Riddle of the Crypt	Serling, R.
The Right Thing	Andrew, W.
The Rim of Morning	S635.
Ring Around the Redhead	MacDonald, J.
The Rip Van Winkle Caper	Serling, R.
Risk	Asimov, I.
Rite of Passage	Oliver, C.
River of Riches	Kersh, G.
Riya's Foundling	Budrys, A.
The Roaches	Disch, T.
The Road of the Eagles	Howard, R.
Road to Nightfall	Silverberg, R.
The Road to the Sea	Clarke, A.
The Roads Must Roll	Heinlein, R.
Roads of Destiny	Henry, O.
Robbie	Asimov, I.
Robin Hood, F.R.S.	Clarke, A.
Robing	Holmes, H.
Robot AL-76 Goes Astray	Asimov, I.
The Robot and the Man	G825.
The Robot Who Wanted to Know	Boyd, F.
The Robotniks	Bakhnov, V.
Robots Don't Bleed	Groves, J.
Robots Have No Tails	Padgett, L.
Robot's Return	Williams, R.
The Rocket	Bradbury, R.
The Rocket Man	Bradbury, R.
The Rocket of 1955	Kornbluth, C.
Rocket Summer	Bradbury, R.
Rocket to the Sun	Van Dresser, P.
The Rocketeers Have Shaggy Ears	Bennett, K.
Rockets to Where?	Merril, J.
The Rocking-Horse Winner	Lawrence, D.
Rod Serling's The Twilight Zone	S490.
The Roger Bacon Formula	Pratt, F.
Rogue Leonardo	Lack, G.
Rogue Ship	Van Vogt, A.

TITLE	AUTHOR
Rogues in the House	Howard, R.
Romance in a 21st Century Used Car Lot	Young, R.
The Room	Russell, R.
The Root of Ampoi	Smith, C.
Rope Enough	Collier, J.
Rope's End	De Ford, M.
A Rose by Any Other Name	Anvil, C.
A Rose for Ecclesiastes	Zelazny, R.
Rossum's Universal Robots	Capek, C.
A Round Billiard Table	Hall, S.
Round the Moon	Verne, J.
Round Trip to Esidarap	Biggle, L.
A Rover I Will Be	Courtney, R.
Rule Golden	Knight, C.
Rule of Three	Sturgeon, T.
The Rulers	Van Vogt, A.
The Rull	Van Vogt, A.
Rump-Titty-Titty-Tum-TAH-Tee	Leiber, F.
Runaround	Asimov, I.
The Runaway Skyscraper	Leinster, M.
Rundown	Lory, R.
Russian Science Fiction	M275.
Russian Science Fiction 1968	M277.
Rust	Kelleam, J.
Rustle of Wings	Brown, F.
The Ruum	Porges, A.
SF 1956-1959	Merril, J.
SRL AD	Matheson, R.
S Is For Space	B835.
Sacheverell	Davidson, A.
The Sack	Morrison, W.
The Sad Story of a Dramatic Critic	Wells, H.
Sail On! Sail On!	Farmer, P.
Saline Solution	Laumer, K.
The Saliva Tree	Aldiss, B.
Sam Hall	Anderson, P.
The Samaritan	Harper, R.
Sanctuary	Galouye, D.

TITLE	AUTHOR
The Science-Fiction Year	Dikty, T.
The Science-Fictional Sherlock Holmes	S420.
"Scientists Are Stupid!"	Campbell, J.
The Screaming Woman	Bradbury, R.
Sculptors of Life	West, W.
Sea Bright	Moore, H.
The Sea Raiders	Wells, H.
The Sealman	Masefield, J.
Search	Brown, F.
The Search	Simonds, B.
The Search	Van Vogt, A.
Searchlight	Heinlein, R.
The Sea's Furthest End	Broderick, D.
Seat of Judgment	Del Rey, L.
Second Chance	Finney, J.
Second Chance	Kubilius, W.
Second Childhood	Simak, C.
Second Dawn	Clarke, A.
The Second Galaxy Reader of Science Fiction	G145.
Second Genesis	Russell, E.
Second Night of Summer	Schmitz, J.
Second Orbit	D655.
Second Sight	Nourse, A.
The Second Trip to Mars	Moore, W.
Second Variety	Dick, P.
The Secret Place	McKenna, R.
The Secret Songs	Leiber, F.
Security Check	Clarke, A.
See?	Robles, E.
See No Evil	Pierce, J.
See You Later	Padgett, L.
The Seed from the Sepulcher	Smith, C.
Seedling of Mars	Smith, C.
Seeds of the Dusk	Gallun, R.
The Seeds of Time	W995.
Seeker of the Sphinx	Clarke, A.
The Seekers	Tubb, E.
The Seekers	Williams, R.

TITLE	AUTHOR
The Seesaw	Van Vogt, A.
Selection from the London Times	Twain, M.
Selections from Science Fiction Thinking	C835.
Self Portrait	Wolfe, B.
The Sellers of the Dream	Jakes, J.
Semper Fi	Knight, D.
Sense from Thought Divide	Clifton, M.
The Sense of Wonder	Moskowitz, S.
The Sensible Man	Davidson, A.
Sentence	Brown, F.
The Sentimentalists	Leinster, M.
The Sentinel	Clarke, A.
A Serious Search for Weird Worlds . . .	Bradbury, R.
The Servant Problem	Tenn, W.
Service First	Keller, D.
The Settlers	Bradbury, R.
Seven Come Infinity	C840.
Seven-Day Terror	Lafferty, R .
Seven Science Fiction Novels of Wells	W460.
Seven Trips Through Time and Space . .	C843.
The Seven Wonders of the Universe . .	Mallette, M.
Seventeen Times Infinity	C845.
The Seventh Galaxy Reader	G170.
The Sex Opposite	Sturgeon, T.
The Shadow and the Flash.	London, J.
The Shadow Kingdom	Howard, R.
The Shadow Lay	Fitzpatrick, E.
Shadow on the Moon	Henderson, Z.
The Shadow out of Time	Lovecraft, H.
Shadow Show	Simak, C.
Shadows of the Past	Yefremov, I.
Shamar's War	Neville, K.
Shambleau	Moore, C.
The Shape of Things	Bradbury, R.
The Shape of Things That Came	Deming, R.
Shark Ship	Kornbluth, C.
She Only Goes Out at Night	Tenn, W.
She Who Laughs	Phillips, P.

TITLE	AUTHOR
The Shed	Evans, E.
The Shelter	Serling, R.
Shepherd's Boy	Middleton, R.
The Sheriff of Canyon Gulch	Anderson, P.
Sherlock Holmes and Science Fiction	Boucher, A.
The Shining Ones	Clarke, A.
The Ship Sails at Midnight	Leiber, F.
The Ship That Turned Aside	Peyton, G.
Shipshape Home	Matheson, R.
Shock	Kuttner, H.
Shock Treatment	McComas, J.
The Shoddy Lands	Lewis, C.
The Shopdropper	Nelson, A.
The Shore	Bradbury, R.
The Shoreline at Sunset	Bradbury, R.
The Shores of Night	Scortia, T.
Short in the Chest	Seabright, I.
The Short Life	Donovan, F.
The Short Ones	Banks, R.
The Short-Short Story of Mankind	Steinbeck, J.
Shortsighted	Hoyle, F.
Shotgun Cure	Simak, C.
Shottle Bop	Sturgeon, T.
The Shout	Graves, R.
The Show Must Go On	Causey, J.
Showdown with Rance McGrew	Serling, R.
The Sickness	Tenn, W.
Sidewise in Time	Leinster, M.
Siema	Dnieprov, A.
Sierra Sam	Dighton, R.
A Sigh for Cybernetics	Lamport, F.
Silence Please	Clarke, A.
Silent Brother	Budrys, A.
The Silent Towns	Bradbury, R.
Silenzia	Nelson, A.
The Silk and the Song	Fontenay, C.
The Silken-Swift	Sturgeon, T.
The Silkie	Van Vogt, A.

TITLE	AUTHOR
The Silly Season	Kornbluth, C.
The Simian Problem	Alpert, H.
Simple Way	Simak, C.
Simworthy's Circus.	Shaw, L.
The Singers	Walter, W.
The Singing Wall	Asimov, I.
Single Combat	Abernathy, R.
A Singular Case of Extreme Electro-Lyte. . .	Tschirgi, R.
The Singular Events Which Occurred. . .	Davidson, A.
Sinister Journey	Richter, C.
A Sinister Metamorphosis	Baker, R.
Sirius	Stapledon, O.
Sit by the Fire	Benedict, M.
The Sitters	Simak, C.
Sitting Duck	Galouye, D.
Sitting Duck	Saari, O.
Six Cubed Plus One	Rankine, J.
Six-Fingered Jacks	James, E.
Six Fingers of Time	G210.
The Six Fingers of Time.	Lafferty, R.
Six Great Short Novels of Science Fiction	C850.
Six Great Short Science Fiction Novels.	C855.
Six Haiku [Poems].	Anderson, K.
Six Matches	Strugatsky, A.
The Sixth Galaxy Reader	G165.
The Sixty-Four Square Madhouse. . . .	Leiber, F.
Skag with the Queer Head	Leinster, M.
Skeleton Men of Jupiter	Burroughs, E.
Skirmish	Simak, C.
The Sky Is Burning	Ellison, H.
Sky Lift	Heinlein, R.
The Sky People	Anderson, P.
Slan	Van Vogt, A.
The Slave	Kornbluth, C.
Sleight of Wit.	Dickson, G.
A Slight Case of Limbo	Biggle, L.
A Slight Case of Sunstroke	Clarke, A.
A Slip under the Microscope	Wells, H.

TITLE	AUTHOR
The Slithering Shadow	Howard, R.
Slow Tuesday Night	Lafferty, R.
The Sly Bungerhop	Morrison, W.
The Small Assassin	Bradbury, R.
The Small World of M-75	Clinton, E.
The Smallest Moon	Wilcox, D.
The Smile	Bradbury, R.
Smoke Ghost	Leiber, F.
The Snowball Effect	MacLean, K.
Snuffles	Lafferty, R.
Snulbug	Boucher, A.
So Proudly We Hail	Merril, J.
Socrates	Christopher, J.
Softly While You're Sleeping	Smith, E.
Solar Plexus	Blish, J.
Soldier	Ellison, H.
Soldier Boy	Shaara, M.
Soldier from Tomorrow	Ellison, H.
Solipsist	Brown, F.
Sol's Little Brother	Elam, R.
Some Live Like Lazarus	Bradbury, R.
Somebody to Play with	Williams, J.
Someday	Asimov, I.
Something	Drury, A.
Something Bright	Henderson, Z.
Something Else	Tilley, R.
Something for Nothing	Sheckley, R.
Something Green	Brown, F.
Something in a Cloud	Finney, J.
Something Invented Me	Phelan, R.
Somewhere Not Far from Here	Kersh, G.
Somnium	Kepler, J.
The Song of the Pewee	Grendon, S.
The Songs of Distant Earth	Clarke, A.
Sonny	Raphael, R.
The Soothsayer	Bennett, K.
The Sorcerer's Apprentice	Jameson, M.
Soul Mate	Sutton, L.

TITLE	AUTHOR
The Sound	Van Vogt, A.
Sound Decision	Garrett, R.
The Sound of Bugles	Williams, R.
The Sound of Summer Running	Bradbury, R.
A Sound of Thunder	Bradbury, R.
The Sound Sweep	Ballard, J.
The Sources of the Nile	Davidson, A.
Souvenir	Ballard, J.
Soviet Science Fiction	D980.
Space	Buchan, J.
The Space-Crime Continuum	Ellis, H.
Space Fix	Richardson, R.
Space Jockey	Heinlein, R.
Space Lane Cadet	Hallstead, W.
Space on My Hands	B885.
Space Pioneers	N880.
Space Police	N885.
Space Rating	Berryman, J.
Space Secret	Sambrot, W.
Space Service	N890.
Space, Space, Space	S640.
Space Steward	Elam, R.
Space, Time and Crime	D310.
Space Time for Springers	Leiber, F.
Space War	Ley, W.
Space War Tactics	Jameson, M.
The Spaceman Cometh	Felsen, H.
Spacemaster	Schmitz, J.
Spacemen Live Forever	Page, G.
Sparkie's Fall	Hyde, G.
Special Aptitude	Sturgeon, T.
Special Delivery	Clarke, A.
Special Delivery	Knight, D.
Special Feature	De Vet, C.
Special Flight	Berryman, J.
Specialist	Sheckley, R.
Spectator Sport	MacDonald, J.
The Specter General	Cogswell, T.

TITLE	AUTHOR
Spectrum I-V	Amis, K.
Spell My Name with an S.	Asimov, I.
Splice of Life	Dorman, S.
Spontaneous Reflex	Strugatsky, A.
Spud and Cochise	La Farge, O.
Spud Failure Definite	Peart, N.
Spy Story	Sheckley, R.
Stair Trick	Clingerman, M.
The Star	Clarke, A.
The Star	Wells, H.
Star Begotten	Wells, H.
Star Bright	Clifton, M.
The Star Ducks	Brown, B.
The Star Dummy	Boucher, A.
The Star Gypsies	Gresham, W.
Star Light	Asimov, I.
Star-Linked	Fyfe, H.
Star Maker	Stapledon, O.
Star Mouse	Brown, F.
Star of Stars	P765.
Star of Wonder	May, J.
The Star Party	Lory, R.
Star Science Fiction Stories I-3	Pohl, F.
Star Short Novels	Pohl, F.
Staras Flonderans	Wilhelm, K.
Starbride	Boucher, A.
Starlight, Star Bright.	Bester, A.
The Stars Are Calling, Mr. Keats	Young, R.
The Stars Are the Styx	Sturgeon, T.
The Stars, Like Dust	Asimov, I.
The Stars My Destination	Bester, A.
The Starting Line	Clarke, A.
Startling Stories	S795.
Status Quondam	Miller, P.
Steel	Matheson, R.
Steel Brother	Dickson, G.
The Stentorii Luggage	Barrett, N.
Stevie and the Dark	Henderson, Z.

TITLE	AUTHOR
Stickeney and the Critic	Clingerman, M.
Still Life	Russell, E.
The Still Waters	Del Rey, L.
Stimulus	Brunner, J.
Stitch in Time	McIntosh, J.
Stitch in Time	Wyndham, J.
The Stolen Bacillus	Wells, H.
The Stolen Body	Wells, H.
Stolen Centuries	Kline, O.
A Stone and a Spear	Jones, R.
Stone from the Stars	Zhuravleva, V.
Stories for Tomorrow	S645.
Stories of Scientific Imagination	G225.
Storm	Zhuravleva, V.
Storm Warning	Wollheim, D.
The Story of a Panic	Forster, E.
The Story of Davidson's Eyes	Wells, H.
A Story of the Days to Come	Wells, H.
The Story of the Last Trump	Wells, H.
The Story of the Late Mr. Elvesham	Wells, H.
A Story of the Stone Age	Wells, H.
The Story-Teller	Saki.
The Strange Case of Dr. Jekyll and Mr...	Stevenson, R.
The Strange Case of John Kingman	Leinster, M.
The Strange Flight of Richard Clayton	Bloch, R.
The Strange Girl	Van Doren, M.
Strange Harvest	Wandrei, D.
The Strange Men	Elam, R.
The Strange Orchid	Wells, H.
Strange Signposts	M940.
Stranger from Space	Lees, G.
Stranger Station	Knight, D.
Strangers in the Universe	S610.
The Strawberry Window	Bradbury, R.
The Street Walker	Tucker, W.
Strikebreaker	Asimov, I.
Student Body	Wallace, F.
The Stutterer	Merliss, R.

TITLE	AUTHOR
Subcommittee	Henderson, Z.
Subjectivity.	Spinrad, N.
Sub-Lim	Roberts, K.
The Subliminal Man	Ballard, J.
The Sublime Vigil	Cuthbert, C.
Submerged	Doyle, A.
The Sub-Standard Sardines	Vance, J.
The Substitute	Henderson, Z.
Subterfuge	Bradbury, R.
Suburban Frontiers	Young, R.
A Subway Named Mobius	Deutsch, A.
The Subways of Taboo	Kapp, C.
Success Story	Goodale, E.
Such Interesting Neighbors	Finney, J.
Such Stuff	Brunner, J.
Sucker Bait	Asimov, I.
The Sudden Afternoon	Ballard, J.
The Summer Night	Bradbury, R.
Summer Wear	De Camp, L.
Summertime on Icarus	Clarke, A.
Sun and Shadow	Bradbury, R.
A Sun Invisible	Anderson, P.
The Sun Maker	Williamson, J.
Sunfire!	Hamilton, E.
Sunjammer	Clarke, A.
Sunjammer	Anderson, P.
Sunken Universe	Blish, J.
Sunout	Williams, E.
The Sunset Harp	Bradbury, R.
Sunward	Coblentz, S.
Superiority	Clarke, A.
Surface Tension	Blish, J.
Survival	Wyndham, J.
Survival Ship	Merril, J.
The Survivor	Moudy, W.
Susan	Bevan, A.
Susceptibility	MacDonald, J.
Swenson, Dispatcher	Miller, R.

TITLE	AUTHOR
Sword of Tomorrow	Kuttner, H.
Swordsman of Lost Terra	Anderson, P.
Swordsman of Varnis	Jackson, C.
Swordsmen in the Sky	W885.
Symbiosis	Leinster, M.
Symbiotica	Russell, E.
Symposium of the Gorgon	Smith, C.
Synchromocracy	Cawood, H.
Syndrone Johnny	Dye, C.
Synth	Roberts, K.
System	Capek, K.
Taboo	Leiber, F.
The Tactful Saboteur	Herbert, F.
The Tail-Tied Kings	Davidson, A.
Take a Deep Breath	Clarke, A.
Take a Deep Breath	Thorne, R.
Take a Seat	Russell, E.
Take Wooden Indians	Davidson, A.
Takeover Bid	Baxter, J.
Tale of a Chemist	Anonymous.
A Tale of Negative Gravity	Stockton, F.
A Tale of the Thirteenth Floor	Nash, O.
Talent	Sturgeon, T.
Tales of Conan	H860.
Tales of Science and Sorcery	S650.
Tales of Ten Worlds	C635.
Tales of the Distant Past	Podolny, R.
Tales of Three Planets	B990.
The Talking Stone	Asimov, I.
Tanar of Pellucidar	Burroughs, E.
Tangle Hold	Wallace, F.
The Tangled Web	Schmitz, J.
Target Generation	Simak, C.
The Taxpayer	Bradbury, R.
Tea Tray in the Sky	Smith, E.
Technical Error	Clarke, A.
Technical Slip	Beynon, J.
Teen-Age Science Fiction Stories	E375.

TITLE	AUTHOR
Teen-Age Super Science Stories	E380.
The Teeth of Despair	Davidson, A.
Teething Ring	Causey, J.
Temple of Despair	Pease, M.
The Temptation of Harringay	Wells, H.
10:01 AM	Malec, A.
Ten-Story Jigsaw	Aldiss, B.
The Tenants	Tenn, W.
The Tenth Galaxy Reader	G185.
Tepondicon	Jacobi, C.
Terminal	Goulart, R.
Terminal Beach	B190.
Terminal Quest	Anderson, P.
The Terra-Venusian War of 1979	Neyroud, G.
The Terrible Intruders	Hinrichs, J.
Territory	Anderson, P.
The Terror of Anerly House School	Lawrence, M.
Terror Out of Space	Brackett, L.
The Test	Matheson, R.
Test	Thomas, T.
Test Piece	Russell, E.
Test Stand	Stine, G.
Test-Tube Terror	Standish, R.
Testament	Baxter, J.
Testament of Andros	Blish, J.
Texas Week	Hernhuter, A.
That Low	Sturgeon, T.
That Only a Mother	Merril, J.
That Share of Glory	Kornbluth, C.
Thaw and Serve	Lang, A.
The Theft of the Thirty-Nine Girdles	Smith, C.
Theory of Rocketry	Kornbluth, C.
There Is a Tide	Aldiss, B.
There Is a Tide	Finney, J.
There Shall Be Darkness	Moore, C.
There Will Come Soft Rains	Bradbury, R.
There's a Starman in Ward 7	Rome, D.
They	Heinlein, R.

TITLE	AUTHOR
They Don't Make Life Like They Used To	Bester, A.
Thin Edge	MacKenzie, J.
The Thing in the Woods	Pratt, F.
Thing of Beauty	Knight, D.
A Thing of Custom	De Camp, L.
Thing-Thing	Malec, A.
Things	Henderson, Z.
Things	Janvier, I.
Things of Distinction	Crossen, K.
Things Pass By	Leinster, M.
Thiotimoline and the Space Age	Asimov, I.
The Third Expedition	Bradbury, R.
Third from the Sun	Matheson, R.
The Third Galaxy Reader	G150.
The Third Level	Finney, J.
Third Offense	Pohl, F.
Thirteen O'Clock	Kornbluth, C.
Thirteen Science Fiction Stories	K715.
The Thirteenth Story	Serling, R.
Thirty Seconds-Thirty Days	Clarke, A.
This Earth of Majesty	Clarke, A.
This Is the House	Padgett, L.
This Is the Land	Bond, N.
This One's On Me	Russell, E.
This Side Up	Banks, R.
This Star Shall Be Free	Leinster, M.
Those Among Us	Kuttner, H.
Those Who Can, Do	Kurosaka, B.
Thou Good and Faithful	Brunner, K.
Though Dreamers Die	Del Rey, L.
The Thousand-and-Second Tale of Scheherazade	Poe, E.
Thread of Life	Safronov, Y.
The Three Brothers	Russell, W.
Three by Heinlein	H500.
The Three-Cornered Wheel	Anderson, P.
Three for Carnival	Shepley, J.
Three for the Stars	Dickinson, J.
Three Martian Novels	B995.

TITLE	AUTHOR
Three Novels [by Damon Knight]	K720.
Three Portraits and a Prayer	Pohl, F.
Three Prologues and an Epilogue	Dos Passos, J.
Three Prophetic Novels [by H.G. Wells]	W465.
Three Stories by Murray Leinster [et al]	L540.
The Threepenny-Piece	Stephens, J.
Through a Window	Wells, H.
Through Channels	Matheson, R.
Through Time and Space with F. Feghoot	Briarton, G.
Throwback	De Camp, L.
Throwback	De Ford, M.
Thunder and Roses	Sturgeon, T.
The Thunder-Thieves	Asimov, I.
Thuvia, Maid of Mars	Burroughs, E.
Ticket to Anywhere	Knight, D.
The Tiddlywink Warriors	Anderson, P.
The Tide of Death	Doyle, A.
Tiger by the Tail	Henderson, G.
Tiger by the Tail	Nourse, A.
The Tiger God	Serling, R.
Time and Stars	A575.
Time Bum	Kornbluth, C.
Time Enough	Knight, D.
Time Heals	Anderson, P.
Time in the Round	Leiber, F.
Time in Thy Flight	Bradbury, R.
Time Lag	Anderson, P.
Time Locker	Padgett, L.
The Time Machine	Bradbury, R.
The Time Machine	Wells, H.
The Time of Going Away	Bradbury, R.
The Time of the Eye	Ellison, H.
Time to Rest	Harris, J.
Time Probe	C640.
Time to Come	D445.
Time to Rest	Wyndham, J.
The Time-Tombs	Ballard, J.
Time Travel and the Law	Kornbluth, C.
Time Travel Happens!	Phillips, A.

TITLE	AUTHOR
Time Waits for Winthrop and Four Other Novels	G215.
Time Waits for Winthrop	Tenn, W.
Time's Arrow	Clarke, A.
Tin Lizzie	Garrett, R.
The Tinkler	Anderson, P.
Tiny and the Monster	Sturgeon, T.
The Tissue-Culture King	Huxley, J.
Title Fight	Gault, W.
To Avenge Man	Del Rey, L.
To Change Their Ways	Martino, J.
To Each His Own	Sharkey, J.
To Explain Mrs. Thompson	Richardson, R.
To Fell a Tree	Young, R.
To Follow Knowledge	Long, F.
To Here and the Easel	Sturgeon, T.
To Marry Medusa	Sturgeon, T.
To Relieve the Sanity	Malec, A.
To Serve Man	Knight, D.
To the Chicago Abyss	Bradbury, R.
To the End of Time	S790.
To the Pure	Knight, D.
To Walk the Night	Sloane, W.
To Worlds Beyond	S590.
Tobermory	Saki.
Tolliver's Travels	Fenton, F.
The Tomb-Spawn	Smith, C.
Tomorrow and Tomorrow and Tomorrow	Vonnegut, K.
Tomorrow Is Here to Stay	Crossen, K.
Tomorrow the Stars	H505.
Tomorrow's Children	A865.
Tongue of Beast	Claudy, C.
Too Far	Brown, F.
Tools of the Trade	Jones, R.
The Tooth	Dewey, G.
Top Secret	Grinnell, D.
A Touch of Immortality	Mackelworth, R.
A Touch of Strange	Sturgeon, T.
The Touch of Your Hand	Sturgeon, T.

TITLE	AUTHOR
Touchstone	Carr, T.
Tough Old Man	Hubbard, L.
The Tourist Trade	Tucker, W.
The Tower of the Elephant	Howard, R.
The Town Where No One Got Off	Bradbury, R.
The Toy Shop	Harrison, H.
Trade-in	Sharkey, J.
Trader to the Stars	Anderson, P.
Trail Blazer	Gallun, R.
Trail to the Stars	Leyson, B.
Trainee for Mars	Harrison, H.
Training Talk	Bunch, D.
Transcience	Clarke, A.
Transfer Point	Boucher, A.
Transition-from Fantasy to Science	Clarke, A.
The Trap	Bennett, K.
Travelers by Night	D450.
Travelers of Space	G830.
Traveler's Rest	Masson, D.
Treasure Hunt	Green, J.
The Treasure in the Forest	Wells, H.
A Treasury of Great Science Fiction v.1-2	Boucher, A.
The Treasury of Science Fiction	C870.
The Treasury of Science Fiction Classics	K950.
Treat	Kerr, W.
Treaty in Tartessos	Anderson, K.
The Tree Men of Potu	Holberg, L.
Tree Trunks	Gallagher, J.
The Trematode	Bester, A.
Trends	Asimov, I.
Trespass!	Anderson, P.
Triad	V190.
The Trial of Tantalus	Saparin, V.
Triangle	A870.
Trick or Treaty	Laumer, K.
A Trick or Two	Novotny, J.
Trigger Tide	Guin, W.
Triggerman	Bone, J.

TITLE	AUTHOR
Trip One	Grendon, R.
Trip to the City	Laumer, K.
Trip, Trap	Wolfe, G.
The Triumphs of a Taxidermist	Wells, H.
The Trolley	Bradbury, R.
Trouble on Tantalus	Miller, P.
The Trouble Twisters	Anderson, P.
The Trouble with Emily	White, J.
The Trouble with H.A.R.R.I.	Macklin, E.
The Trouble with Telstar	Berryman, J.
Trouble with the Natives	Clarke, A.
Trouble with Time	Clarke, A.
Trouble with Water	Gold, H.
Troubling of the Water	Henderson, Z.
True Confession	Tremaine, F.
A True History	Lucian.
True Self	Borgese, E.
The Truth about Cushgar	Schmitz, J.
The Truth about Pyecraft	Wells, H.
Try and Change the Past	Leiber, F.
Try to Remember	Herbert, F.
Tryst	Baxter, J.
The Tunesmith	Biggle, L.
The Tunnel under the World	Pohl, F.
Turn the Page	Henderson, Z.
Turning on	K725.
Turning Point	Anderson, P.
2066: Election Day	Shaara, M.
Twenty Thousand Leagues under the Sea	Verne, J.
28 Science Fiction Stories of H.G. Wells	W475.
The Twerlik	Sharkey, J.
Twice Bitten	Malcolm, D.
Twice Twenty-Two	B840.
Twilight	Stuart, D.
The Twilight Zone	S490.
Twin's Wail	Borgese, E.
Two Dooms	Kornbluth, C.
Two Face	Long, F.
237 Talking Statues, etc.	Leiber, F.

TITLE	AUTHOR
Two Letters to Lord Kelvin	Jarry, A.
The Two Shadows	Temple, W.
Two Weeks in August	Robinson, F.
The Twonky	Padgett, L.
Two's a Crowd	Gilien, S.
Two's Company	Rankine, J.
Tyrannosaurus Rex	Bradbury, R.
The Ugly Little Boy	Asimov, I.
Ugly Sister	Struther, J.
Uller Uprising	Piper, H.
Ultima Thule	Russell, E.
The Ultimate Catalyst	Bell, E.
Ultimate Construction	Shackleton, C.
The Ultimate Egoist	Sturgeon, T.
The Ultimate Melody	Clarke, A.
Ultimatum	Laumer, K.
Una	Wyndham, J.
Uncle Einar	Bradbury, R.
Under the Knife	Wells, H.
Under the Sand-Seas	Saari, O.
Underground Movement	Neville, K.
The Underprivileged	Aldiss, B.
The Unfortunate Mr. Morky	Aandahl, V.
Unfortunate Passage	Tubb, E.
Unhuman Sacrifice	MacLean, K.
Unite and Conquer	Sturgeon, T.
University	Phillips, P.
Unknown Quantity	Phillips, P.
The Un-Man	Anderson, P.
The Unpleasantness at Carver House	Jacobi, C.
Unready to Wear	Vonnegut, K.
Unreal Estates	Lewis, C.
The Unremembered	Mackin, E.
The Unsafe Deposit Box	Kersh, G.
The Untimely Toper	De Camp, L.
Unto the Fourth Generation	Asimov, I.
Unwelcome Tenant	Dee, R.
The Up-to-Date Sorcerer	Asimov, I.

TITLE	AUTHOR
Voice from the Gallery	Brownlow, C.
The Voice in the Earphones	Schramm, W.
The Voice in the Garden	Ellison, H.
The Voice of the Dolphins	Szilard, L.
The Voice of the Lobster	Kuttner, H.
Voices from the Cliff	Leahy, J.
The Voices of Time	Ballard, J.
The Volcano Dances	Ballard, J.
Volpla	Guin, W.
The Vortex Blasters	Smith, E.
The Voyage of the Space Beagle	Van Vogt, A.
The Voyage That Lasted Six Hundred Years	Wilcox, D.
Voyage to Sfanomoe	Smith, C.
Voyage to the Moon	Rostand, E.
Voyagers in Time	Silverberg, R.
The Wabbler	Leinster, M.
The Wages of Synergy	Sturgeon, T.
The Wait	Reed, K.
Wake for the Living	Bradbury, R.
The Waker Dreams	Matheson, R.
Waldo	Heinlein, R.
A Walk in the Dark	Clarke, A.
Walk Like a Mountain	Wellman, M.
Walkabout	Earl, S.
Walking Aunt Daid	Henderson, Z.
The Wall	Saxton, J.
The Wall Around the World	Cogswell, T.
Wall of Crystal, Eye of Night	Budrys, A.
The Wall of Darkness	Clarke, A.
The Wall of Fire	Kirkland, J.
The Walls	Laumer, K.
Wanted—An Enemy	Leiber, F.
The War Against the Moon	Maurois, A.
The War in the Air	Cassill, R.
The War in the Air	Wells, H.
The War of the Worlds	Wells, H.
Warm	Sheckley, R.
The Warning	Phillips, P.

TITLE	AUTHOR
Warrior	Dickson, G.
Waste Not, Want Not	Atherton, J.
Wasted on the Young	Brunner, J.
Watch This Space	Clarke, A.
The Watchers	Bradbury, R.
The Watchers	Brode, A.
The Watchers	Deutsch, R.
The Watchers in the Glade	Wilson, R.
The Water Eater	Marks, W.
Water Is for Washing	Heinlein, R.
The Watery Place	Asimov, I.
The Waveries	Brown, F.
A Way Home	S950.
Way in the Middle of the Air	Bradbury, R.
Way of Escape	Temple, W.
A Way of Life	Bloch, R.
A Way of Thinking	Sturgeon, T.
The Wayfairing Strangers	Tucker, W.
The Wayward Cravat	Friedberg, G.
"We Also Walk Dogs"	Heinlein, R.
We Are Alone	Sheckley, R.
We Can Remember It for You Wholesale	Dick, P.
We Didn't Do Anything Wrong, Hardly	Kuykendall, R.
We Don't Want Any Trouble	Schmitz, J.
We Guard the Black Planet!	Kuttner, H.
We Kill People	Padgett, L.
We Mourn for Anyone	Ellison, H.
We Never Mention Aunt Nora	Flehr, P.
We The People	Moore, W.
We Would See a Sign	Rose, M.
The Weapon	Brown, F.
The Weapon Shops of Isher	Van Vogt, A.
The Weather in the Underworld	Free, C.
The Weather Man	Thomas, T.
The Weigher of Souls	Maurois, A.
The Weissenbroch Spectacles	De Camp, L.
Welcome to Slippage City	Hoyle, F.
The Well-Oiled Machine	Fyfe, H.

TITLE	AUTHOR
Where Is Everybody?	Bova, B.
Wherever You May Be	Gunn, J.
The Whisperer in Darkness	Lovecraft, H.
The White Army	Dressler, D.
White Mutiny	Jameson, M.
The White Pinnacle	Jacobi, C.
Who Can Replace a Man?	Aldiss, B.
Who Dreams of Ivy	Worthington, W.
Who Goes There?	Stuart, D.
Who Knows His Brother	Doar, G.
Who Needs Insurance?	Scott, R.
Who Shall Dwell	Neal, H.
Who Shall I Say Is Calling?	Derleth, A.
The Whole Truth	Serling, R.
Who's Cribbing?	Lewis, J.
Who's in Charge Here?	Blish, J.
Who's There?	Clarke, A.
Wicker Wonderland	Laumer, K.
The [Widget], the [Wadget], and Boff	Sturgeon, T.
Wild Flower	Wyndham, J.
The Wild Man of the Sea	Hodgson, W.
A Wild Surmise	Kuttner, H.
The Wild Wood	Clingerman, M.
The Wilderness	Bradbury, R.
Wilderness	Henderson, Z.
The Will	Miller, W.
Will You Wait?	Bester, A.
"Will You Walk a Little Faster?"	Tenn, W.
The Willow Tree	Rice, J.
Win the World	Oliver, C.
The Wind from Nowhere	Ballard, J.
A Wind Is Rising	O'Donnevan, F.
The Wind People	Bradley, M.
The Windows of Heaven	Brunner, J.
The Winds of Time	Schmitz, J.
The Wines of Earth	Seabright, I.
Wingless Victory	Heard, H.
The Wings of a Bat	Ash, P.
The Wings of Night	Del Rey, L.

TITLE	AUTHOR
Winner Lose All	Vance, J.
Winner Take All	Rocklynne, R.
Winthrop Was Stubborn	Tenn, W.
Wireless	Kipling, R.
Witch War	Matheson, R.
The Witches of Karres	Schmitz, J.
With Folded Hands	Williamson, J.
With Redfern on Capella XI	Pohl, F.
With Redfern on Capella XII	Satterfield, C.
With These Hands	Kornbluth, C.
Within the Pyramid	Miller, R.
The Witness	Russell, E.
The Wizard of Venus	Burroughs, E.
The Wizard of Pung's Corners	Pohl, F.
Wolf Pack	Miller, W.
Wolfshead	Howard, R.
A Woman's Place	Clifton, M.
The Wonder Horse	Byram, G.
The Wonderful Dog Suit	Hall, D.
The Wonderful Ice-Cream Suit	Bradbury, R.
The Wondersmith	O'Brien, F.
The Word	Clingerman, M.
Word of Honor	Bloch, R.
The Words of Guru	Kornbluth, C.
A Work of Art	Blish, J.
A World by the Tale	McKettrig, S.
The World Is Mine	Padgett, L.
The World of A	Van Vogt, A.
The World of Myrion Flowers	Pohl, F.
World of Wonder	P910.
The World That Couldn't Be	Simak, C.
The World That Couldn't Be	G220.
The World Well Lost	Sturgeon, T.
World without Children	Knight, D.
Worlds Apart	W755.
World's Best SF: 1965-67	Wollheim, D.
The Worlds of Clifford Simak	Simak, C.
The Worlds of Robert F. Young	Y750.